The Nightwatches of Bonaventura

TRANSLATED BY GERALD GILLESPIE

University of Chicago Press × Chicago and London

GERALD GILLESPIE is professor emeritus at Stanford University and a former president of the International Comparative Literature Association.

The University of Chicago Press, Chicago 60637
The University of Chicago Press, Ltd., London
© 1971, 2014 by Gerald Gillespie
All rights reserved. Published 2014.
Printed in the United States of America

23 22 21 20 19 18 17 16 15 14   1 2 3 4 5

ISBN-13: 978-0-226-14142-8   (cloth)
ISBN-13: 978-0-226-14156-5   (paper)
ISBN-13: 978-0-226-17753-3   (e-book)
DOI: 10.7208/chicago/9780226177533.001.0001

Library of Congress Cataloging-in-Publication Data

Bonaventura, author.
   [Nachtwachen. English]
   The nightwatches of Bonaventura / translated by Gerald Gillespie.
     pages cm
   Includes bibliographical references.
   ISBN 978-0-226-14142-8 (cloth : alk. paper) — ISBN 978-0-226-14156-5
(pbk. : alk. paper) — ISBN 978-0-226-17753-3 (e-book)
   I. Gillespie, Gerald, 1933-   II. Title.
   PT1823.B65N313 2014
   833'.6—dc23

                                                    2014008635

♾ This paper meets the requirements of ANSI/NISO Z39.48-1992
(Permanence of Paper).

Contents

Preface

This new edition of *The Nightwatches of Bonaventura* is intended for native speakers of English and for those who use English as a lingua franca to gain access to a diverse range of world literature. It will especially interest readers curious about ties between English and German culture in the transition from the eighteenth to the nineteenth century and about the return of troubling insights from that age. A prominent feature of the *Nightwatches* is its obsessive attention to the arts as indicators of stages in human consciousness from ancient beginnings to the crisis of modernity. Hence it is no wonder that a variety of artists as well as critics have responded to the novel's provocative treatment of romantic aspirations; for many it seems, generation by generation, to foreshadow aspects of expressionism, existentialism, and postmodernism. The broader story of reception—both in critical discourse and in literary, pictorial, theatrical, and musical expression—will be treated in an afterword. The introduction deals with the contents of the *Nightwatches* from a present-day standpoint. The aim is to explain for the general reader why certain motifs and themes born out of a negative romanticism now seem ancestral to our literature of the absurd.

A swarm of editions of the *Nightwatches* at the start of the twentieth century, climaxing in Raimund Steinert's almost reverential bibliophile edition during World War I (1916), marked a turning point, for Bonaventura was now to gain currency among adherents of the ascendant expressionist movement as a prophet of the debacle of Western culture and of the need for a new art; he seemed to exemplify their own moral anguish and cry for rebirth. Though the full impact of Bonaventura was not yet felt, this burst of interest was comparable to the naturalists' rediscovery of Georg Büchner preceding World War I. Then, following World War II, critical attention gradually shifted from identifying the author of the *Nightwatches* to dealing more intensively with the significance of the novel's contents. Today numerous critics regard the *Nightwatches* as more than a program of rebuke and defiance. Rather, it seems a manifesto of a new start for altered consciousness, and therein resides its modernity—whether pernicious or not.

Perhaps no single metaphor among the many on which the book is patterned reveals this better than the frequent references to digestion. Because thorough assimilation is equated to artistic prowess, we are justified in regarding the poetic principle of the whole novel to be a relentless processing of materials. Bonaventura gives us as his explicit model the hateful worm, borrowed from Shakespeare, that finally feasts on all us human actors and on our brains teeming with sentiments and ideas. What we discover ourselves to be experiencing is how the narrator's mind slowly converts illusion (life) into truth (life thought through).

The new introduction and afterword attempt to do justice to the wealth of Bonaventura commentary over the past generation. This renascence was stimulated especially by the identification of the author as the theater director, playwright, critic, and novelist August Klingemann in the 1970s. Readers of German can consult the select bibliography for leads on the European side, but readers of English, too, will find adequate references because the critical story has clearly become international.

My translation of Bonaventura is based on the original German edition of 1804, specifically the copy held by Yale University in the Beinecke Rare Book and Manuscript Library under signature Zg 19/B 6371/805n; on Hermann Michel's critical centenary edi-

tion, *Nachtwachen. Von Bonaventura* (Berlin: B. Behr, 1904); and on
Raimund Steinert's bibliophile edition, *Nachtwachen. Von Bonaventura. Nach Rahel Varnhagens Exemplar [. . .]* (Weimar: Gustav Kiepenheuer, 1916). My English version of the *Nightwatches* was first
published by University of Texas Press (1971) and Edinburgh University Press (1972). I appreciate their agreement to my reiterating
points and passages extensively under my extant copyright.

I am grateful to the cultural critic Nick Herman (Los Angeles)
for his encouragement of my reissuing the *Nightwatches* and for
his bringing to my attention a number of US-based contemporary
visual artists who have felt attracted to Bonaventura. I thank the
art editor Axel Lapp (Berlin), who kindly informed me of the relevance of Bonaventura for the contemporary German artist Cornelia Renz.

I have invented the term "tantric romanticism" as a special label for the kind of anguish Bonaventura experiences in making the
transition from the bright hopes of the Enlightenment into a perplexing new world of subjectivism, and in undertaking a journey
into the interiority of the self that finally becomes unfathomable.

Introduction

It was a dangerous and turbulent time. The disorders of the French Revolution had given rise to the Reign of Terror, which ended after the execution of its central figure, the righteous dictator Maximillien de Robespierre, in 1794. The young general Napoleon Bonaparte rapidly rose to control the nation's destiny. His efforts to redirect the energies of the revolution entailed continuing to send French armies and their allied forces throughout Europe to consolidate French power. Finally, with his coronation in 1804, he formally converted the new republic into an empire. This larger historical drama overlapped with the rise of romanticism in Britain and Germany and the spread of the new subjectivist philosophy expounded most notably by Immanuel Kant.

The anonymous *Nightwatches of Bonaventura* appeared late in the year of Kant's death, also in 1804. It belongs among German and British works of the ending eighteenth and beginning nineteenth centuries that seem still impassioned about Enlightenment causes yet bear unmistakable traits of gothic anxiety and slip inexorably into romanticism. What sets the German first-person *Nightwatches* apart is how its strange narrator, the night watchman Kreuzgang, probes the story of his own fall from revolutionary aspirations and poetic heights, navigates his way through the deconstruction of newly triumphant romantic tenets, and at his story's end plunges into an abyss of the mind as reliable values collapse. The *Nightwatches* reveals a remarkable economy in the way it presents a fictional biography purposely out of order so as to exhibit a discovery process, a general indictment against the age's decadence, and a manifesto of an art of despair.

Insofar as the satirist Kreuzgang, the narrator, rails against his world, endangered values momentarily appear to be affirmed. But we sense a palpable tension between his moral anger and his existential despair as a disillusioned, fallen poet. This has produced a long-lasting split in critical approaches down to the present. Some critics persist in arguing that Kreuzgang's often wild, theatrical exposure of societal ills characterizes the *Nightwatches* as an extremely grim example of satire rooted mainly in eighteenth-century moral outrage, such as we find in a writer like Jonathan Swift or a painter like William Hogarth. The latter artist, in fact, exercised a powerful influence that the anonymous Bonaventura explicitly acknowledges in the novel. Emphasizing the narrator's intense distress only as an expression of Enlightenment protest, however, requires that we avoid evaluating the impact of the newer romantic subjectivism, even though the novel directly treats this as something that could spawn both high expectations and existential dread. Through Kreuzgang we experience how romantic irony could turn on romanticism itself and yield not a reaffirmation of progress but an alternative nihilistic vision. The critic Richard Brinkmann formulated the drastic pattern trenchantly in an essay during the flare-up of fresh interest in Bonaventura after World War II: "Everything in the *Nightwatches*, not least Romanticism and finally the narrator himself, succumbs to irony" (Brinkmann 1966, 8 [trans. GG]).

Despite many attempts, until the 1970s no one ever convincingly identified the author of the bitter and bizarre work. A few notable writers noticed the book upon its appearance and lent it an underground reputation over the ensuing decades. It is thus a mark of the novel's unusual power that it eventually entered the German literary canon of the twentieth century when, as the then unknown Bonaventura predicted, there would be a general turning to the grotesque and absurd out of the logic of modern cultural development. The book's eventual breakthrough to canonical status occurred in the traumatic aftermaths of two world wars separated by only twenty uneasy years. In the afterword I will discuss the protracted search for the author and the expressionist, existentialist, and postmodernist phases of modern critical reception.

Since the *Nightwatches* draws the gloomiest consequences inherent in romantic pessimism and radically attacks all German idealism, it is justifiable to attach Mario Praz's well-known phrase "the romantic agony" to this most agonized of the many black outpourings of that age in Germany. The term is more than approximately suited to an odd narrator whose name, Kreuzgang, from the crossroads where he was found as a baby, is one of several punning allusions to his cross or anguish. Whatever disagreements still may arise over puzzling moments in the book, it is clear today, beyond the waning of postmodernism, that we get nowhere by attempting to judge Bonaventura by the literary values which he himself dismisses, even if we personally may cherish them. "Humanity" Bonaventura exposes as a tragic lie; despite its perplexing splendors, "nature" comes to possess no ultimate meaning for him except as a model of horror. To conclude that the *Nightwatches* presents simply a disjointed turmoil of diatribes and ghastly scenes, merely a harsh satirical tour, amounts to a misleading truism.

Replete with images of death, disintegration, and entropy, this book is no longer moored in the Enlightenment bedrock of theodicy and reason. Rather, Bonaventura's oppositional attitude has its own coherent aesthetic that anticipates traits we encounter in expressionism and existentialism. Many things converged to foster Bonaventura's anguish: the above-mentioned epochal disorder of the French Revolution was at hand, exhibited in the Terror and the Napoleonic wars; the flowering of individualism climaxed in the new Kantian subjectivist philosophy; romantic thinkers soon were elaborating a modern psychology that featured the concept of the unconscious, while the fear persisted that human beings might be mechanical entities, as, for example, materialists like Julien

Offray de La Mettrie had asserted in the treatise *L'homme machine* (1748), and therefore be will-less and soulless puppets.

I propose the term *tantric romanticism* to distinguish Bonaventura's response to his times and his inability to believe in the age's proclamation of human progress. The *Nightwatches* independently admitted the presence of monstrosities, such as those that the painter Francisco de Goya feared were emanating from our dream world as the Enlightenment waned. Bonaventura did not know Goya's etching *The Sleep of Reason Produces Monsters* from 1797–99, but as we see in climactic Nightwatch 16, he was deeply affected by Hogarth's famous last work, *The Tailpiece*, filled with apocalyptic imagery of decline and disintegration.

We may reject Bonaventura's "tantric" vision on religious or philosophic grounds as perverse and therefore unacceptable as genuine art. The historical impediments to receptivity of Bonaventura are less weighty. Each reader will grasp features of the work's structural complexity according to his or her own familiarity with literature of the period that gave it birth; however, because romantic themes and devices have so deeply affected modern writing, most details in the *Nightwatches* today possess a basic resonance. The work is obviously a mosaic, but it is not necessary to know about romantic adulation of the fragment as a formal principle in art to sense how Bonaventura, through skillful arrangement, produces turbulence, irregularity, and anxiety, a jaggedness that is the objective correlative to the flow of events in a chaotic universe and mirrors the quirky logic of Kreuzgang's perceptions. Even the work's idiosyncratic punctuation, with its frequent use of dashes (—) and leaders (. . .), often in combination with a semicolon or comma, to indicate shift of focus or trailing off of a thought, contributes to the sense of following the movement of a mind. (In the English version, these combinations will be reduced to a dash or leaders only.) There is no simplistic plot line, but the development of interlocking motif patterns provides a narrative rhythm. Initiated readers will recognize further that this motivic variation also permits a running commentary on romantic and earlier thought, for the work almost bursts with allusions, parodies, paraphrases, quotations, and names, bits and pieces of cultural heritage. These appear as elements subordinate to the narrator's mentality. Here we detect the deep structural impact of Laurence Sterne's influential first-person novel *The Life and Opinions of Tristram Shandy, Gentleman* (1759–67). Except that in the case of the *Nightwatches*, such subjective control by the unknown author finally excludes peace of mind.

In assembling a repertory of literary and artistic expression, the narrator Kreuzgang creates a theory of stages in the evolution of culture that bears a formal likeness to the philosopher Giambattista Vico's concept in *The New Science* (*La scienza nuova*, 1720s), which became very influential during modernism through writers like James Joyce. However, in Bonaventura's version of cultural development, as expressed in Kreuzgang's thought, while indeed a foundational theocratic age is succeeded by an aristocratic or heroic age, and then a democratic age, there is no *ricorso* or reconstitution of culture once human consciousness has descended all the way down from the lofty plane of the gods to the banal reality of humankind; rather, dissolution is final. For Bonaventura the world-historical axial figure in the downward career of the human race is Shakespeare, and the ultimate incarnation of his voice according to the *Nightwatches* is the clown as successor to Hamlet. Bonaventura is among the important romantics who analyze the early-modern protagonists Faust, Hamlet, and Don Juan alongside ancient protagonists like Oedipus as mythic figures through whom we may gain insights into mankind. His bleakness and social conscience also made him anticipate the late romantic Georg Büchner (1813–37) and thus be accepted as congenial to the German expressionists. Viewed in a longer trajectory, his sardonic anger at the cruelty and corruption of human society furthermore foreshadowed in a general way the raging of anarchic nihilists like the novelist Céline (Louis-Ferdinand Destouches) in the mid-twentieth century.

The sixteen "vigils" or "nightwatches" fall roughly into a series of groups, each progressing from satire to despair and tragedy, while the work as a whole intensifies cycle by cycle with unrelenting consistency toward the spiritual catastrophe in its final chapter. In the earlier chapters, the narrator is noticeably more a commentator on happenings he witnesses, or acts as a listener while others relate various stories. But he becomes increasingly involved with, and speaks more and more of and for himself, so that the work as a whole progressively turns into a self-revelation. Jeffrey Sammons sees "a kind of structural counter-point"—on the one hand "as an external form a cyclical movement boring ever deeper into the empty core of the universe," and on the other, "the convergence of two lines of presentation: the intellectual content . . . and the personality of the watchman" (Sammons 1965, 102). The narrator's ironic distance and personal alienation go together, because the *ego* is one of the book's chief subjects, as well as its principal instrument for probing the nature of existence. While the naive and innocent suffer pain, the misanthropes and cynics in the *Nightwatches* who do exchange a few signs of recognition share only their knowledge of the world's perversity. Otherwise the watchman, like the subnarrators, really engages in a lonely monologue, as the final page drastically under-scores. What is more, the oppressive twinned realities of transi-toriness and eternity shape the meaning of any sentimental devel-opment; the entire pattern of individuation and the ages of Man is reduced to truncated segments in a nightmare. The juxtaposition of these facts in a kind of spatial arbitrariness expresses the aimless, crushing monotony of existence.

If we feel Bonaventura's despair to be genuine, one of the first questions must then be why this impulse did not disrupt his book—an attempt, after all, at communication, from which we could perhaps infer some hope for meaning. If he was trying to test the reality of divine love through negation, did he drift from an eschatological yearning into nihilistic despair as his subject over-whelmed him? Should we regard the *Nightwatches* as an artistic failure if the author was defeated in his purpose and lured into the abyss? It so happens that Kreuzgang consistently defines the true artist's role otherwise under the baleful star of the modern age, overturning the traditional assumption that every artist sets out, necessarily and properly, to express final trust in a higher order. We could not imagine a spokesman more ready and able to expose the deficiencies of his own viewpoint, more bent on unmitigated disillusionment.

Indeed, Kreuzgang—so far as we can tell by internal evidence—is the highest ironist in the book's world, and the cause of his suffering is that he cannot honestly detect the sway of any supreme Author worthy of reverence. English-speaking readers will be interested in his frequent allusions to the darker insights of Shakespeare. It would be no exaggeration to define the art of the *Nightwatches* as an attempt to portray life as "a tale told by an idiot, full of sound and fury, signifying nothing." The particular character of that Nothing which obsesses Bonaventura requires careful scrutiny. Notable in this connection is that he never despises genuine artists, of whom he mentions more than a dozen in passing; true artistry is virtually the only value he respects. And since the sixteen nightwatches formulate their message in large measure by means of literary quotation and reference to the arts and the artist problem, creative consciousness may be regarded as the strong framework containing the author's nihilism. On one level, the book tells of the narrator's struggle against prosaic life. Neither Bonaventura as author nor Kreuzgang as fictive speaker, however, aims simply at manifesting his own artistic sovereignty over a world his mind invents or interprets. Apparent arbitrariness may be the compositional method, but romantic irony is not the final rationale; such a triumph of the creative ego, posited by leading romantics around 1800, is denied as a delusion. I shall now trace the main steps in this simultaneous statement on delusion and disillusionment.

THE FICTION OF KREUZGANG'S EXPERIENCE
AND CONSCIOUSNESS

If we reconstruct the rough chronology of experiences to make it clear in prosaic terms—an act that naturally contravenes the spirit as well as actual sequence of the work—we gain this approximate picture: The narrator was conceived on Christmas when his Gypsy mother and necromancer father fatefully interrupted the latter's conjuration of the devil. His mother put him in a casket at a crossroads so that a gullible, pious shoemaker would find him while treasure hunting. Raised in the image of the mystic Jacob Boehme and the mastersinger Hans Sachs, both cobblers (and folk figures idealized by the German romantics), young Kreuzgang begins to lose his innocence through over-acute intellect. His social satire as a budding poet lands him rather soon in the madhouse. There he succumbs to love for Ophelia, the insane actress who had once played opposite him in *Hamlet* but lost her own identity and became her role. Her death in childbirth on a ghostly storm-lit night elicits one of the two tears that the narrator ever manages to shed. The next drops for the confiscated puppet Hanswurst (Jack Sausage or Clown), with whom he associates himself while employed as a marionette master after his release from the asylum. The authorities disband the troupe as a political threat during the unrest attending the French Revolution, for the traditional puppet play of Judith and Holofernes incites the peasants to violent rebellion.

At this juncture, the defeated poet takes a steady job as night watchman, in which we actually first meet him in the book's opening chapters, where he becomes involved in the struggle between a confident dying atheist and a cruel, corrupt church. It is during the poet's career as watchman that the various minor stories occur or are told. There is his interference with an adulterous couple, whom he turns over to the pedantic husband, an execution-loving judge, in revenge for the hollow romantic clichés they use to mask their lust; his hearing of the story of the incestuous fratricide Don Juan, and retelling of it; the piteous suicide of the town's unsuccessful poet, who hangs himself with the cord from the returned manuscript of his tragedy titled *Man*; the secret live burial of an Ursuline nun who has borne a child, followed by the history of the once blind young father, who curses his own recovery of physical sight, which helped precipitate the disaster; the attempt to dissuade from suicide a person who proves to be an actor diligently studying his part; a visit to an art museum, with sardonic commentary on modern adulation of antiquity; and finally, Kreuzgang's discovery of his own ancestry and opening of his father's grave. The above condensation regrettably must omit many choice details, of which there is a rewarding abundance.

The culmination of nihilistic despair in the birth and death trauma of Nightwatch 16 would, in this heavy-handed reconstruction, ordinarily be expected to fall at the beginning or furnish a starting point with powerful memories. But Bonaventura carefully deprives us of any feeling of continuity such as might govern a sentimental tale. While he constantly drops storytelling hints that show he is in total control, many sudden shifts occur in season, hour, and environment, and the work is interrupted over and over again for harangues, monologues, and observations given or reported by the watchman. These features reflect especially the influence of the then-popular novelist Jean Paul Richter, as numerous critics have noted. Events are often related through projection into other art forms, such as woodcuts, paintings, sculpture, or drama. Thereby Bonaventura counteracts the mesmerizing effect of romanesque flow and creates a new narrative ambience that serves his view of art. Even a cursory reading suffices to reveal that Night in the *Nightwatches* is not simply a phase of time but a medium for a particular revelation of truth. Of course, there are many echoes of the romantic discovery of night as a special realm of the mind and spirit. But Bonaventura very explicitly controverts the recently deceased poet Novalis's approach to immortality through it, or any connection with love and faith as final references. This is evident in the final Nightwatch 16, when a bereft lover (whose behavior travesties Novalis's biography) attempts to retain his beloved's image in a tryst at the cemetery; but as in the case of all the dead, her wraith—obviously only a poetic memory—dissolves away into nothingness.

Nightwatches 4 and 5 define this new "antiromantic" or disillusionistic function of night, and show beyond a doubt that the stage props of lightning, swirling wind, obscuring clouds, and other imagery of terror or sudden illumination in the book serve a purposely harsh black-and-white technique. Toward the end of Nightwatch 4, the watchman observes a cloaked figure enter the gloomy cathedral and try to kill himself with a dagger. It is an entertaining spectacle of tragic nobility, and the delighted narrator has no desire at all to intervene. But when the stranger remains frozen at the stroke of midnight, unable to stab, Kreuzgang asks for his story, which is forthwith told in the form of a puppet play, to the imaginary accompaniment of Mozart, played badly by village musicians. This is a sardonic double reference to the Don Juan problem and to the hopeless confusion of a divine spark in human nature—themes that recur throughout the book. The clown Hanswurst romps about functioning as Fate and chorus. Two nameless brothers, one using prose, the other poor verse, come on stage, then a *commedia dell'arte* Columbine and a page. The prosaic brother thumps his wooden chest at the sight of her and starts using verses, but Hanswurst arbitrarily crashes into him when he attempts to pursue her. Next Columbine appears in a duet with the other brother, whereupon Hanswurst leads the disappointed one on stage and, to his surprise, now finds a real heart under the flap on the latter's wooden chest. When the two brothers meet and Columbine is introduced as the other's wife, the one with a heart falls in a heap. In the last act, he tries to explain to Columbine that the director confounded things and mistakenly gave her to her own brother. But being rejected in his sinister advances, he tricks the husband, his brother, into killing her, their sister, and the innocent page for suspected adultery. He is just about to follow his brother in suicide, when a wire snaps and his hand is left dangling forever. Hanswurst consoles with the remark that one should not take farce for anything higher than farce, and the wooden clowns praise the director for abolishing Greek Fate and introducing a moral order with freewill in the theater—one of many slaps at the ethical pretensions of German classical drama.

The puppet story in Nightwatch 4 actually constitutes a denial of freewill. Under the spell of multiple satire (for instance, among other things the plot probably parodies Friedrich Schiller's recent tragedy *The Bride of Messina* [1803]), the impact of this negation is still somewhat delayed. But in the course of the work, we begin to recognize that Bonaventura's mockery rests on no positive convictions. Nightwatch 9, set in the insane asylum, underscores the lack of any supreme model of order through its depiction of a Creator who is at best an incompetent meddler and bungler. Kreuzgang himself cannot believe in the reality of a morality or justice that would be the implicit ideal normally held by a satirist who scourges the world's deceivers and fools for their deviation therefrom. Laughter proves here to be not a corrective instrument but a defense against meaninglessness. As a result of the midnight encounter in Nightwatch 4, the watchman finds himself uncomfortably awake at morning in hated daylight and resolves to apply the following soporific in Nightwatch 5:

> Thus I had nothing better to do than to translate my poetically mad night into clear boring prose for myself, and I brought to paper the madman's life, well motivated and reasoned, and had it printed for the amusement and pleasure of the judicious day-wanderers. Actually, however, it was only a means to tire myself, and I wanted to read it aloud to myself on this nightwatch so as not to have to deal with prose and the day a second time.

Night, then, is the sphere of poetry and truth, while day is the sphere of prose and deception. Nonetheless, what follows in the retelling can easily startle or confuse us, for what we read is a carefully drawn story of the flesh-and-blood brothers Juan and Ponce, in an omniscient third-person account expounding the consequences of the former's insanely jealous love for Ines, whom he eventually discovers to be his sister. All the marionettes from the puppet play acquire personal names and individual coloration, and the action springs from their character and motivation. The clowns have disappeared who personified abstract forces. Juan's evident repression of his unconscious recognition of kinship, and its inexorable deformation into crime as it rises to the surface, could delight any present-day reader familiar with Freudian patterns. Unfortunately, however, the narration in Nightwatch 5 is explicitly intended to contrast with Nightwatch 4 as a lesser with a greater form. Kreuzgang actually tells us point blank that the psychological and sentimental realism of his second version lacks the veracity of the savage mechanical farce. This assertion predates by almost a century the absurdist playwright Alfred Jarry's ostentation of the monstrous consciousness of Père Ubu in place of older European tragedy. I shall return to this matter. Suffice it for now to point to the consistency between the conception of farce and the stark black-and-white ambience of night.

Bonaventura's obsession with the possibility man is only a machine and his concern over attaining truth intensify grippingly in Nightwatch 14. This episode of the watchman's struggle against love comes late in the book as it gets deeper into the heart of the crisis—his tormentingly ambivalent attitude toward human emotions under the threat of their probable meaninglessness. Kreuzgang's attraction to the illusion in which his feminine counterpart, the actress, lives is recounted in fragmentary notes, that is, in the quirkish prose-poems he relates he found himself composing, and the letters they exchanged as Hamlet and Ophelia. In order to "communicate," the watchman has simply had to accept her view of him as "really" Hamlet. Another sign of the momentary breakdown of his studied isolation from humankind is his idea of propagating a race of "fools" like himself to oppose bourgeois civilization. This amounts to a sentimental rationalization—as we soon learn.

The pair's odd love letters examine the whole question of identity, while jabbing at various German philosophers. Ophelia still seeks reassurance in the depth of delusion, using the onion metaphor of self-analysis, that is, peeling away all attributes to reach a true visage beneath the masks of an actor in a dreamlike play: "See, now I will never be able to find out whether I am a dream—whether it is merely play or truth, and whether the truth in turn is more than play—one shell covers the next, and I am often on the verge of losing my mind over this." Ophelia would like to rehearse her way out of mere role back to herself: "Help me read my role backwards, till I reach myself, . . . See, there I am trying to catch myself, but I am always running ahead of myself and my name behind, and now in turn I am renouncing the role—but the role is not I."

A rather self-serving Hamlet replies that she should not brood on such matters as "to be or not to be," since there is nothing but dust and hellish mockery behind the role, but should seal a reasonable match. And she accepts him, because—in her own words—he is written into her role as a cue. Dying after bearing his dead child, the actress who thought she was Ophelia emerges from her obsession in an eloquent disillusionment that, like Don Quixote's at the conclusion of Cervantes's novel, is a moving act of faith:

> The role comes to an end, but the I remains, and they bury only the role. Praise God that I am coming out of the play and can put aside my assumed name; after the play the I commences! . . . There it is, already standing back of the wings and waiting for its cue; when only the curtain is first all the way down! —Ah, I love you! That is the final speech in the play and it alone do I seek to retain from my role—it was the most beautiful passage! The rest they may bury!

Her confidence in her own permanent identity grows out of the (for her) meaningful encounter with a "thou," another's existence. Witnessing her brave interpretation of the world theater does not, however, alter the watchman's atheism. Rather, this loss crushes him as an enormous failure, aggravates his loneliness, and forces him into further defensive solipsism, for he has now personally experienced the entrapment of people by the devices of nature.

After Ophelia's death, Kreuzgang-Hamlet probes the nature of laughter as an expression of despair and misanthropy and recognizes his own counterpart in the clown Hanswurst in Nightwatch 15. Even before Ophelia's death in Nightwatch 15, the love union ("exchange of selves")—which he passes over as if such memories are too painful in their deceiving beauty—has caused terrible anxiety in him, the nightmare of having forever and inexorably an identity. An eternity of isolation with the self is now a horrifying prospect indeed:

> Then I saw myself with me alone in the Nothing, only the late earth was still flickering far out in the distance, as an extinguishing spark—but it was only a thought of mine which was just ending. A single tone quavered gravely and earnestly through the void—it was time chiming out, and eternity now set in. I had now ceased

thinking everything else, and was thinking only myself! No object was to be found round about but the great dreadful I which feasted on itself and in devouring constantly regenerated itself. I was not sinking, for there was no longer space; just as little did I seem to float upward. Variety had disappeared simultaneously with time, and there reigned a horrible, eternally void tedium. Beyond myself I tried to annihilate myself—but I remained and felt myself immortal!

It is therefore a relief to believe there is nothing after death. Here a peculiar shift occurs in romantic thought—a change I will relate below to Bonaventura's treatment of cosmological metaphors rooted in German and European literary tradition. He recognizes that the post-Kantian idea of the ego or subject as a creative consciousness or a supreme and transcendent entity, out of which all else emanates, is a model for a universe. But that universe would be at war with itself, condemned to be itself, to feed on and bring forth itself only.

The opening episode of the atheist in Nightwatch 1 seemed momentarily to promise some affirmation of life in and of itself as a value, in opposition to a spurious afterlife. By this juncture in the book, however, the unshakable freethinker and sincere family in Nightwatches 1, 2, and 3 acquire a definite structural function of picturing the marvelous vernal state of any absolute faith, though it be engulfed by a threatening world. The arrangement allows readers to appreciate the fundamental experience or discovery that the delusion of faith is always "retrospective" to real consciousness. This lost state of faith the watchman once knew himself—and the book opens after his own fall, a fact that is unknown to us readers in the initial pages. The Ophelia tragedy is not narrated until Nightwatch 14, but Kreuzgang-Hamlet has already suffered it when we first encounter him. His exile from childhood piety and this drastic confirmation of life's deception in the case of Ophelia, both happenings as yet unmentioned, generate the strange tension we immediately sense in the words of the odd voice that addresses us in the book's first pages.

Hence, too, the puzzling, tender comparison of the atheist with the great baroque mystic Jacob Boehme in the last paragraph of Nightwatch 1. At the start, atheism has the force of a noble sentiment and comforting doctrine, a guaranty of eternal bliss, that is, extinction. But the celestial "music" that the dying atheist hears in Nightwatch 1 devolves into a mocking echo of the watchman's self by Nightwatch 13, when he asks nature for an answer to the fragmentary riddle of man: "I hear nothing but echo, echo of my own speech—am I then alone?" The lack of any answer except the echo of the question is in this case the answer. And as the *Nightwatches* closes, the narrator has just watched his dead father's hand, symbolic vestige of Faustian defiance, crumble to dust. The cult of Titanism, too, is suddenly rendered insignificant, for no kind of rebellion alters man's futility one iota. Neither does any attempted spiritualization. Therefore Kreuzgang utters the last words of the book with agonized finality:

> I strew this handful of paternal dust into the air and it remains—
> Nothing!
> On the grave beyond, the visionary is still standing and embracing Nothing!
> And the echo in the charnel house cries for the last time NOTHING!

DISTURBING IDEAS / HISTORICAL TRAUMA: BIRTH PANGS OF (TANTRIC) ROMANTICISM

Nightwatch 13 prepares us for this nadir of despair in the cry "Nothing!" through its "Dithyramb on Spring," which invokes the romantic metaphor complex of rebirth, inherited from Renaissance cosmology, but reaches disturbing conclusions through it. As (for example) in Novalis's novel *Heinrich von Ofterdingen*, published posthumously in 1802 and obviously known to Bonaventura, we witness how a frozen world is redeemed at springtime by the power of light and fire. The sun, playing the role of the Divine Father or creative ether, inspirits life in its bride the earth. At this point, however, the watchman interrupts with the unanswerable question of why man has the misfortune of appearing as observer-participant in this colossal drama under the ultimate sign of entropy. For once we accept that the cosmos is running downhill toward extinction, nature is only a cruel sketch, a fragment broken off without meaningful continuation; and because man has lost his primitive protective naiveté, all he can now know is the echo of his own thoughts trapped within a dying system. The book fully grants the existence of a *natura naturans*, but its whole motion is unmasked as a nightmare.

In the final chapter, the watchman rails against the creation such as he views it: "These myriads of worlds roar through all their heavens only by the gigantic force of nature, and this terrifying spawner who has spawned everything and herself with it, has no heart in her own breast, but for a pastime only forms little ones which she passes around." As I have suggested, the similarity of attributes (terrible, monstrous, self-generating, and self-consuming) indicates that the ego is now a model for the entire universe in Bonaventura's eyes. His several references to evolution never affirm even remotely the idea of an expansion of consciousness within the whole of created nature as a gradual triumph of the spirit; rather, he views the overall organic development of consciousness simply as a by-product of an enclosed system, somewhat in analogy to individuation within one's skin. The human beings who appear with "hearts" are simply outgrowths of evolution. That the development of sentiments means useless tragedy is only an unfortunate fact of no consequence to the system. With a lack of concern equal to that of a puppet master in assigning destinies (or playing out stories), nature has spawned hearts.

Bonaventura's gaze into the abyss of nature remarkably resembles the anguished perception by Johann Wolfgang von Goethe's Werther, in the letter of August 18 in *The Sorrows of Young Werther* (1774), concluding (trans. GG): "My heart is undermined by the consumptive power which lies hidden in the entirety of nature; which has formed nothing that did not destroy its neighbor, destroy itself. And so I reel anguished. Heaven and earth and their interacting forces about me: I see nothing but an eternally devouring, eternally regurgitating monster." The related fear that life is a ridiculous puppet spectacle occurs in Werther's letter of January 20: "I play away, rather I am played with like a marionette and sometimes grasp my neighbor by his wooden hand and recoil shuddering."

Bonaventura does not try to evade this threat to the Sturm und Drang confidence in nature felt by Goethe and, next, faced by romantic spirits. Rather than mitigate the primal horror of existence, which is ordinarily subordinated in the standard German poetic cosmology of organic development, he calls into question any rationalization of suffering endured by the "heart." Thus the theosophist mystic Jacob Boehme's concept of a contest in the very processes of the universe between Love and Anger may be as familiar in the *Nightwatches* as it is generally in German romanticism and among many English romantics like William Blake. But instead of hinting at some ultimate transfiguration of life that is being worked out, Bonaventura announces a triumph of darkness and hate. One of the watchman's more elaborate references to this struggle within his own personality is another perverse variation upon the metaphor of the marriage of heaven and earth. He muses "that the very devil himself, in order to play a trick on heaven, slipped into the bed of a just canonized saint during a dark night and inscribed me there as it were as a *lex cruciata* for our Lord God, over which he should break his head on Judgment Day."

Lex cruciata refers to the law of biological inheritance and is, of course, another pun on *cross*, for Kreuzgang. In the grisly recognition scene of the final Nightwatch 16, of which I intend to speak again, the narrator hears from his Gypsy mother the maxim of their kind. It is a total reversal of romantic values and of the sense of the romantic vision of evolution as an upward striving: "It is greater to hate the world than to love it." This negativism appears logically in the several models for the supreme artist of such a vexatious creation. One of the God-figures is the aforementioned inmate at the insane asylum in Nightwatch 9 who thinks he is the Creator. On several levels of meaning, the madhouse is a representation of micro- and macro-cosmic relationships. In the "Monologue of the Insane Creator of the World," a pathetic, indecisive person expresses views that are, ambiguously, acknowledged products of mental aberration. Reviewing his work, this self-appointed God is sorry that he created the world in which man is a misfit by virtue of endowment with a misleading, hurtful spark of divinity. But though he admits that he has bungled, he is equally confused as to what remedy to apply, beyond letting the race muddle along with its delusions in the chaos until he can bring himself to appoint a day of final judgment—that is, ultimate extinction. The idea of having to grant human beings their overweening dream of immortality and therefore tolerate them for eternity frightens the mad creator. He is already quite annoyed that humanity's inquisitive probing through science encroaches on his lordly prerogatives. The other important God-figure is the marionette director, who can quite arbitrarily pull a wire and decide a destiny. By contrast, he appears to be a powerful, indifferent demiurge; his theater is characterized by the ridiculous gestures and harsh laughter of clowns. Nonetheless, like the frustrated town poet, he kills himself over the loss of his private universe, which gets out of control, that is, which mirrors the primitive relationships of the larger world accurately enough to trigger violence, with its repercussions.

Nightwatch 11 closes with the recognition that the dream of life and love brings unbearable pain and that mother nature herself actually is suffering. What is crucial in Kreuzgang's passing allusion to Napoleon at the opening of Nightwatch 12 ("Who does not know the solar eagle who soars through recent history! . . .") is its anguished doubleness. On the one hand, the amazing rise of Napoleon stokes the Promethean dream inherited from Sturm und Drang; Napoleon epitomizes the individual who is achieving virtually divine status in his world through sheer daring and genius. Among contemporary artists whom Kreuzgang could have cited, Ludwig van Beethoven initially reacted by dedicating a symphony to Napoleon; later Beethoven famously recanted in disappointment. As Kreuzgang already understands must happen and says in this nightwatch, unless a shining hero dies quite soon, his luster invariably tarnishes and he must resort to blinding his fellow men to maintain his status, for inevitably "the egoist returns" and has recourse to oppression. In the yearning of would-be self-empowering individualists to burst the limits of their world, Bonaventura detects the explosive turmoil and torment that is manifested in the violence of the times. Yet the Promethean pretense running through the culture contrasts poorly with the mediocrity of the majority, as he illustrates. As the narrator examines the age's hopelessly contradictory emotions, we sense the emergence of existential nausea over the prevailing phoniness in people and society.

DISCOVERY OF A DANGEROUS PSYCHOLOGICAL KEY

Shifting our focus slightly, we can consider the hypertropic egos of the madhouse and regular society also as variations upon the ego-model in Kreuzgang's nightmare. On one level, each figure's story is a case of extreme loneliness, an exclusion from and of "normal" life—which they bitterly expose. On another level, the suicide or insanity of each indicates the direction in which consciousness develops as it expands in the drive for absolute supremacy. The trend is toward perversion and even annihilation—all creation is tragic through its own inherent principle. The idea of entropy seems to imply the correlative of suicide for the self-labeled identity within its universe. In this sense, the final cry of the book is a moment when Nothingness overwhelms Kreuzgang and when his mind merges with the universal process and end of being.

Obviously, we are dealing here with a complex picture, because the *Nightwatches* repeatedly portrays persons as helpless dolls and the narrator himself often feels like a puppet. In the dense space of some 150 pages Bonaventura incorporates all important phases in the development of the marionette theme in German since the reaction to Enlightenment rationalism. Scorning popular and lower forms of theater, including puppet plays and fairytales, as manifestations of the barbaric, retrograde, and superstitious in the folk, rationalist critics such as Johann Christoph Gottsched (1700–1766) had tried to banish Hanswurst from the stage. It seemed necessary if they were to lift art to a classical, ethical, progressive plane. But the German preromantics soon rallied to the defense of folk theater and the clown. For young Goethe and Sturm und Drang authors generally, the puppet acquired new literary value as a symbol variously of an outside, dead society or of elementary vitality and the frustrated genius and the arbitrariness of the powers of fate operating against his freedom. In Ludwig Tieck's novel *William Lovell* (1795-96) and in early romanticism, the marionette expressed a subjective fatalism on the part of the aspiring class of artists—their fear of the existence of a mechanical world instead of one governed by the dynamic natural processes with which their creative theory was linked. The marionette play thus provided a pattern of gestures for a new kind of style.

Finally, the romantic concept of the "organic" began to exclude the idea of a dynamic or irrational unfolding in favor of transcendental significance in art. Mature romantic irony, or the control by art over life, introduced a perspective for the genius not as a Sturm und Drang Prometheus in chains but as a sublime puppeteer. The primitivism of the marionette form permitted allegorical manipulation of the author's creatures. Eventually, it became evident that such an emphasis upon a shaping idea or authorial mind would tend to equalize necessity and freedom for a fictive protagonist. This meant the inevitable nullification of the tragic hero's individualism based on dynamic qualities, and here was one basis in German literature for the gradual growth of the late-romantic "fate drama" (*Schicksalstragödie*) in which man is a pawn of dark forces. The English gothic mode, too, fed into this tendency. To name a prominent example: we encounter the persistence of gothicism and the blending of the British and German romantic streams in the verse drama *Death's Jest-Book* (1829) by Thomas Lovell Beddoes, who was attracted to Germany to study medicine and subsequently spent most of his life in Europe. The attitude behind such plays exhibiting fate or a curse also contributed its measure to the eventual formation of European naturalist drama in the later nineteenth century, for it was easy to leap from invoking inherently obscure factors such as a curse to invoking various allegedly scientific factors of determinism.

Problematic was that the basis for the dignity of the tragic hero was eroded. Thus—as Bonaventura precociously says in several places, overleaping naturalistic realism and adumbrating theater of the absurd—comedy logically replaces tragedy; and as a corollary, the puppet becomes the highest form of actor, for his wooden gestures are closest in essence to those of ancient masked drama. In this connection, I shall now turn to that aspect of Bonaventura's work which may most intrigue many present-day readers. They cannot fail to notice that he develops the story of Don Juan's incestuous and fratricidal mania in Nightwatch 5 explicitly on the Oedipal pattern and arrives at the watchman's birth trauma in a circuitous approach to the root of evil deep in the self. In the grisly discovery of Nightwatch 16, the narrator exclaims: "What a clear light dawned in me after this speech, that only psychologists can imagine; the key to my Self was tendered me, and for the first time I opened with astonishment and secret trembling the long-barred door—the inside looked like Bluebeard's chamber, and it would have strangled me had I been less fearless. It was a dangerous psychological key!"

This weird final nightwatch is intended to symbolize the embodiment of the contesting forces in Kreuzgang rather than be a confessional revelation. Throughout the book sexual drives are regarded as among the mechanisms that make puppet-humanity perform its farcical tragedy. It is plain that Bonaventura had absorbed many implications of general romantic psychology, on which Sigmund Freud and Carl G. Jung and others later built with slight modifications, the way Charles Darwin and the naturalists built on romantic biology with its thesis of evolution. In fact, the two fields of study were already unified in advanced romantic thought, as the intellectual historian Henri Ellenberger has shown. An outline must suffice here. The idea that individuation recapitulated and continued evolution was widespread around 1800. Leading scientists accepted the appearance of matter out of the void, organic life out of matter, and spiritual life within organic nature as a meaningful process. Many regarded the growth of the human being as an analogous pattern of emergence from unconsciousness to consciousness. The opening sentence of the treatise *Psyche: Zur Entwicklungsgeschichte der Seele* (1846; Psyche: The developmental history of the soul) by the eminent biologist and psychologist, as well as art critic, Carl G.

Carus can serve to illustrate the widespread understanding of this relationship in high romanticism: "The key to cognition of the nature of conscious psychological life lies in the region of unconscious psychological life" (trans. GG).

The important point is that Bonaventura is not novel because he recognizes the existence of shaping impulses behind the facade of the ego, but because he casts doubt on the meaningfulness of the whole evolutionary scheme of life from top to bottom and bottom to top. He certainly senses the depths of the mind—but as an abyss. Hence although the book's structure suggests formally the psychoanalytic release of repressed materials, it advances to an outcome that is precisely opposite of the one expected of a therapeutic process. The acquisition of self-knowledge cannot effect any conventional normalization here, since in learning to hate a hateful universe, paradoxically, the watchman exemplifies its very perversity. He himself grasps the strange unity of defiance and defeat, while denying that unity tragic stature in the final analysis. The romantic quest for a key to both inner and outer knowledge led many, like the subjective idealist Friedrich Schelling (whom some of the earliest connoisseurs suspected might be Bonaventura), through nature philosophy to metaphysical symbolization. But among the truly new directions in the early nineteenth century for interpreting the given "facts" about life patterns of the creature *homo sapiens*, the most productive comparisons we can draw are with troubled contemporaries of the romantics such as Heinrich von Kleist and Georg Büchner.

In his famous essay "On the Marionette Theater" (1810), Kleist proposes that man can return to a state of "grace" only by reapproaching himself from his hidden side. The image of the astonishingly agile bear who can outfence a rational opponent is one of his many hints that unconscious factors will restore man's lost balance. He also identifies grace with the unconsciousness of puppets' movements. Their unreflecting physical purity suggests the paradise from which humanity has fallen by virtue of tasting of the tree of knowledge. The paradigm of an ascending restoration is the sequence: "marionette" (total unconsciousness), "man" (sentimental split), "god" (total consciousness indistinguishable from spontaneous nature). Kleist resembles Bonaventura in denying the validity of Kantian moral imperatives arrived at through rational abstraction, but is unlike him in often glorifying nature's deep promptings, laws that (to borrow Nietzsche's terms) are Dionysian rather than Apollonian. While the unconscious is implicit in Bonaventura's model of man as puppet, he envisions no regaining of a golden age through its agency. The story of being ends with *Man: A Tragedy*, as the town poet sums it up before hanging himself in Nightwatch 8. Bonaventura may take for granted that hidden springs impel human beings and that their dreams are distorted releases of inner psychic movement. But just as he is nauseated by modern humanity's sentimental projections into the ruins of a primal era (e.g., Greek antiquity), so he impatiently repudiates psychological realism as a mere deceptive surface and exposes instead the inauthentic view of society of itself as a moral order and of human beings as sentimental personalities. It is a very pained admission.

FOUNDATIONS OF A LITERATURE OF THE ABSURD

Perhaps the only significant moments when Kreuzgang seems to exult in dark impulses are the several anarchistic gestures that he admires or indulges in—for example, there is the boy in Nightwatch 6 who shoots himself during the watchman's false alarm of an onrushing apocalypse, just to see whether he can avoid participating in God's grand finale to time. In brief, Bonaventura regards communal life as an amoral pyramid of structured power, which wears the mask of "society," and human history as a process of deformation from barbaric splendor to grotesque farce. This ethical rage brings him closer to the sphere of Georg Büchner, who also was concerned over the compulsiveness of human actions and the villainous oppression of man by man through manipulation of the natural drives in the social order. Giving way to nihilistic despair, Bonaventura does not, however, balance his own vision of grinding ennui and transitoriness with a program of potential revolutionary redemption. His cry that the clown must replace the tragic victim remains strictly an artistic rather than social manifesto, anticipating certain elements in the aesthetic of the grotesque and absurd today. His puppet theater is a compact and obvious microcosm based on the old theater of the Elizabethan and Jacobean era and Siglo de Oro—over whose metaphors he so often and so negatively broods.

In this respect he draws near to the German romantic founders of theater of the absurd, Ludwig Tieck (1773-1853) and Christian Dietrich Grabbe (1801-36), forerunners appreciated by Alfred Jarry and Luigi Pirandello, among other modernists. But in associating the unconscious or mechanical aspects of existence with an arbitrary assignment of human beings to particular roles, Bonaventura in 1804 already deals a double blow, on the one hand, to theodicy and, on the other, to the concept of progress deriving therefrom under the guise of organic laws or dialectical processes. The secular interpretive problem of the nineteenth century may be illustrated by the quarrel of Herbert Spencer and Thomas Huxley over the meaning of evolution. The former thought its cruel mechanisms should be allowed to operate freely so as to guarantee a "healthy" society through survival of the fittest. The latter held that all vital progress was, on the contrary, based on a struggle for moral evolution against deleterious aspects of greater nature, that civilization was a laboriously cultivated garden cut out of the jungle. Bonaventura, in a third position as skeptical nihilist, neither attempts to justify the laws of the jungle nor can honestly believe that the special garden is anything more than a delusion, a blindness excited by the fundamental natural force for continuing life blindly.

It was noted that the narrator's ramblings and flashbacks, as he reworks the materials of his life, bear some analogy to psychoanalysis. The novel evinces perhaps an even more pertinent foreshadowing of an insight of later psychological thought. Bonaventura gradually defines the emergence in his narrator's tormented intellect of a life-denying force, what Freud famously termed the death wish. In outline, Kreuzgang states that illusion is inherent in life itself; life continues through the masking of things in Apollonian light and color. Truth, he decides, is thus an attack on the deception of being. It is significant that the watchman, as satirist, does not himself escape the trap but must also become ridiculous. His encounter with Ophelia leads to no affirmation of a meaning; rather he admits the folly of his love affair. Similarly, he admits being taken in by the compulsion to talk a seeming suicide out of rejecting life; the party turns out to be an actor practicing his role of despair, for which he lacks any personal feeling. (This instructive moment of attempting to save an actor who is rehearsing suicide recurs in Ingmar Bergman's movie *The Magician* in the late twentieth century.) Such double deceptions only underscore the fraudulence of the world. When the cynic too is so easily victimized, no sure hold is left. The prescription given by the asylum doctor in Nightwatch 9 is less thinking, or none at all.

The mind, in exposing the system of the universe to be empty and absurd, drifts into its fateful orientation to Nothingness, even through its efforts to rebel against its alleged enslavement by vital instincts and drives. The conflict between good and evil or love and hate in the genesis of the watchman is no longer just the familiar theme from Sturm und Drang to explain the turbulence of wild heroes who live out the struggle between nature and perversion. Bonaventura's attitude toward nature is disturbingly ambivalent. Though he acknowledges its often piercing beauty, he is horrified by the grim inevitability of absolute extinction under its vernal mask. Ultimately, the mechanical, heartless, frozen triumphs— and hence Kreuzgang's obsession with motifs of death as rigidity and fragmentation and mutilation, as in his dream of the ancient gods in the museum or his vignette of the dying beggar in winter. The former are called a "torso of gods," the latter a "torso of nature," and the entire novel is riddled with expressions such as "stump" for "limb" and the like. Everything, both biological entities and created works of art, is perceived to be returning to the realm of lifelessness, disorganization. Humankind's works, including the entire glory of Greek civilization, become broken bits and sheer dust in the end.

In view of our actual state of consciousness, so Bonaventura proposes, only a savage marionette play is artistically true. Alfred

Jarry's *Ubu Roi* and Ramón María del Valle-Inclán's aesthetic of the *esperpento* (grotesque-absurd) are independent recapitulations of the same thought in the late nineteenth and early twentieth centuries. Reconsidered in a broader historical framework, however, many current repetitive exponents of absurdity are doing what Bonaventura fiercely denounced about then contemporary sentimental literature—they are providing a warm bath of self-pity, a new commercialized escape for jaded masses robbed of gripping beliefs and any authenticity. Negation of the formal message itself is the logical step that Bonaventura never took. Though numerous modern artists have indeed progressed to the point of halfhearted attempts at creating art that "denies" art, only total silence and abstinence from creative activities would fulfill the nihilistic logic. Even "happenings" and ostentatious "destructions" of work are merely evasions today, without any forthright facing of the dilemma of a dead end. Obviously, as a Kreuzgang might well have noticed were he still among us, the modern artistic community hangs on to its illusions, its life habits; only certain of its members are committing literal or figurative suicide, though many find a solution in insanity, and several tenacious camps of thriving professional "illusionists" can be named who sell the public various stunts of supposed destruction of art.

Bonaventura's rejection of freewill also sets him off, of course, from existentialists who—in agreement with Jean-Paul Sartre—conceive of a godless world but insist that human beings must accept their moral freedom and create values. In Bonaventura, man remains, despite any acquired knowledge of his condition or attempt at meaningful engagement, inevitably and hopelessly the dupe of godless nature. Unlike followers of Bertold Brecht who scourge human criminality and then revert to a faith in an ultimate solution (world transformation through communism)—betraying thereby their underlying kinship with bourgeois idealists—Bonaventura breaks off with an anguished cry but no answer to the reality of bestial habits and decadence. In the case of the *Nightwatches* we may be facing a precocious moment when a writer breaks through the "comforting" shell of gnostic pride in being nobly wounded and forlorn in the world, an attitude all too evident still in postmodernism, and discovers that there is no cruel demigod, instigator of a fallen creation, nor manipulative archons against whom to fight. There is just the Nothing, as the old waiter will think to himself in Ernest Hemingway's much later story "A Clean, Well-Lighted Place."

As many an absurdist such as Friedrich Dürrenmatt has opined, somewhat belatedly a century and a half after Bonaventura, when the world grows absurd in our eyes, tragedy must metamorphose into farce. Hence, as the *Nightwatches* already proposed long ago, Hanswurst eventually replaces Hamlet. Of course, Bonaventura's harsh laughter is a defense against the consequences of a loss of identity. It enables a temporizing retreat from the senseless world into total isolation vis-à-vis chaos. An inversion of positive romantic values must follow such inversion into oneself, into the vast emptiness of the self, so the book concludes.

It is worth returning to the late moment in the novel when the narrator's mother expresses the work's internal logic in this oracular dictum: "It is greater to hate the world than to love it; he who loves desires, he who hates is sufficient unto himself and needs nothing beyond the hate in his breast and no third party." We see here one scary direction that is taken in the aftermath of the Kantian relegation of all authority to the inherent structures of the mind, and of the post-Kantian attempt to create an ego philosophy capable of embracing total responsibility for the patterns of the perceived universe and man's own special situation as the subject beholding his world. The fragmentation process of European individualism is effectively completed in the statement quoted above: the single unit of being is sundered from all organic human relationships that depend on "love," that is, emotional acceptance and involvement. If one thinks "too much," the book shows often enough, it becomes very difficult to submit to the social context or the notions of "health" that social structure imposes. The alienated begin to insist more defiantly on retiring into private mental worlds, many to the extent of being classified as "sick."

Bonaventura knows that romantic introspection is leading to this impasse and that he himself, as a representative analyst of humankind, is penetrating into disagreeable, once better hidden recesses of the human mind. In this sense, his book compresses into a rapid series of scenes and discourses, a set of "discoveries" that, historically, have also occurred in various guises to mystics in different nations and epochs. But a radical "emptying out" of the human mind in order to achieve union with God is not the apparent goal in the *Nightwatches*. Bonaventura's fundamental awareness is that the human self must, in the course of things, discover its own limitations as a speck of consciousness attached to a dying animal within a doomed system. That even the products of the brain, that transitory organ which is the fountainhead of all human achievement, evil, and pretension, constitute only a phantasmagoria without validity or permanence. That humankind brings forth the mysterious script of the world theater through the interaction of minds in a collective tragedy, but both for the single persona and for all dramatis personae during the transitory life of our species, the script is nightmarishly and futilely finite:

> What now is this palace that can enclose a whole world and a heaven; this fairy castle in which love's wonders enchantingly delude; this microcosm in which all that is great and splendid and everything terrible and fearsome reside together in embryo, which brought forth temples and gods, inquisitions and devils; this tail-piece of the creation—the human head!—shelter for a worm! —Oh, what is the world if that which it thought is nothing, and everything in it only transitory fantasy! —What are the fantasies of earth, spring and the flowers, if the fantasy in this little orb is scattered as dust, if here in the inner Pantheon all gods crash from their pedestals, and worms and decay take possession! Oh, do not vaunt to me in any way the autonomy of the spirit—here lies its battered workshop, and the thousand threads with which it spun the tissue of the world are all rent and the world with them.

With this distillation of Shakespearian rants echoing Hamlet, the book reaches an operatic pitch of despair in Nightwatch 16.

In his great treatise *The World as Will and Representation* (*Die Welt als Wille und Vorstellung*, 1818), regarding tragedy as the highest genre, the philosopher Arthur Schopenhauer, a romantic atheist, saw the artist's function as a piercer of the veil of Maya or illusion, as a definer of the idea of Man. In works by the highest artists, consciousness momentarily redeems itself from bondage to life. While Bonaventura ostensibly denies tragedy, he actually substitutes in its place a modern existential anguish. He does not, then, directly anticipate Friedrich Nietzsche's more positive cry for authenticity of suffering in an attempt to transcend even the idea of Man. The sole point of contact is that in both cases the philosophic preparation for any chance for "truth" is the rigorous denunciation and rejection of Man, including the masses of deluded egos in their common separate dreams. This entails the task of exploring the puzzling unreality of human "identity."

Thus Bonaventura differs markedly from two prominent types of atheists of the late eighteenth and early nineteenth centuries. Unlike the Marquis de Sade, he does not make the leap to the proposition that God is dead, therefore all is permitted, and decide to glory in the opportunity for unlicensed self-aggrandizement with fellow "friends of crime" (Sade's "amis du crime") who lord it over normal people who are stupid enough to believe in moral laws and let themselves be enslaved. Nor does he strike the heroic pose of the most famous of all nineteenth-century absolute atheists, Max Stirner, who rejects the idea of Man along with God in *Der Einzige und sein Eigentum* (1844; *The Ego and Its Own*) but proposes a future utopia of cooperation among enlightened anarchs. Nor is there any hint in Bonaventura of a popular work like William Winwood Reade's *The Martyrdom of Man* (1872), which encouraged positivists of the Biedermeier and Victorian period to indulge in self-congratulatory confidence in their role as builders of a secular scientific future, to see themselves as banishing the enslaving phantoms of the past and marching from victory to victory, overcoming war, slavery, and religion.

Applying Northrup Frye's theory of modes (which Frye derives from Vico's views), in the *Nightwatches* we have a seeming dead end in literature, after a long steady descent from high to low mimesis, when protagonists are no longer capable of playing even the roles of "ironic comedy" or of parodying "tragic irony." In Bonaventura, if we apply Frye, "one notes a recurring tendency on the part of ironic comedy to ridicule and scold an audience assumed to be hankering after sentiment, solemnity, and the triumph of fidelity and approved moral standards." But we also already have in the watchman, as of 1804, "a character who, with the sympathy of the author or audience, repudiates such a society to the point of deliberately walking out of it, becoming thereby a kind of *pharmacos* [scapegoat] in reverse"; that is, we witness "an ironic deadlock in which the hero is regarded as a fool or worse by the fictional society, and yet impresses the real audience as having something more valuable than his society has"(Frye 1969, 48).

We are, in short, compelled to take sides by joining in the irony, no matter how ambiguous our position remains on so choosing. There are signs of an urge in such irony for a return to myth, and alienation itself is made into a quester story with enigmatic suggestiveness. Nausea, exile, insanity, rebellion, forlornness, and many other negative attributes invest the new actor with a symbolic aura—even though no one may have a ready key to meaning. This kind of truth shatters old norms. If suffering is to remain authentic and not degenerate into mock sensibility, only sardonic, self-critical art can cope with it. As I have suggested, what is especially puzzling and engaging is that this kind of suffering seems to push beyond gnostic suspicion of the created world and beyond our self-ennoblement as individual strugglers against our fallenness. The Enlightenment critic and dramatist Gotthold Ephraim Lessing (1729–81) had fleetingly probed demonic laughter in his plays as an expression of despair in extremity (Odoardo in *Emlia Galotti*) and misanthropy (Tellheim in *Minna von Barnhelm*), but Bonaventura makes it into a chief weapon with his myth of its invention by the devil, a theme that begins with Bonaventura's contemporary the novelist Jean Paul Richter, recurs in the poet Charles Baudelaire, and passes down to modernist writers. It is given to humankind as a reaction of doubt in the face of absurd facts. The artist is destined to make a pact with the powers of darkness, forced to side against life with its implied subservience to a hypothetical Creator who permits the monstrosities of reality. Hence truth makes common cause metaphorically with the devil, and the artist finds his own face contorted in the grimace of all inmates of hell.

× The Nightwatches ×

First Nightwatch

The night hour struck; I wrapped myself in my quixotic[1] disguise, took in hand the pike and horn, went out into the gloom, and called out the hour, after I had protected myself against the evil spirits with a sign of the cross.

It was one of those uncanny nights when light and gloom alternate quickly and strangely. In the sky the clouds, driven by the wind, flew by like eccentric colossal figures, and the moon appeared and vanished in the swift change. Dead silence reigned below in the streets. Only high above in the air did the storm dwell like an invisible spirit.

That was all right by me, and I took pleasure in my lonely reverberating footsteps, for among the many sleepers I seemed to myself like the prince in the fairytale, in the enchanted city where an evil power had transformed every living being into stone, or like a lone survivor after a universal plague or deluge.

The last comparison made me shudder, and I was cheered to see a single faint lamp still burning high up over the city in a free garret.

I well knew who ruled there so high in the airways. It was an unfortunate poet who was awake only in the night, because his creditors slept then, and the muses alone did not belong among the latter.

I could not refrain from delivering the following harangue to him:

"Oh you who are knocking about up there, I understand you well, for I was once of your kind! But I gave up this occupation for an honorable trade that nourishes its man and that is really in no way devoid of poetry for the person who knows how to discover this in it. I am placed in your pathway as if as a satirical Stentor,[2] and here below on earth regularly interrupt, with a reminder of time and transitoriness, your dreams of immortality that you dream up there in the air. We are truly both night watchmen; only it's too bad that your vigils bring in nothing in these coldly prosaic times, whereas mine always yield something extra. When I was still poetizing in the night like you, I had to go hungry like you and sang to deaf ears; the latter I still do now, to be sure, but people pay me for it. Oh friend poet, he who intends to live nowadays should not make verses. If, however, singing is inborn in you and you absolutely cannot forbear, well then, become a night watchman like me. That is still the only solid post for which you're paid and where people don't let you starve. —Good night, brother poet."

I looked up once more and became aware of his shadow on the wall. He had struck a tragic pose, his one hand in his hair, his other holding the page from which he was apparently reciting to himself his immortality.

I blasted on my horn, called the time to him loudly, and went on my way . . .

Hold! There a sick man is awake—also in dreams like the poet, in true fever dreams.

All along the man was a freethinker, and, like Voltaire,[3] he is holding firm in his last hour. Then I see him through the peephole in the shutters. He gazes palely and calmly into empty nothingness, into which he intends to penetrate after an hour, in order to sleep forever the dreamless sleep. The roses of life have fallen from his cheeks but they blossom round about him on the faces of three gracious boys. Childishly innocent, the youngest frets before his pale, motionless visage, because it will no longer smile as it used to. The others stand observing soberly; they cannot yet imagine death in their fresh life.

In contrast, the young wife, with flowing hair and open, fair breast, looks despairing into the black grave and only now and again, as if mechanically, wipes the sweat from the dying man's cold forehead.

Beside him the priest, glowing with anger, stands with raised crucifix to convert the freethinker. His speech swells mightily as a stream, and he paints the beyond in audacious pictures—not, however, the beautiful aurora of the new day and the budding arbors and angels, but, like a wild hellish Brueghel,[4] the flames and abysses and the whole ghastly underworld of Dante.[5]

In vain! The sick man remains mute and stubborn. With a frightful calm, he sees one leaf after another falling and feels how the icy crust of death draws closer and closer to his heart.

The night wind whistled through my hair and rattled the decayed shutters like an invisible, approaching spirit of death. I shuddered. The sick man looked about with sudden strength, as if through a miracle he were speedily recovering and felt a new, higher life. This quick, bright flaring up of the already extinguishing flame, certain herald of imminent death, simultaneously casts a brilliant light into the night-piece set up before the dying man and shines, swiftly and for a moment, into the vernal world of faith and poetry. It is the double illumination in the Correggio[6] night and fuses the earthly and heavenly ray into one marvelous splendor.

Firm and resolute, the sick man rejected the higher hope and thereby brought about a great moment. The priest thundered angrily into his soul and, like a desperate man, was now painting with tongues of fire and conjuring up all Tartarus[7] into the final hour of the dying. The latter only smiled and shook his head.

I was in this moment certain of his endurance; for only the finite being cannot think the thought of annihilation, while the immortal spirit does not tremble before it, who—a free being—can freely offer himself to it, as Indian women boldly hurl themselves into the flames and dedicate themselves to annihilation.

A wild madness seemed to grip the priest at this sight, and true to his character, he now spoke—since descriptions appeared too feeble to him—in the person of the devil himself, which suited him perfectly. He expressed himself as a master in this role, genuinely diabolical in the boldest style and far from the weak manner of the modern devil.

It became too much for the sick man. He turned away gloomily and looked at the three spring roses that bloomed around his bed. Then the whole hot love flared up for the last time in his heart, and a light redness rushed over his pale visage like a memory. He had the boys held up for him and he kissed them with effort; then he laid his heavy head on the woman's agitated breast, uttered a gentle "Oh!" that seemed more bliss than pain, and fell asleep lovingly in the arms of love.

The priest, true to his devil's role, thundered into his ears—in accordance with the observation that in the case of deceased persons the hearing faculty still remains sensitive a rather long time—and promised him firmly and bindingly that the devil would claim not only his soul but also his body.

With this he burst forth onto the street. I had become confused, in the deception held him truly to be the devil, and set the pike at his breast as he wished to pass by me. "Go to the devil!" he said, snorting. Then I gathered my wits and said, "Pardon, reverend sir. In a kind of possession I held you to be Himself, and for that reason set the pike at your heart, as a 'God-be-with-us.'[8] Excuse me for this once!"

He rushed on.

Oh! There in the room the scene had become more lovely. The fair wife held the pale beloved quietly in her arms like a slumberer; in fair ignorance she did not yet suspect death and believed that sleep would strengthen him for new life—a sweet belief, which did not deceive her in the higher sense. The children kneeled earnestly at the bed, and only the youngest endeavored to wake their father, while their mother, beckoning to him silently with her eyes, laid her hand on his curly head.

The scene was too beautiful; I turned away in order not to see the moment in which the illusion vanished.

With muted voice I sang a dirge under the window in order, through gentle tones, to supplant in the still hearing ear the monk's cry of fire. Music is kindred to the dying; it is the first sweet sound of the distant beyond, and the muse of song is the mystical sister who points the way to heaven. So Jacob Boehme⁹ passed away, while listening to the distant music that none but the dying hear.

Second Nightwatch

The hour called me once more to my nocturnal business; the desolate streets lay before me as if shrouded, and only a sheet of lightning now and then flew through them vaporously and swiftly, and far, far in the distance there was intermittent mumbling as of an incomprehensible incantation.

My poet had extinguished his lamp, because heaven was giving light and he considered this latter kind to be at the same time cheaper and more poetic. He gazed up into the flashes on high, reclining in his window, his white nightshirt open at the chest and his black hair shaggy and disordered about his head. I remembered similar super-poetic hours when there is a storm inside, when the mouth would speak in thunder and the hand grasp the lightning bolt instead of the pen to write fiery words with it. Then the spirit flies from pole to pole, believes it is winging over the entire universe, and when at last it arrives at speech—there is only the childish word, and the hand impetuously tears up the paper.

I banished this poetic devil in me, who in the end had the habit of always laughing sadistically over my weakness, usually through the spellbinding medium of music; now I am accustomed to just blasting shrilly a couple of times on the horn and then everything is soon past.

I can recommend the tone of my night watchman's horn as a genuine *antipoeticum* for anyone anywhere who shies away from similar poetic surprises as from a fever. This remedy is cheap and of the greatest importance as well, since people in the present day follow Plato in considering poetry to be a rage, with the sole difference that he derived this rage from heaven and not from the booby hatch.[1]

But be that as it may, poetizing nowadays is everywhere still in a critical state, because there are so few deranged people anymore and such a surplus of rational ones is on hand that they can, out of their own means, occupy all specialties, even poetry. A sheer madman like me finds no employment under such circumstances, and therefore I'm merely skirting poetry now; that is, I have become a humorist, for which, as night watchman, I have the greatest leisure ...

First, no doubt, I should probably demonstrate in advance my vocation as a humorist; only I'm not going to bother with that, because in general people themselves are not now so strict about vocation but to the contraryare content with position alone. For there are even poets without vocation, through mere position—and herewith I withdraw from the market.

A lightning flash was just flaming through the air; three figures were creeping like carnival masks along the churchyard wall. I called to them, but night had already resumed round about, and I saw nothing but a glowing tail and a couple of fiery eyes, and a voice close by murmured to the far thunder, as if in an accompaniment to Don Juan's,[2] "Do what your job is, night owl; but don't meddle in ghostly work!"

That was just a little too much for me, and I threw my pike in the direction from which the voice came; just then there was another flash—the three had dissolved into the air like Macbeth's witches.[3]

"You don't recognize me as a spirit!"—I called after them, still angry, in the hope that they would hear it—"and yet I was a poet, street minstrel, marionette director, and everything of the like ingenious spirit in turn. I would really like to have known your spirits in life, if you indeed really are already out of it! and to have seen whether mine could not have matched them; or have you acquired an addition of spirit after your death, as we experienced in the case of a number of great men who became famous only after their deaths and whose writings gained in spirit by long lying, like wine, which with increasing age grows more spirited." ...

I had approached to within a few feet of the excommunicated freethinker's dwelling. From the open door a muted glow projected into the night and often strangely commingled with the storm light. A more perceptible mumbling also crossed from the far mountains, as if the spirit realm were seriously thinking of meddling in the game.

The dead man, according to the usual custom, was on open display in the hallway; a few unblessed candles were burning around him, because the priest of devilish memory had denied the blessing. The deceased smiled over this in his fast sleep or over his own foolish delusion which the beyond had controverted, and his smile shone like a distant reflection of life on the rigid death-set features.

Through a long, scarcely lit hall, one looked into a black-draped niche; there the three boys and their pale mother knelt motionless before an altar—the group of Niobe[4] with her children—immersed in mute anxious prayer in order to snatch the deceased's body and soul from the devil, to whom they had been assigned by the priest.

Only the brother of the departed, a soldier, kept watch by the coffin with a firm, sure belief in heaven and in his own courage which would dare to tangle with the devil himself. His glance was calm and expectant, and he looked alternately into the rigid face of the dead man and the storm light that often quivered inimically through the dull glow of the candles; his saber lay drawn on the corpse and, its pommel shaped like a cross, resembled both a spiritual and worldly weapon.

Moreover, deathly stillness reigned round about, and besides the distant growling of the storm and the sputtering of the candles, one perceived nothing.

So things remained until in single solemn strokes the clock announced midnight; —then suddenly the storm wind drove a thunder cloud across like a nocturnal phantom high above in the sky roads, and soon it had spread its grave cloth over the whole sky. The candles around the coffin were extinguished, the thunder roared down angrily like a tumultuous power and summoned those who were fast asleep, and the cloud spewed out flame upon flame, by which alone the dead man's rigid pale countenance was harshly and periodically illuminated.

I saw now that the soldier's saber was glinting through the night and that he was bravely girding himself for battle.

And that came soon enough—the air cast up bubbles, and the three Macbeth ghosts were suddenly visible again, as if the storm wind had whirled them there by their pates. The lightning illuminated twisted devil's masks and snaky hair and the whole hellish contrivance.

At that moment the devil caught me by a hair, and as the ghosts were going up the alley I impetuously mixed in with them. They were stunned over the fourth, unbidden party who ran into them as if they were walking on evil pathways. "What, the devil! Can the devil too walk on the paths of goodness!" I cried out, laughing wildly. "Then don't be confused that I meet you on evil ones. I am of your ilk, brothers, I'll make common cause with you!" ...

That really made them disconcerted. The one blurted out, "God be with us!" and crossed himself, which surprised me, and on this account I exclaimed: "Brother devil, don't fall so crudely out of character; I might otherwise almost despair of you and take you for a saint, at least for ordained. —If, however, I reflect on the matter more maturely, then I must rather congratulate you on finally also having digested the cross and, though by origin a devil incarnate, having developed, at least in appearance, into a saint!"

By my talk they probably finally hit on the fact that I was not one of their kind, and they all three went at me and now spoke in a genuinely clerical tone of excommunication and the like if I should disturb them in their business.

"Don't worry," I replied; "up to now I really haven't believed in the devil, but since I've seen you, he's become transparent to me, and I am certain that you will qualify for his gang. Settle your affairs, for no poor night watchman can tangle with hell and the church."

And they went that way, into the house. I followed cautiously after.

It was a frightening spectacle. Stroke by stroke, lightning and night alternated. Now it was bright and one saw the three scuffling over the coffin and the flashing of the saber in the iron-nerved warrior's hand, in between which the dead man gazed as motionless as a mask from his pale rigid face. Then it was deep night again and, far off, a dull shimmer in the recesses of the niche, and with her three children the kneeling mother wrestling in desperate prayer.

Everything occurred quietly and without words; however, now there was a sudden loud crumpling noise as if the devil had gained the upper hand. The lightning flashes became sparser, and it remained night for a longer time. After a little while, nonetheless, two emerged quickly at the door, and then I saw through the darkness by the shining of their eyes—that they actually were carrying a dead man off with them.

There I stood at the door cursing at myself; it was quite gloomy in the hall, no soul stirred, and I believed the valiant warrior too had at least had his neck broken.

In this instant a violent thunderbolt flashed, with which the storm cloud completely discharged itself and remained, as it were, like an erected torch, a space of time in the air without extinguishing. Then I saw the soldier, standing again calmly and coldly by the casket, and the corpse was smiling as before—but, oh wonder! Right next to the smiling death's-head, a devil's mask was grinning, but the torso was missing to complete the whole, and a purply red stream of blood stained the white winding sheet of the sleeping freethinker ...

Shuddering, I wrapped myself in my cloak, forgot to blow and sing out the hour, and fled to my hut.

Third Nightwatch

We night watchmen and poets care little indeed about the doings of men in the day; for by this time it belongs among the settled truths that when they *act*, men are very much creatures of daytime, and one may gain some interest in them at best when they *dream*.

For this reason, then, I learned only disconnected things about the outcome of that occurrence which I intend to communicate in a similarly disconnected way.

People broke their heads mostly over the head, for it was no usual type but a true devil's head. Justice, to whom it was presented, dismissed the matter, opining that heads really didn't fall in its province. It was indeed a bad business, and people even got to quarreling over whether they should proceed *criminaliter*[1] against the soldier, for committing manslaughter, or rather have to canonize him because the slain person was the devil. Out of the latter point issued in turn a new ill; indeed for several months absolution was no longer desired, because people now denied the devil's existence point blank and cited in evidence the head taken into custody. The priests were screaming themselves hoarse from their pulpits and insisted without further ado that a devil could exist even without head, of which they were ready to adduce proofs from their own resources.

Of the head itself one could in fact not quite make heads or tails. The physiognomy was of iron; but a clasp that was located on the side almost led to the supposition that the devil had hidden yet another head under the first, which he perhaps saved only for special feast days. Worse was that the key to the clasp, and therefore also to this second face, was missing. Who knows what kind of frightening remarks about devil physiognomies could otherwise have been made, since, in contrast, the first was only an everyday face that the devil wears in any woodcut.

In this general confusion, and with the uncertainty whether one had a genuine devil's head before oneself, it was decided that the head would be sent to Dr. Gall in Vienna,[2] so that he might hunt out the unmistakable satanic protuberances on it; but then the church suddenly meddled in the game and declared that it was to be regarded as the first and last instance for such determinations. It had the skull handed over to itself, and soon thereupon, the way it was told, this had disappeared, and several of the ecclesiastical gentlemen claimed to have seen the devil himself in the night hours as he carried off with him the head he was missing.

Therewith the whole matter remained as good as unexplained, all the more so since the sole person who in any case could yet have shed some light, that same priest who had pronounced the anathema over the freethinker, had suffered sudden death by an apoplexy. So at least said rumor and cloistered gentlemen; for no profane person had seen the corpse itself, since, on account of the warm season, it had had to be interred quickly.

The story kept revolving in my head during my nightwatch, for up to now I had believed in only a poetic devil, in no way whatsoever in the real. As regards the poetic, it is certainly a great shame that people now neglect him so extremely and, instead of an absolute evil principle, prefer the virtuous scoundrels in the manner of Iffland[3] and Kotzebue,[4] in which the devil appears humanized and man satanized. In a vacillating era people are shy of anything absolute and autonomous; for this very reason, then, we no longer care to tolerate either genuine fun or genuine earnest, either genuine virtue or genuine malice. The character of the times is patched and pieced together like a fool's coat, and worst of all, the fool buttoned in it would like to appear serious ...

As I was engaging in these observations, I had posted myself in a niche before stony Crispin,[5] who wore just such a gray cloak as I. Suddenly a feminine form and a masculine form moved there right before me and almost leaned on me, because they held me to be the blind and deaf-mute one of stone.

The man was quite absorbed in rhetorical bombast and spoke in one breath of love and troth; the womanly figure, in contrast, credulously doubted and managed a lot of artificial handwringing. Now the man impudently made an appeal to me and swore he stood unchanging and inflexible as the statue. Then the satyr awoke in me, and when he laid his hand on my cloak as it were in protestation, I shook myself a little maliciously, over which both were astonished; but the paramour took things very lightly and thought the block under the statue had sunk, whereby it had lost some of its equilibrium.

He now forswore his soul in the guise of ten characters from the newest dramas and tragedies one after another, should he ever be faithless; in the end, he even spoke in the manner of *Don Giovanni*, which he had attended that evening, and closed with the significant words: "This stone shall appear as a fearful guest at our nightly meal if my intentions are not honorable."

I took note of this, and listened further as she described the house to him and the secret lever on the door by which he could open it, and at the same time fixed the midnight hour for the banquet.

I was at the place a half-hour early, found the house, the door, along with the secret lever, and slipped softly up several back staircases to a room in which there was dim light. The light fell through two glass doors; I neared one and glimpsed a creature in its nightgown at a worktable, about whom at the start I remained in doubt as to whether it was a human being or a mechanical figure, so very much was everything human in it erased, with only the expression of work remaining. The creature wrote while buried in piles of documents, like a Laplander interred alive. It struck me as if it wanted to sample living and lodging under the earth already, in advance, for everything passionate and sympathetic was extinguished on its cold wooden forehead and the marionette sat lifelessly erect in its document coffin full of bookworms. Now the invisible wire was pulled and the fingers clicked, grasped the pen, and signed three papers in a row; I peered more acutely—they were death warrants. On the table lay the Code of Justinian[6] and the criminal code, as it were, the personified soul of the marionette.

I could find no fault here; but the cold, righteous man appeared to me like a mechanical death machine that prostrates blindly; his worktable like the place of judgment on which in a minute he had with three strokes of the pen carried out three death sentences. By heaven, if I had had the choice between the two, I would rather be the living sinner than this dead righteous one.

It gripped me still more when I saw his well-struck counterfeit embossed in wax sitting motionlessly opposite him, as if one life-less copy were not sufficient and a double were needed in order to show the dead oddity from two different angles.

Now the lady from earlier stepped in, and the marionette took off its cap and laid it at its side, anxiously expectant. "Not yet gone to sleep?" she said. "What a wild kind of life you are leading! Always exerting your fantasy!" —"Fantasy?" he asked, puzzled. "What do you mean by that? I so seldom understand the new terminology with which you talk now." —"Because you have no interest in anything higher; not even for the tragic!" —"Tragic? Ay, of course!" he answered complacently; "look here, I'm having three delinquents executed!" —"Oh woe, what sentiments!" —"How's that? I thought this might give you a little pleasure, because in the books you read, so many lose their lives. And therefore to surprise you, I have set the executions for your birthday!" —"My God! My nerves!" —"Oh woe, you get this attack so often now that I start feeling anxious in advance every time!" —"Oh well, unfortunately there is nothing you can do about it. Just go, I pray, and lie down to sleep!"

The conversation was at an end and he went, drying the sweat from his forehead. I decided in this instant, devilishly enough, to deliver his wife over to him, if possible this very night, under criminal jurisdiction, so that she would be under his power.

And it was not at all long until my Mars crept to his Venus. Since I limped by nature and didn't have the best appearance, as Vulcan I really lacked little more than the golden net. Nonetheless, in the absence of this, I determined to apply a few golden truths and moral axioms. At the start things went quite tolerably; my fellow was sinning merely against poetry through a too-material tendency in his depictions; he painted a heaven full of nymphs and teasing love gods on the baldachin under which he thought to rest. The way there he strewed with trick roses, which he cast in numbers from himself in ornate figures of speech, and the thorns, which now and again were about to wound his feet, he avoided with light, frivolous turns.

When the sinner had now, however, so translated himself into a poetic element and, according to the spirit of the newest theories, had completely dismissed morality, when the green silk drape rolled down in front of the glass door and the whole place began to resemble a play behind curtains, I instantly applied my *antipoeticum* and blasted shrilly on the night watchman's horn, then swung myself up onto an empty pedestal that was intended for the statue of Justice (who was till now still being worked on) and stood quietly and motionlessly.

The fearsome tone had shocked the two from poetry and the husband from sleep, and all three suddenly hurried at the same time out of two separate doors.

"The guest of stone!"[7] the paramour cried, shuddering, when he spied me. "Ah, my Justice!" the husband, "has she finally been finished; how unexpectedly you have surprised me with this, darling!" —"Pure error," I said; "Justice is still lying over at the sculptor's and I have only placed myself on the pedestal provisionally so that it won't be totally empty on especially important occasions. To be sure, I will ever remain but an expedient, for Justice is as cold as marble and has no heart in its stony breast; I, however, am a poor rogue full of sentimental tenderness and even now and then am somewhat in a poetic mood; nonetheless, in usual cases for this house I may still be good enough and, when necessary, play a stone guest. Such guests have this in their favor, that they don't join in the eating and also don't warm themselves when that could cause hurt; in contrast, the others easily catch fire and impudently make it hot for the master of the house, for which I have the immediate example." —"Ay ay, my God, what's this then?" stammered the husband.

"That the dumb begin to speak, do you mean? That flows from the frivolity of the age. One should never speak of the devil. Our young worldly gentlemen, however, go beyond that and misuse the like against weak souls in order to show themselves from the heroic angle. I have now taken my man at his word there, although I actually don't belong here but stand outside in the marketplace in my gray cloak as St. Crispin of Stone."

"God, what is one to think of this!" he continued, alarmed. "It's not at all according to regulations, and an unheard-of case!"

"For the learned jurist certainly! This same Crispin was a cobbler but, out of an unusual piety and a real surplus of virtue, devoted himself to thievery and stole leather in order to make shoes for the poor with it. What can be decided there, just speak! I see no other way out than to hang him first and canonize him afterward. One would have to proceed on similar grounds, for example, against adulterers who, merely to maintain peace in the house, offend against the laws; the animus here is obviously praiseworthy; and in general, this is really the crux of the matter. How many a woman would not torment her husband to death if such a house friend did not turn up and turn into a scoundrel out of pure morality! Here I am really getting to my theme, and we can now in God's name open the book of criminal jurisdiction. —But I see that the suspects are already lying unconscious; so we must have a recess in the trial!"

"Suspects?" the husband asked mechanically. "I don't see any; that woman there is my better half!" ...

"All right then, in the first place let's stay with her. Better half! Quite right! That means the cross or the torment in marriage—and truly that marriage is already exemplary when this cross amounts to only a half. If you now, as the second half, are the marriage blessing, then your marriage is really heaven on earth."

"Marriage blessing!" he said with a deep sigh.

"No sentimental marginal gloss, dear friend; let's rather cast our glance here upon the second suspect who is lying unconscious, likewise out of terror over the stone guest. If we could by right derive mitigating grounds for people from moral principles, then I would like to be his defender and at least try to avert for him the punishment of beheading that the *Lex Carolina*[8] imposes on him—especially because in the case of such malefactors beheading can be applied only in effigy, since for them, speaking seriously, there can be no talk of a head!" ...

"That Karolina[9] should all at once have become so horrible!" he said quite confused. "Just a short time ago, she was shuddering when I spoke of execution!" ...

"I don't blame you," I answered, "for confusing the one Karolina with the other; for your living Karolina, as marriage cross and torture, is easily to be confounded with the penal one, which likewise doesn't deal with a bed of roses. Indeed, I might almost assert, such a matrimonial one is much worse yet than the imperial, since in the latter at least there is no talk in a single instance of lifelong torment." ...

"But my god, it can't go on this way, though!" he said suddenly, as if coming to himself. "One no longer really knows whether one's waking or dreaming; indeed, I would like to pinch myself just to see whether I was waking or sleeping, if I didn't want to swear to the fact of actually having heard the night watchman beforehand!" ...

"Ay, my God!" I exclaimed. "Now I awake; you have called me by my name, and it is my further good fortune that I don't find myself too high just now, for example, on a roof or in a poetic ecstasy, so as to break my neck in falling down. Thus, however, I luckily am not standing higher than Justice should stand here, and so I remain human still and among men. You stare at me and don't know what to make of it; but I'll solve the matter for you at once. I am night watchman here and at the same time sleepwalker, apparently because both functions can be comprehended in one person. Whenever I now perform my office as night watchman, I often get the desire to betake myself as sleepwalker to sharp points, such as roof peaks or other critical places, in this fashion; and so apparently I have even gotten onto the pedestal of Themis[10] here. It's a desperate humor that may yet cost me my neck; nonetheless, it often happens that I have thereby in my own way safeguarded the good inhabitants of this city against thefts just because I am in the habit of crawling into every corner, and precisely those thieves are the most harmless who only go about outside exercising their handiwork on shops with crowbars. This point, I believe, excuses me; and I herewith wish you well!"

I withdrew and left behind in astonishment the husband and the other two who also had come round again now. How they may still have conversed afterward with one another, I don't know.

Fourth Nightwatch

Among the favorite places in which I am accustomed to stop during my nightwatches is the ledge in the old Gothic cathedral. Here I sit by the dusky glow of the single ever-burning lamp and often even appear to myself like a night spirit. The place induces contemplation; today it led me to my own story, and, as it were out of boredom, I thumbed through the book of my life, which is written confusedly and madly enough.

Right on the first page, things look worrisome, and page five treats not of my birth but of digging treasure. Here one sees mystic signs from the Kabbalah[1] and, on the explanatory woodcut, a not very usual shoemaker who wants to give up shoemaking to learn how to make gold. A Gypsy woman[2] stands nearby, yellow and unrecognizable, with her shaggy hair tousled about her forehead; she's instructing him in treasure digging, gives him a divining rod, and also points out precisely the spot where in three days he is to raise a treasure. Today I simply am in the mood to pause over the woodcuts in the book, and so I turn to the

Second Woodcut.

Here is the shoemaker again without the Gypsy. This time the artist has managed his face far more expressively. It has strong features and shows that the man hasn't kept merely to his feet but has gone *ultra crepidam*.[3] He is a satirical contribution to the blunders of genius and makes evident how that person who might have become a good hatmaker must turn out a bad shoemaker, and also the contrary, if one turns the example on its head. —The locale is a crossroad; the dark lines are to make the night perceptible, and the zigzag in the sky indicates a lightning bolt. It is clear any other honorable man with a trade would run away from such surroundings. But our genius doesn't let himself be disturbed. He has already raised a heavy chest out of a cavity, and has already even come to the point of opening his captured little treasure casket; but, oh heaven, its content should probably be termed a treasure for the curious amateur alone—for I myself am located bodily in the little casket and indeed sans all movable property, already a quite complete citizen of the world.

What kind of observations my treasure hunter may have engaged in concerning his find—of that nothing stands in the woodcut, because the artist has not wished to overstep the boundaries of his art in the slightest.

Third Woodcut.

Here a skilled commentator is needed. —I am sitting on a book, I am reading from one. My adoptive father is busy with a shoe but seems to make room at the same time for some observations on immortality. The book on which I am sitting contains Hans Sachs's Shrovetide plays,[4] and that from which I read is Jacob Boehme's *Aurora*;[5] they are the nucleus of our house library because both authors were guild-member shoemakers and poets.

I don't care to go further in this account, because there is too much talk of my own originality in the woodcut. I prefer therefore to read to myself in the stillness the hereto pertaining

Third Chapter.

It is composed by my shoemaker, who, so far as it went, himself continued sketching my career, and starts thus:

"I very often get a peculiar feeling when I observe Kreuzgang."[6]

For according to custom, the place where I was found had stood godfather to me at my baptism. —"I cannot regard him as an ordinary shoe, for there is something extravagant in him, perhaps as in the old Boehme, who was also already early engrossed in thought over shoemaking and chanced upon the mystery. Likewise he; for quite ordinary things appear to him most extraordinary, as for example a sunrise, which takes place day in and day out, and in the case of which we other human beings are simply accustomed to think nothing peculiar. So also the stars in the sky and the flowers on the earth, which he often lets deliberate with one another and carry on most wonderful communication. For he has recently made me quite confused over a shoe, in that he asked me at the beginning about the constituent parts of the same and, when I had given an answer and talk on that, suddenly demanded explanation for every single substance, soared ever higher and higher, first into the natural sciences by tracing leather to the ox, then still further, until at last I found myself high above in theology with my shoe and he told me straight from this that I was a bungler in my line, because I could not give him information right down to the last rudiments on it. Similarly, he often calls the flowers a script that we simply do not know how to read, likewise also the varicolored stones. He still hopes one day to learn this language and promises then to communicate through it most wonderful things. Often he listens quite secretly to the midges or flies when they are buzzing in the sunshine, because he believes them to be conversing about important subjects of which, up to now, no man has yet had any inkling. When he prattles like this to the journeymen and apprentices in the workshop and they laugh at him, he very seriously declares them to be blind men and deaf, who neither saw nor heard what was taking place around them. Now he sits day and night with Jacob Boehme and Hans Sachs, the two of whom were quite peculiar shoemakers, whom even in their time no one could get to the bottom of ...

"Thus much is as clear as the sun: this Kreuzgang is not a usual human being, for I did not come by him in any usual way.

"The evening will never slip from my mind, when disgruntled over my scant earnings I had fallen asleep on the tripod—that it had to be precisely a tripod, as they tell me, is not supposed to have been without influence. —I dreamed that I found a treasure in a sealed chest, but I was commanded not to open this chest any earlier than the time that I would be awakened. That was all so clear and self-evident, since dream and waking were obviously so different from one another, that I could never again get it out of my head, and I finally made the acquaintance of a Gypsy woman in order to really undertake the experiment.

"Everything went according to plan; I raised the chest I had seen in the dream, deliberated in advance whether I was really awake, and then opened it; but instead of the gold that I expected, I had raised this prodigy from the earth.

"In the beginning I was somewhat disconcerted over this, because such a living treasure must at the least be accompanied by a dead one, if anything to spare is to come out of it all, and the boy was stark naked and, in addition, even laughed about it when I looked at him in that state. When I had reflected, however, I regarded the matter more deeply and had my own thoughts about it, for which reason I providently bore my treasure home."

So far my honest shoemaker, when I was suddenly interrupted by an unusual occurrence. A tall manly figure, wrapped in a cloak, strode through the arch and stood on a gravestone. I crept softly behind a pillar that I was close to; then he cast back his cloak, and I espied, behind black hair falling down over his forehead, a gloomy inimical countenance with a southern pale gray complexion.

I always step before an alien unusual human life with the same feelings as before a curtain behind which a Shakespearean drama is to be produced; and I like it best if the former as well as the latter is a tragedy, for, besides genuine seriousness, I can suffer only tragic jest and such fools as in *King Lear*, precisely because these alone are truly audacious and carry on their clownery *en gros*, and without regard, over the whole of human life. The little jokers and good-natured composers of comedies, on the other hand, who only bash about in families and do not, as Aristophanes, dare to make merry over the very gods, are heartily repugnant to me, just as are those weak, sensitive souls who, instead of shattering an entire human life in order to raise man himself above it, are occupied only with petty torment and have the doctor standing by their torture victims to determine the precise degree of torture for them, so that the poor rogue, although virtually mangled, still can escape with his life; as if life were the highest thing and not rather man, who goes further than life, which makes up merely the first act and the inferno in the *Divine Comedy* through which, in order to seek his ideal, he is traveling ...

My man, who was kneeling here close before me on the gravestone, in his hand a brightly polished dagger that he had drawn from a beautifully worked sheath, seemed to me to be of a genuinely tragic nature and chained me to his presence. I didn't even have an urge to sound the alarm in case he undertook something serious, and I had just as little desire to stand as confidant in the wings so as to be ready on cue in the fifth act to hold my hero's arm at the right time; for his life appeared to me as being like the beautifully worked sheath in his hand that concealed the dagger in its gay shell, or like Cleopatra's flower basket, among whose roses the poisonous snake lay in wait, and when the drama of life has once so constellated itself, one must not try to avert the tragic catastrophe.

When I was still marionette director, I had a King Saul whom he resembled to a hair, even in all his manners—just such wooden, mechanical movements, and such a petrified ancient style, by which marionette troops distinguish themselves from living actors, who nowadays don't even understand how to die the right way in our theaters.

Everything had already been finished, right up to the falling of the curtain, when the man's arm, already lifted for the fatal stroke, suddenly grew rigid, and he knelt like a stone memorial on the gravestone. Between the dagger point and his breast, which it was to cut through, there remained scarcely the space of a hand, and death stood right up against life, but time seemed to have stopped and refused to jog forward any further, and the one moment seemed to have become eternity, which forever suspended all change.

I began to feel quite uneasy; I looked up in fright toward the face of the church clock; here, too, the pointer stood still, exactly at midnight's number. I felt lamed, and everything was motionless and dead around me: the man on the grave, the cathedral with its rigid high columns and monuments, and the kneeling stone knights and saints round about, who seemed to tarry motionlessly in expectation of a new time breaking and a progression in the same, whereby they would be released.

Now it was over, the gears of the clock came unstuck, the pointer moved on, and the first stroke of the midnight hour reverberated slowly through the desolate vault. As if through the marching on of the clock, the man on the grave seemed to receive movement again; the dagger rolled rattling over the stone, and broke.

"Cursed be this benumbment," he said coldly, as if he were already used to it; "it never lets me carry out the blow!" —With this he stood up as if nothing more had occurred and was about to withdraw again.

"You please me," I cried, "for there is character in your life and genuine tragic calm. I love the grand classical dignity in man which despises many words when so much should be done; and such a *salto mortale*[7] as that for which you were just prepared is certainly no small thing and belongs to those trump points that one saves up till the last." ...

"If you can assist me to this leap," he said morosely, "then it is well; otherwise don't go to any further effort in eulogies and remarks. On the art of living more than too much is written, but I have been forever seeking in vain for a treatise on the art of dying; and I cannot die!" ...

"Oh, if only some of our beloved professional writers possessed this talent of yours!" I exclaimed. "It would not matter if their works remained ephemera, were they themselves immortal and able to continue their ephemeral authorship eternally and remain beloved up to the Last Judgment. Unfortunately for them, the hour comes only too soon in which they, and their one-day flies with them, must die. —Oh friend, could I but raise you in this moment to a Kotzebue, this Kotzebue would then never go under, and even at the end of all things his last works would still be present in the Hogarthian tailpiece,[8] and time could fire the last pipe it smokes here with a scene from his last drama and, thus inspired, pass over into eternity!"

The man wished now to exit quietly, without holding another powerful tirade at the conclusion, as a bad actor would; I, however, held him by the hand and said: "Not so hastily, friend, it's really not necessary, since you always have time, if moreover there can even be any talk of time at all; for, judging by your words, I take you to be the wandering Jew[9] who, because he blasphemed the immortal, has for punishment already become immortal here below, where everything passes away around him. You are morose, you singular person whose life the pointer of time shall never cut through, that pointer which flies around on the clock's face like a sharp sword never ceasing from murder and which cannot pass away before time's iron wheelworks themselves are demolished. Take the matter on its lighter side; for it is amusing and worth the effort to attend this great tragicomedy, world history, as spectator up to its last act, and you can give yourself that unique pleasure finally, when at the end of all things, as sole survivor, you stand above the general deluge upon the last projecting mountain peak to hiss the entire production on your own hook, and then wild and angry, a second Prometheus,[10] hurl yourself into the abyss."

"Hiss I will," the man said defiantly. "If only the poet had not woven me, too, into the play as dramatis persona; that I'll never forgive him!"

"All the better!" I cried, "for there's probably going to be yet, once and for all, a revolt in the play itself, and the first hero rebels against his author. For that's not even rare in the little imitation of the great world comedy, and the hero gets out of the poet's control in the end so that he can no longer master him.[11] —Oh, I would enjoy listening to your story, you eternal traveler, in order to split my sides with laughter; just as I often will laugh valiantly at a genuinely serious tragedy and, in contrast, now and then must weep at a good farce, since the truly bold and great can always be comprehended from these two opposite aspects simultaneously!" ...

"I understand you, buffoon," the man said, "and feel just wild enough now to laugh and tell you my story. But, by heaven, don't let me catch you pulling any serious faces, otherwise you'll render me mute in an instant!" ...

"Don't worry, comrade, I'll laugh with you," I answered, and he sat down beneath a baronial family of stone praying on their own grave and commenced:

"It is, you will concede, damned boring to unroll one's own story from period to period so nicely and agreeably. I therefore prefer to convert it into action and produce it as a marionette play with Clown;[12] thus the whole thing becomes more self-evident and comical.[13]

"First there is a Mozart symphony executed by bad village musicians; that fits perfectly with a bungled life and lifts the heart by great thoughts, while, at the same time, with such scratching one might well go to the devil. —The Clown comes and excuses the marionette director for having disposed things like our Lord God and entrusted the most important roles to the least talented actors; precisely from this, however, he deduces in turn the advantage that the play must turn out movingly, just as is the case with great tragic materials that have been worked over by petty, ordinary poets. He makes the most insipid remarks about the life and the character of the times: that both are now more moving than comic and that one now has less cause to laugh over men than to weep—for which reason then even he himself has become a moral and grave fool and shows himself only in the noble genre where he might earn much applause.

"Thereupon the wooden puppets themselves come forward; two brothers without hearts embrace, and Clown laughs over the clattering together of their arms and over the kiss for which they are not able to move their stiff lips. The one wooden brother remains in marionette character and expresses himself with infinite stiffness, even frames long, dry periodic sentences, into which no life at all can intrude, and which therefore form a model of prosaic style. The other puppet, however, would like to affect a living actor and speaks now and again in bad iambs, at times even rhyming the final syllables, and Clown nods all the while with his head and gives a speech on the warmth of feeling in a marionette and on elegant delivery of tragic poems. —Hereupon the brothers shake each other's wooden hand and go off. Clown dances a solo into the bargain, and then in the entr'acte Mozart again speaks through the village musicians.

"Now things progress. Two new puppets come forward, a Columbine with a page who spreads an umbrella over her; the Columbine is the company's prima donna and, without flattery, the model maker's masterpiece. Truly Grecian contours, and everything about her worked over to the ideal. The one brother comes, he who previously spoke in prose; he espies her, strikes himself on the place for the heart, hereupon suddenly speaks in verses, rhymes all end syllables, or applies assonance with *a* and *o*, so that Columbine is frightened at this and runs off with the page. The brother tries to rush after her. However, because the marionette director makes a slip here, he bangs solidly against Clown, who now makes extempore a very nasty satirical speech in which he sets forth to him that it does not please his creator—namely the marionette director—to allot the lady to him and that the play should therefore become quite mad and comical, since a melancholy fool furnishes the drollest person in a farce. —The other puppet bursts into curses, even blasphemes in despair against the director, over which, for laughter, tears stream from the onlookers' eyes. Finally, however, the marionette still clutches the hope of finding the lady again and decides at least to search through the whole theater. Clown accompanies it.

"In the third act Columbine appears again and acts very nicely with the other brother marionette; they also sing a tender duet with one another and exchange rings right then, whereupon an old officious Pantaloon arrives with musicians who play through much merry music, in whose course, however, one does not hear any notes, which makes an odd impression on the viewers. Finally, there is a dance to this mute music, and Pantaloon makes rather good remarks about his musical hearing, and also defends the fable that the notes froze at the North Pole and would thaw out and become audible again only in the warm south. That is all so strange that one simply doesn't know whether one is supposed to take it seriously or jokingly; some clever people in the audience even think it mad.

"When those first two have finally gone to bed, Clown comes back with the other brother. The latter tells how he has made far journeys from one pole to the other and yet never found Columbine, on account of which he is ready to despair and take his own life. Clown opens a flap on the marionette's chest and to his surprise now actually finds a heart in it, over which he grows concerned and in his anxiety gets a number of clever ideas, for example, that everything in life, the pain as well as the joy, is mere appearance, in which regard the one bad point is merely that the appearance itself never comes to appearance, on account of which the marionettes have also never suspected that someone had the best of them and was playing with them merely for amusement, but rather fancy themselves to be very serious and important persons. —At this juncture he tries to make comprehensible for him the essence of a marionette itself, but constantly confounds himself in the process and, after a long, very droll speech, at the end again stands right where he began. —Now he laughs maliciously and quietly into his sleeve and goes off …

"In the fourth act the two brothers meet, and while he with the heart is speaking, the mute tones from the previous act suddenly become audible and accompany his words, over which the brother without heart grows quite confused. Harlequin now also joins in and jeers at love, because it is not a heroic sentiment and cannot be used to promote the general good. He calls upon the director to abolish it completely in the sequel and introduce pure moral feelings in his troupe. Finally he presses for a revision of the human race and for some highly necessary world repairs; he also insists very obstinately on knowing why he has to play the fool for a public not of his acquaintance.

"Now a tragic situation is very poorly executed. For the beautiful Columbine appears, and when the brother without heart presents her to the other as his wife, the latter falls down without speaking a word, most clumsily banging his wooden head on a stone. The former two run off to get help; Clown, however, lifts him up and, in wiping his bloody forehead, quite calmly asks him to kindly strike the stone as well as the entire story out of his head, since there are no things in themselves. He also praises the director for having abolished Greek fate and introduced in its place a moral theatrical order, according to which everything has to turn out well in the end.

"The last act now makes one laugh oneself quite to death. First, silly waltzes are played in order to soothe the mind; then the marionette with the heart appears and proves to Columbine through syllogisms and sophistries that the director has confused the puppets and given her in error to his brother, since in accordance with the comic outcome of the play she belongs to him himself. Columbine seems to believe him but is unwilling, out of morality and respect toward the marionette director, to accept this, whereupon he falls into despair and makes preparations to abduct her. She repels him scornfully; now he behaves like a raving maniac, runs his wooden forehead against the wall, and applies assonance in *u*. Finally he dashes out and next, as the handsome page from the second act, overcome by sleep, is just going by in his nightshirt, hurls him into the room and closes the door behind himself.

"After a short pause he appears again with the brother-marionette, who holds a drawn dagger in his hand and, after a short, stiff tirade, cuts down first the page, then Columbine, and finally himself. The brother stands quite vacant and dumb among the three wooden puppets who lie round him on the ground; then, without speaking a further word, he snatches the dagger to dispatch himself after them for good and all; but in this moment the wire, which the director is drawing too tightly, breaks, and the arm cannot carry out the blow and dangles motionlessly; finally it is as if a strange voice speaks from the puppet's mouth and calls, 'Thou shalt live eternally.' ...

"Now Clown appears again to soothe and console him and, when he carries on too grossly, points out among other things how silly it is whenever it occurs to a marionette to reflect about itself, since it simply must comport itself in accordance with the whim of the director, who puts them back in his chest when it pleases him. Then he also says some good things about freedom of will and about the insanity in a marionette brain, which he treats quite realistically and reasonably. All this in order to prove to the puppet how mad it really is to take things of this sort so loftily, since in the end the whole affair amounts to buffoonery and since, basically, Clown plays the only rational role in the entire farce, just because he doesn't take the farce for anything loftier than a farce."

Here the man paused a second and then said in a really lustily wild mood: "There you have the whole Shrovetide play in which I myself have portrayed the brother with the heart. I find it, moreover, quite pleasant to carve one's story into wood thus and play it out; one can in the process be quite ill-natured without the moralists being able to object to it and call it a blasphemy. Also everything seems to be so very sublimely unmotivated, as is really the case in the original circumstances, although we silly men like to motivate in miniature. In contrast, our director doesn't at all and gives no account of his reasons for being unwilling to strike out so many botched roles, like mine for example, in his Shrovetide play. Oh, for many ages of man already I have been striving to vault out of this play and give the director the slip, but he doesn't let me go, however cunningly I may initiate my move. But the most wearisome part of this is the ennui that I feel more and more; for you should know that I have already served many centuries here below as actor and am one of the standard Italian masks that never step down from the stage.

"I have attempted to in every way. In the beginning I turned myself in to the courts as a great villain and triple murderer. They investigated and finally rendered the verdict: I would have to remain alive, since it followed from my defense that I had not commissioned the murder in definite and express words and it was to be reckoned against me at the most as an intellectual action, which did not belong before a *forum externum*.[14] I cursed my defense attorney, and the consequence was a minor trial for damages, with which they let me go.

"Thereupon I entered into military service and missed no battle; but fate had inscribed my name on not a single bullet, and death embraced me on the great field of slaughter among a thousand dying men and tore up his laurel crown to share it with me. Indeed, I now even had to assume a splendid hero's role in the detested drama and, with gnashing teeth, cursed my immortality which blocked my path on all sides.

"A thousand times I lifted the poisoned beaker to my lips, and a thousand times it tumbled from my hand before I could empty it. At every midnight hour I emerge from my concealment like the mechanical figure on the face of a clock in order to execute the death blow; like it, however, I step back each time, when the last stroke has faded, in order to return and exit immediately into the infinite. Oh, if I only knew how to seek out this perpetually rushing wheelhouse of time itself so as to hurl myself in and tear it apart or let myself be crushed. The yearning to carry out this intent often brings me to despair; indeed, as in a state of insanity, I form a thousand plans to make it possible—then, however, suddenly I peer deeply into myself as into an unfathomable abyss in which time is rumbling on as a never-exhaustible subterranean stream, and out of the gloomy depths the lonely word *eternal* reverberates upward, and I start back, shuddering at myself and yet never able to escape myself." ...

Here the man ended, and the burning desire rose in me to proffer the wretched insomniac beneficent opium with my own hand and bring him the long, sweet sleep for which his burning, exhausted eye vainly pined. But I feared that at the decisive moment, his insanity could subside in him and he, dying, might again learn affection for life just on account of its transitoriness. Oh, out of this contradiction is man indeed created; he loves life for the sake of death, and he would hate it if that which he fears had vanished before him.

Thus I could do nothing for him and left him to his insanity and his fate.

Fifth Nightwatch

The previous nightwatch lasted long; the result, as in that man's case, was sleeplessness, and I was compelled to stay awake through the bright prosaic day, which, according to habit, I otherwise make into night as the Spaniards do, and to be bored in the midst of bourgeois life and its many waking sleepers.

Thus I had nothing better to do than to translate my poetically mad night into clear, boring prose for myself, and I brought to paper the madman's life, well motivated and reasoned, and had it printed for the amusement and pleasure of the judicious day-wanderers. Actually, however, it was only a means to tire myself, and I wanted to read it aloud to myself on this nightwatch so as not to have to deal with prose and the day a second time.

This, then, is just what now quite plainly takes place, as follows:

Don Juan's fatherland was hot, fiery Spain, in which trees and people unfold far more luxuriantly and the whole of life assumes a more ardent coloration. However, he alone seemed to be transposed like a Nordic rock into this eternal spring; he stood there cold and inflexible, and only now and then did an earthquake course under him, so that peopletook fright and felt something uncanny in his presence.

His brother Don Ponce, in contrast, was virginally gentle, and when he spoke, his words blossomed forth as flowers and twined themselves about life, through which he wandered as through a greenly veiled enchanted garden. All loved him. Juan did not hate him but was repelled by his expression, because he did not know how to take anything calmly and grandly but diminished everything through overladen embellishments, and first had to crudely paint his garish flourishes everywhere in order to take pleasure in things, like bad poets who attempt to deck out luxuriantly rich nature for a second time, instead of creating a new, independent one through their own power.

They lived side by side without sympathy, and when they embraced, they seemed like two stiffened corpses on the St. Bernard Pass leaning breast to breast, so cold were their hearts in which neither hate not love ruled; only Ponce held its unchangeably smiling mask before his face and lavished many kind words in an innocent, pleasant manner without genial hardness or cordial rudeness. Juan then became only more reserved and rejecting, and the severe north wafted inimically through the mild south, so that the affected flowers were quickly shorn of petals.

Fate seemed to be provoked over the indifference of two kindred hearts, and malevolently cast hate and dissension between them so that they who had disdained love might draw close to each other as angry enemies ...

It happened at Seville as an indifferent Juan was attending a bullfight. His glance strayed from the arena, ascending row by row over the banks of onlookers, and fixed less on the living crowd than on the gay, fantastic decorations and the embroidered rugs that covered the balustrades. Finally he noticed a single still-empty lodge, and he stared mechanically toward it as if the curtain of the true drama would first be raised here for him. After a long pause, there appeared a single tall, feminine form quite enveloped in a black veil and, behind her, a most handsome page who protected her from the heat with an opened umbrella. She remained standing motionless on the tribune, and just as motionless, Juan stood across from her;

it was as if the riddle of his life were hidden behind these veils, and yet he feared the moment when they would fall as though a bloody ghost of Banquo should rise from them.

Finally the moment came, and a bewitching feminine form blossomed out of this raiment like a white lily; her cheeks seemed without life, and her scarcely colored lips were closed in tranquillity; thus she was more like the significant image of a wonderful superhuman being than an earthly woman.

Juan felt simultaneously dread and hot, wild love. There was deep confusion in him, and a loud cry was the sole expression that escaped his lips. The unknown woman looked swiftly and acutely toward him, closed her veils in the same moment, and disappeared.

Juan hurried after her and did not find her. He combed Seville—in vain; anxiety and love drove him back and forth, and yet in isolated, quickly fleeting seconds, the moment when he would find her seemed to him just as frightful as desired; he endeavored to hold fast this premonition for a single instant in order to comprehend it, but it rushed quickly by him like a nocturnal dream every time, and whenever he deliberated everything was obscure again and extinguished in his memory ...

He had circled through the whole of Spain three times without ever again encountering the pale countenance that, deadly and loving at the same time, seemed to peer into his life; finally an irresistible nostalgia drove him back to Seville, and the first person he encountered there was Ponce.

The two brothers seemed startled, for both had grown so strange to each other as to be mutual riddles. Juan's hardness had disappeared, and he stood all in flames like a volcano, through whose millenary layers the inner fire all at once had found its vent; but in his presence things now seemed only all the more dangerous. Ponce's former gentleness had, in contrast, turned into reserve, and he stood there cold next to his ardent brother; all false trumpery had dropped from his life, and he was like a tree that, robbed of its transitory vernal embellishment, stretches its naked branches stiff and bewildered into the breezes. —Thus the same lightning flash ignites a forest for it to illuminate the horizon a thousand nights through, while it travels fleetingly over the heath and singes the meager flowers for them to wither and leave no trace behind.

With cold courtesy Ponce bade Don Juan accompany him to his dwelling so that he could present his wife to him. Juan followed mechanically. It was just siesta time; the brothers stepped into a pavilion enveloped by a thick wine arbor—there on a marble memorial the pale figure rested slumbering and motionless next to the stony genius of death, whose inverted torch touched her breast. Juan stood rigid and rooted; the dark premonition rose swiftly before his mind and did not disappear again but became fearfully clear, like the riddle of Oedipus suddenly resolving itself. Then his senses left him, and he sank down unconscious on the stone.

When he awoke again, he found himself alone, and only the page, a mute, serious youth, had remained behind with him. Storm and tumult inside of him, he plunged out into the open ...

And everything was transformed round about him and had become different; old time seemed to regenerate, and gray fate awoke out of its deep sleep and ruled again over heaven and earth. A fury pursued him like Orestes at every step and often maliciously lifted her snaky hair and showed him her lovely countenance ...

Ponce had to leave Seville for a rather long time; now Don Juan crept forth from his deep concealment like a criminal shy of the light. In his soul everything was fixed and determined, yet he fled his own company in order not to give expression to the dark feeling and not have to account to himself for himself. Thus a mystery to himself, he sought out Ponce's country estate and entered Donna Ines's room; she recognized him instantly, and for the first time the white rose blossomed fiery red, and love vivified Pygmalion's cold miraculous image. The evening sun was burning through foliage and blossoms, and childishly innocent Ines held up her ruby cheeks to the sky's fire that beamed on her. Then, trembling, she grasped the harp, and as Juan, on the flute, accompanied her playing, the forbidden conversation commenced without words, and the notes confessed and rejoined love. So things stood, till Juan became bolder, disdained the mystic hieroglyph, and revealed the beautiful secret sin in clear speech. Then twilight faded for the guiltless girl. She seemed only now to recognize everything about her as by an inimical torchlight and for the first time, shuddering and terrified, named the name: "Brother!"

The sun sank in the same moment, and her even now still flushed countenance was swiftly pale again as before.

Juan grew mute; Ines drew a bell cord, and that same page, handsome as the god of love, stepped into the room. —Juan withdrew without speaking a word.

It was already quite gloomy out in the forest; he walked ahead void of thoughts; suddenly Don Ponce stood right before him; instantly he drew his dagger and directed a wild blow. —Now he came to his senses; the dagger was stuck deep in the branch of a tree, and only his fantasy had committed the fratricide.

Ponce finally returned, but Ines made no mention of the event in his presence and veiled love and transgression deep in her breast. Juan hated the day and thenceforth lived only in the night, for what was taking place in him shunned the light and was dangerous. Each night as soon as it became dark, he would wander from the place he haunted to Ponce's estate and look toward Ines's windows, but with the gray of morning he withdrew again, wild with rancor. Once he saw Ines and the page in the lamplight, and his fantasy created a fairytale of how Ines had rejected him on the youth's account and secretly dedicated the sweet hours of the night to the latter alone; then in wild jealousy he swore death to the handsome boy and determined to seize the first opportunity to carry it out. —The light in her room did not go out; he imagined the page to be still at her side; he waited trembling with rage and love right up to the hour of midnight; then, no longer in control of himself, half-crazed, he crept out up to the door of the house and found it only latched. With uncertain, staggering steps he moved forward and came to Ines's room—a swift turn, and it was open.

The pale girl lay there as on the sarcophagus again; her nightgown was only lightly wound about her, and her brown locks twined in the strings of the harp that, still slumbering, she pressed to her breast. His brother's name involuntarily escaped Juan's lips.

Then he thought he suddenly saw in the sleeper a fury who had ascended between them, and the locks trembling about the beautiful face seemed to metamorphose into snakes. But then, once more, she was the woman he loved, and he sank down at her feet, beside himself, and pressed his hot lips on her breast. In fright, she reeled to her feet, recognized him by the glow of the night lamp, and pushed him from her with violent force; her look expressed horror and revulsion.

That single look shattered him, but his evil demon was quickly aroused, and he burst forth not conscious of what he intended to do—a bloody design lay darkly before his soul.

Wakened by the noise, the page staggered, drunken with sleep, out of a room in the outer hall; Juan clutched him and said hurriedly: "Your mistress is calling for you; she wants to attend early mass!" The page rubbed his eyes; he looked after him and was still watching as he disappeared into Ines's room. Fate had malevolently prepared the catastrophe: Don Juan found his brother's bedchamber, tore him from first slumber, and cried out to him his wife's faithlessness. Ponce started up instantly and demanded explanation, but he dragged him along violently and on the way just pressed his dagger into his hand; then he shoved him into the room.

It was deathly still around Don Juan; he stood frightfully lonely in the night and searched, teeth chattering, in dim anxiety for the weapon he had just given away. Now a noise arose, and the door flew, as by itself, off its hinges.

There the terrible nightpiece was illuminated. The handsome boy already lay in a fast death's slumber on the floor, and from Ines's breast the purply red stream was flowing and stuck to her snow-white veil like pinned-on roses.

Juan stood as rigid as a statue; Ines looked at him fixedly, but her pallid lips remained closed and revealed nothing; then deep sleep descended softly over her eyes.

Ponce awoke only when she died, and now for the first time he seemed to love, because he had lost love, and to feel a loving heart so as to pierce it through. Silently he was remarried to Ines.

Don Juan stood mute and insane among the dead.

Sixth Nightwatch

What wouldn't I give to be able to narrate with the same nice coherence and directness as other honest Protestant poets and magazine writers, who become great and splendid in so doing and exchange their golden ideas for golden realities. It simply has not been granted to me; the brief, simple murder story has cost me sweat and toil enough and, nonetheless, still looks quite shaggy and motley.

Unfortunately I was corrupted in my young years, and as it were already in the bud, for in contrast to the way other scholarly boys and promising youths make it their business to become more and more clever and reasonable, I have constantly had a special predilection for folly and tried to bring about absolute confusion in myself so as to achieve, like our Lord God, a fine and complete chaos, out of which afterward opportunely, whenever it occurred to me, a tolerable world could be arranged. —Indeed, in overexcited moments it sometimes strikes me that the human race has botched even chaos and been too precipitate in organizing; and on this account, then, nothing can come to rest at its appropriate place, and as soon as possible the Creator will have to set about deleting and nullifying the world as a miscarried system ...

Ah, this idée fixe has brought me ill enough and once almost might even have cost me my night watchman's post, because it occurred to me in the final hour of the century to portend the Last Judgment and to cry out eternity instead of time, over which many ecclesiastical and worldly gentlemen leaped in fright from their feathers and into perplexity, since they were not prepared for anything so unexpected.

The scene unfolded drolly enough at this false Last Judgment alarm, during which I played the sole calm onlooker, whereas all others had to serve me as passionate actors. —Oh, you should have seen what a pushing and shoving arose among these poor human beings and how the nobility ran in fearful confusion and yet still sought to maintain proper ranks before their Lord God; a crowd of judicial and other wolves wanted to shed their skins and in complete despair endeavored to change themselves into sheep, here by granting large pensions to the widows and orphans dashing about in heated fear, there by publicly quashing unjust sentences and vowing to pay back, immediately after the outcome of the Last Judgment, the stolen monies through which they had made the poor devils into beggars. Thus many a bloodsucker and vampire denounced himself as worthy of hanging and beheading and urged that the sentence against him be carried out with dispatch here below, in order to avert punishment by a higher hand. For the first time the proudest man in the state, with his crown in his hand, stood humble and almost crawling and exchanged polite hesitations over precedence with a tattered fellow, because the dawn of a general equality seemed possible to him.

Offices were resigned, ribbons and decorations were taken off by unworthy possessors with their own hands; pastors solemnly promised to give their flocks in the future, in addition to good words, a good example into the bargain, if only the Lord God would this one time rest satisfied with their return to reason.

Oh, how can I describe how before me on the stage the people ran into one another and in confusion and fear prayed and cursed and moaned and howled; and how the disguise fell from the countenance of every mask on this great ball, collapsed by the trumpet's summons; and how people discovered kings in beggars' clothes and the reverse, weaklings in knights' armor, and so almost always contrast between dress and man.

I was happy that through colossal fear they did not even notice the delay of divine criminal justice for a long while, and residents of the whole city had time to uncover all their virtues and vices and to expose themselves completely, as it were, before me, their last co-citizen. There was only a single genial little drama, and that was perpetrated by a satirical boy who was already previously determined out of ennui not to migrate into the new millennium and, in the final hour of the old, shot himself as an experiment to see whether, in this moment of indifference between death and resurrection, dying might for an instant still be possible, so that he would not have to cross forthwith into eternity bearing the whole enormous monotony of life.

Besides me, moreover, there was only one other calm person, and he was of course the city poet who scornfully looked down from his garret window into the Michelangelo painting[1] and seemed to intend to take even the end of the world poetically from his poetic height.

An astronomer near me finally noticed that this great *actus solemnis* was somewhat too long delayed and that even the fiery sword in the north was probably to be taken as a mere aurora borealis instead of the sword of judgment. In this decisive moment, since some of the wretches already wanted to stick their heads up again, I considered it of utility to attempt to hold them fast in their abjectness at least for the space of a short edifying address, and I began in the following manner:

"Beloved fellow citizens!

"An astronomer cannot be regarded as a competent judge in this case since such an important phenomenon as seems to descend over us in the sky can in no way be reckoned as an insignificant comet and occurs only once during the whole of world history; let us therefore not so idly give up our solemn mood, but rather engage in a few observations important and purposeful from our standpoint.

"What indeed is of greater moment for us on the day of world judgment than a backward glance at the planet reeling under us, which is about to collapse with its paradises and dungeons, with its crazy houses and scholars' republics; do let us for this reason in this final hour, when we are about to close off world history, review briefly and summarily what we have engaged in and carried out here since this earthly sphere rose forth from the chaos. It has been a long sequel of years since Adam's day—even if we are unwilling to accept the Chinese reckoning of time as the valid one; what, however, have we accomplished in it? —I maintain: nothing at all!

"Don't look at me so astonished; this present day simply is not appointed for making oneself important, and it is vital that we seek to occupy ourselves precipitately with modesty a little while yet.

"Tell me, with what kind of a face do you want to appear before our Lord God, you my brothers, princes, usurers, warriors, murderers, capitalists, thieves, state officials, jurists, theologians, philosophers, fools, and of whatever office or trade you may be; for today no one has a right to be missing from this general national convention, although I notice that several of you would like to get on your feet in order to take to your heels.

"Pay honor to truth; what have you achieved that might have been worth the effort? You philosophers, for example, have you up to now said anything more important than that you are capable of saying nothing? —The actual and most manifest result of all previous philosophies ! —You scholars, what has your scholarship ever purposed other than a disintegration and dissipation of the human spirit, so that you could attach yourselves finally with ease and naive importance to the *caput mortuum*[2] that is left? —You theologians, who would so much like to be numbered among the divine household, yet while ogling and fawning upon the Almighty have instituted a miserable den of assassins here below and, instead of uniting men, have churned them apart in sects and, as malicious friends of the house, forever torn asunder the beautiful general estate of brotherhood and family. —You jurists, you semihuman beings, who actually should constitute only one person with the theologians, but instead of that separated yourselves in a cursed hour from them, so as to execute bodies as the latter do intellects. Oh, only on the execution block before the poor sinner on the seat of judgment do you brotherly souls take one another's hands yet, and the spiritual and worldly hangmen appear worthy side by side! ...

"What can I even say of you, you statesmen, who reduced the human race to mechanical principles? Can you stand before a heavenly review with your maxims, and now that we are about to make the transition into a realm of spirits, how do you intend to consign those plundered shapes, of which as it were you only knew how to use the stripped-off skin, since you killed the spirit in them? —Oh, and what thoughts do not obtrude on me respecting the giants standing alone, the princes and rulers, who pay with people instead of with coins and engage in the most shameful slave trade with death.

"Oh it has made me mad and wild, and as I see the brood of earth creeping around before me now with their merits and virtues, I would like to be the devil at this general world judgment just for an hour, merely to give you a still stronger talk! ...

"The solemn action is still delayed, as I see, and some room yet is given you for conversion; so pray and howl then, you hypocrites, as you're accustomed to do shortly before death, when you don't know how to employ your bungled life more profitably and have become incapable of sinning any longer.

"Behind you lies the whole of world history like a silly novel, in which there are some few tolerable characters and a legion of wretched ones. Ah, your Lord God made a mistake only in this one regard, that he did not himself elaborate it but left it up to you to write in it. Tell me, will he indeed consider it now worth the effort to translate the botched thing into a higher language, or must he not rather, when he sees it lying before him in its whole shallowness, tear it to shreds in wrath and deliver you with all your plans over to oblivion? I can't see it any other way! For can you, as I glimpse you here, can you all lawfully really make claim to heaven or hell? For the former you are too bad; for the latter, too boring! ...

"The preparations for judgment are being protracted, but I advise you, don't relax; rather, pull yourselves together in order to have taken a few nice steps forward in mortification before everything crashes beneath us. I will break off with the most cogent arguments: The Lord once spared Sodom and Gomorrah for the sake of a single just man, but you could be insolent enough to conclude that he would harbor with himself an entire globe full of hypocrites for the sake of a few sufferable pious people. Let someone among you make but a single reasonable suggestion as to what place one should consign you! The late Kant[3] has already demonstrated to you how time and space are merely forms of sensual perception; now you know, however, that neither occurs any longer in the spirit world. So I ask you, you who live and move in sensualism alone, how do you expect to find space there where there no longer is any space? —Indeed, whatever do you expect to begin when time comes to an end? Even applied to your greatest wise men and poets, immortality in the final analysis still remains but an inappropriate expression; what is it to mean for you poor devils, who have practiced no other business than that of selling wares and know no other spirit than in wine, through which your poets induce in themselves an analogy to inspiration? —Let somebody then give some tolerable advice; I at least don't know what the devil I am to do with you!" ...

Here I noticed an uneasiness in the assembly before me and also heard quite plainly how some young freethinkers, who are now synonymous with *thoughtless*, were boldly maintaining that the whole affair had only been a false alarm. One person in the assembly had already put his crown on again, and the high council, which had denounced itself before, opined angrily that playing comedy with an entire respectful city merited a severe penalty and that they would have to hold on to me as the first alarm instigator.

I now meekly conceded and, turning to the man with the crown, requested only a further moment's hearing, whereupon I made the following remark: That such an announcement of Judgment Day, even though a false alarm, could still be of some use, and it would even be desirable on the part of the state to make such a ghostly warning regularly through physical experiments and a few hundredweight of flash power to be sent down in flaming bolts from the heights and towers, so that the man wearing the crown, who is in no case omniscient, could now and again thereby institute a general reform of the state and perceive the state itself *in puris naturalibus*⁴ with all its failings, since otherwise it was always presented to him only in gala array, deceptively decked out by the state tailors or clippers, the favorites and councillors. Indeed, I myself was applying to have a patent issued for my invention of this state experiment, simply to draw into my purse the incidental law fees that fall on such a pseudo-Last Judgment—the blessings of the poor devils helped up again, the curses of the toppled saints, and the like.

Indeed, made more audacious by the dead stillness around me, I finally dared to note how, through my fire alarm, I myself had today already instituted such a revision, and it would not be a bad idea to proceed immediately with modest repairs and anchor the shifted state structure tolerably in place again through some dismissals from office, executions, and so forth.

No one spoke a word when I finished, and the man shoved the crown on his head back and forth as if he were irresolute; the final outcome was, nonetheless, that my invention was rejected as inapplicable; further, I was regarded out of highest mercy only as a fool, and this one time more the dismissal from office entered against me was to be suspended.

So that a similar alarm need not again be feared later, however, the watchman's noctuaries invented by Samuel Day* were introduced by a cabinet order, whereby I was demoted from a singing and trumpeting night watchman to a mute one, in support of which they argued that through my blowing and calling I betrayed myself to the night thieves and therefore this had to be suppressed as unsuitable.

The day thieves were thus at a stroke removed from my vigilance,

---

*These night-clocks are so arranged that the night watchman each time, as proof that he has gone around according to regulation, inserts a card in a previously concealed slot that moves forward only at the precise hour. In the morning a police officer unlocks the clock to see whether a card is present in each single slot.

and I now wander around mute and sad through the desolate streets in order to shove my card into the nightclock on every hour. Oh, it is unbelievable how much sleep has been promoted since then and how, since my trumpet blast of doom has been broken, many a person who in secret sinning feared nothing but the Last Judgment lies calm and fast asleep on his pillows.

Seventh Nightwatch

Well, so I've touched on my madcap deeds; but then, the worst of them all is my life itself, and tonight I want to continue in the recapitulation of the same, since I'm no longer allowed to pass the time for myself with trumpeting and singing.

I've already often made a start, sitting before the mirror of my imagination, at passably portraying myself; I have always, however, bashed in the damned countenance when I finally found that it resembled a puzzle painting that, regarded from three different standpoints, presents one of the Graces, a monkey, and *en face* the devil. I then became bewildered over myself and assumed hypothetically as the final ground of my existence that the very devil himself, in order to play a trick on heaven, slipped into the bed of a just canonized saint during a dark night and inscribed me there as it were as a *lex cruciata*[1] for our Lord God, over which he should break his head on the Judgment Day.

This cursed contradiction in me goes so far that, for example, the pope himself cannot be more devout in praying than I am in blaspheming, and if I'm perusing really good, edifying works, then I absolutely cannot refrain from the most malicious thoughts. If other reasonable and feeling people wander out into nature in order to erect poetic tabernacles and shrines[2] there for themselves, I prefer to gather together choice and long-lasting building materials for a general fools-house, in which I would like to lock up prose stylists and poets side by side. People chased me a few times from churches because I laughed there, and just as often from houses of pleasure because I wanted to pray in them.

The possibilities are in stark contrast: either people are standing on their heads or I am. If a majority vote is to decide here, then I am utterly lost.

Be that as it may, and whether my physiognomy may turn out ugly or handsome, I intend to copy away at it faithfully for a little hour. I will not flatter, because I paint at night, when I cannot employ the dissembling colors, and must limit myself to strong shadows and sharp emphases.

At first a few poetic broadsheets, which I let fly from my shoemaker's workshop, gave me a tolerable name; the first contained a funeral oration that I wrote down when a little boy was born to him, and by now I remember just the beginning, which went approximately thus:

"They are dressing him for his first coffin until the second, in which his deeds and follies are to be entombed, has been made ready; just as one is accustomed to lay princely corpses first in a provisional casket, until they then later carry the metal one down into the grotto, which is worthily ornamented with trophies and inscriptions, and encoffin the cadaver for a second time. —And do not trust, I pray you, the glow of life and the roses on the boy's cheeks; that is the art of nature, whereby she like a skilled doctor preserves the embalmed body a longer time in a pleasant deception; decay is already gnawing on his insides, and if you wanted to uncover the fact, you would actually see the little worms developing out of their embryos, the joy and pain that quickly gnaw their way through so that the corpse disintegrates into dust. Ah, only when he was not yet born did he live, just as happiness consists in hope alone but as soon as it is realized destroys itself. He is now only just situated on the bed of state, yet the flowers you strew on him are autumnal flowers for his winding cloth. In the distance the pall bearers, who are going to carry away his joys and him himself, are already gathering in readiness, and the earth is already preparing his tomb in order to receive him. Everywhere mere death and decay greedily stretch out their arms after him, to consume him little by little, in order at last, when his pains, his ecstasy, his memory and his dust have wafted away, to rest on his empty tomb, tired from killing. His ash nature has by then already long since used up again on new death flowers for new mortals." ...

The rest of the speech I've forgotten. They thought the overall effect was not bad and only the title was a mistake, since obviously "deathday" should stand instead of birthday; it was even so used then in cases involving children's corpses ...

An author making his debut has to struggle against great difficulties, since in general he first must make himself known through his works; in contrast, once he has arrived and been applauded, he makes works famous through his name; since people can never convince themselves that great poets and great heroes have hours in which they bring to light worse works and worse actions than the worst of other extremely quotidian sons of earth. Height and depth exist only reciprocally; on a flat plane, on the other hand, a plunge is not to be feared.

Luck pursued me meanwhile in a proper fashion, and I received almost more rhymes than shoes to patch together, so that we were able to restore the old Hans Sachs shingle over our workshop and amalgamate two arts important for the state. In addition, I received almost more pay for a poem than for a shoe, for which reason the old master allowed the loose trade to make its way in alongside the staple trade without raillery, and my Delphic tripod to stand next to his of public utility.

I regard it, moreover, as a reasonable regulation of Providence that a number of people are locked into a wretchedly narrow circle of activity and four walls, where in the stifling dungeon air their light can flare up only dully and harmlessly, so that at the most they see by it that they are located in a dungeon—as otherwise, in freedom, it would burst into flames like a volcano, setting everything round about on fire. —In my case things were now already beginning to spit and to spark; nevertheless, nothing more than poetic flares for reconnoitering the terrain were able to put in an appearance, no bombs to blast it apart and ravage it. A terrible anxiety often seized me, like that of a giant who has been walled into a low space when a child and who now grows up and wishes to stretch himself and stand upright, without being able to do so, and can only squash his brain in or press himself together into a disjointed deformity.

Men of this stripe, if they prospered, would express themselves with hostility and go among the folk as a plague, an earthquake, or a storm, and eradicate and burn to powder a good part of the planet. But these sons of Anak[3] are usually well placed, and there are mountains thrown over them as over the Titans,[4] under which they can only shake themselves in fury. Here their fuel is gradually reduced to charcoal, and only seldom do they succeed in finding a vent and angrily hurling their fire out of the volcano heavenward.

Meanwhile I was already bringing the people into an uproar through my mere pyrotechnics, and my desultory satirical speech of a jackass on the theme of why jackasses must exist in the first place created a prodigious row. I had, by God, intended little mischief by it and had relegated the whole matter to mere generalities; but a satire is like a touchstone, and every metal that brushes against it leaves behind the token of its worth or worthlessness; this was the case here too. — Mr. X had read the pamphlet and found everything exactly fitting himself, for which reason they locked me up without further ado in the tower, where I had leisure to become wilder and wilder. In the course of this, moreover, my misanthropy progressed like that of princes, who are beneficent to individual men and massacre them only in whole hosts.

Finally they let me loose when the outside payment ceased, for my old master had gone death's way, and I now stood all alone in the world as if I had fallen from another planet. Now I really saw how man no longer has any value as man and possesses nothing on earth beyond what he can buy or fight for. Oh, how furious I was that beggars, vagabonds, and other poor devils such as I am let the law of the jungle be taken from them and accorded to only the princes, who now exercise it on a grand scale, as pertaining to their royal prerogatives; for I truly could find no little plot of earth to settle myself on, so thoroughly had they divided and carved up among themselves every handbreadth and absolutely refused to hear anything about natural law, as the sole general and positive law, but had their special law and their special belief in every little corner. In Sparta they sang the praises of the thief in accordance with how artfully he knew how to steal; and nearby in Athens they strung him up.

I had to seize hold of something, nonetheless, in order not to starve, for they had usurped all the free common wealth of nature, including the birds below heaven and the fish in the water, and were unwilling to grant me a kernel of grain without good payment in cash. I chose the profession in which I could best celebrate their doings and became a rhapsodist like blind Homer, who also had to go about as a ballad singer.

Blood they love beyond measure, and whenever they themselves may not be spilling it, they delight to see it flowing everywhere in pictures, in poems, and in life itself—particularly in great battle scenes. I therefore sang tales of murder to them and made my livelihood that way; indeed, I began to number myself among the useful members of the state, that is, among the fencing masters, gun manufacturers, powder producers, ministers of war, doctors, et cetera, who all obviously work in death's cause, and acquired a good reputation for myself by endeavoring to harden my listeners and pupils and accustom them to bloody events.

Finally, however, the smaller death scenes began to repel, and I tried my hand at greater ones—killings of the soul by church and state, for which I chose good materials from history; I also now and again mixed in more trifling murder delights, as, for example, of honor by insidious good repute, of love by cold, heartless fellows, of loyalty by false friends, of justice by courts of law, of sound reason by censors' edicts. But then the whole thing was over, for in short order more than fifty damage suits were brought against me. I appeared before court as my own *advocatus diaboli*.[5] Before me at the table sat half a dozen men with juridical masks before their countenance, under which they concealed their own scoundrel's physiognomy and the other half of their Hogarth face. They understand the art of Rubens, with which he transformed a laughing face into a weeping one by means of a single stroke, and apply it to themselves as soon as they have settled upon their judge's chairs, so that one might not be inclined to regard these as poor-sinner stools. —After a strict warning to tell the truth regarding the complaints lodged against me, I began thus:

"Most wise ones! I stand here before you as an accused slanderer, and all *corpora delicti* speak against me, among which I am even of a firm will to count you yourselves, since one could regard as *corpora delicti*[6] not only the objects from which one can draw conclusions respecting a certain crime (crowbars, cat ladders, and the like) but also the bodies themselves in which the crime resides. Now it would not, however, be amiss for you yourselves to become acquainted with the crimes, not only as good theoreticians but also to know how to commit them as worthy practitioners; just as a number of poets earnestly complain that their reviewers are themselves not capable of framing a single verse and yet presume to judge verses— and what objection could you raise, wise ones, if a thief, adulterer, or any other sort of mean cur of this gang over whom you would pass judgment were to give you, in accordance with the analogy, a similar nut to crack and refuse to recognize you as competent reviewers in your department because you yourselves have achieved nothing at all yet *in praxi*?[7]

"The laws, too, indeed seem to point in this direction and in many cases exonerate you of crimes as persons of the court, as, for example, you may put to death with impunity, strike about with the sword, hack down with clubs, burn, drown in a sack, bury alive, quarter, and wrack—sheer gross offenses that one would never take from anyone except you. Indeed in minor trespasses too, and namely in the case in which I now find myself here as defendant, the laws absolve you; thus *lex* 13, *para*. I and 2, *de iniuriis* allows you outright to slander those whom you yourselves hold captive in your judicial net for slander.[8]

"It is unbelievable what advantages could accrue to the state from this arrangement; would not, for example, a multitude of crimes be sooner brought to light, if respective justices visited the houses of pleasure in their own person and consummated the pleasure in order to convict the inculpated immediately without further ado; if they likewise mixed as thieves among thieves simply to have their comrades hanged; or if they themselves committed adultery in order to make the acquaintance of whatever adulteresses and such as take pleasure and delight in this crime and are to be regarded as pernicious members of the state?

"Good heavens, the beneficial aspect of such an arrangement is so clear that I may add nothing further at all and should have earned my acquittal merely on account of this unauthoritative recommendation.

"I pass, nonetheless, to my defense, wise ones! The charge of an *iniuria oralis*, and in fact according to subcategory beta a *sung* injury, has been placed here against me. I might already find a ground for the nullity of the complaint in that singers obviously belong to the caste of the poets and, precisely because according to the newest school they have no purpose in view, the latter should be permitted to slander and blaspheme in their inspiration just as much as they like. Indeed, for this reason alone this crime could not be imputed to a poet and singer, because inspiration is to be equated with drunkenness which, without further ado, absolves of punishment if the drunken person has not gotten himself into this condition *culpose*,[9] which obviously is not to be assumed in the case of an inspired man, since inspiration is a gift of the gods. —Nonetheless, I am going to formulate my defense still more cogently and therefore direct your attention to the writings of our most outstanding newer legal scholars, in which it is cogently demonstrated that justice has absolutely nothing to do with morality and that only an action transgressing *external* rights can be imputed as a crime under law. But now I have only injured and wounded morally and therefore dismiss the complaint before this court as insufficient, in that I as a moral person stand under the *foro privilegiato*[10] of another world.

"Indeed since (according to Weber[11] on slander in the first section, page 29) no injury can be committed against those persons who have renounced their right to honor, so I too must infer, by analogy, that I may here in the open place of judgment overwhelm you with all possible moral injuries, since you have automatically cut your ties with morality as *icti* and members of the court; indeed, if I dare to call you cold, heartless, immoral, albeit most wise and just lords, that is to be taken more as an apology than as an injury, and I simply reject as insufficient any judicial demands subsequently issuing herefrom." ...

Here I paused, and all six looked at one another awhile without coming to a decision; I waited calmly. If they had decreed as punishment for me the strappado, the squirrel cage,[12] the Spanish cape,[13] slow roasting, leather thongs, or even disemboweling, which is considered very honorific in Japan, it would have pleased me, compared with the malice that the first friend of justice and chairman perpetrated when he rendered the verdict that I could absolutely not be held responsible for the crime, since I was to be numbered among the *mente captis*[14] and my offense had to be considered as the result of a partial insanity, for which reason they would have to deliver me over to the madhouse without further ado. It is too much; I don't care to recapitulate anymore today, and I'm going to lie down and sleep.

Eighth Nightwatch

The poets are a harmless little folk, with their dreams and raptures and heaven full of Greek gods that they carry about with them in their fantasy. But they become wicked as soon as they presume to hold their ideal up to reality and then flail the latter angrily, when they should have nothing at all to do with it. They would, nevertheless, remain harmless if they were only granted their free little place in reality undisturbed and not compelled through crowding and pressure to cast a backward glance at it. Everything must turn out too petty against the measure of their ideal, for it reaches beyond the clouds, and they themselves cannot survey it all and must cling to the stars as provisory border points, of which, however, who knows how many are yet today invisible, their light still in the process of journeying down to us.

The city poet up in his garret room also belonged to those idealists who had been converted into realists under duress through hunger, creditors, forced labor, et cetera, as Charlemagne drove the heathens before his sword into the river so that they should be baptized there as Christians. I had made the acquaintance of this night owl, and after I had shoved my card into the night-clock for a time stamp, I would often run up to him in order to watch his seething and blustering, when he inveighed against men up there as an inspired apostle with the tongue of flame crowning him. His whole genius was concentrated on the completion of a tragedy in which the great spirits of mankind (whose body and mere outward shell, as it were, it constituted), love, hate, time, and eternity appeared as lofty arcane figures, and through which, instead of the chorus, there ran a tragic clown, a grotesque and fearful mask. With an iron fist this tragedian held the beautiful countenance of life unflinchingly before his great concave mirror, in which it was distorted into wild features as though it manifested its abysses in the furrows and ugly wrinkles that dropped into the beautiful cheeks; thus he drew its sketch.

It is well that many did not understand this, for in our opera-glass age the greatest objects have become so remote that at the most one still recognizes them only unclearly in the distance through magnifying lenses; in contrast, the small are very thoroughly cultivated, because shortsighted people see all the more acutely close up.

He had already ended the whole thing and hoped that the gods, whom he had invoked for the occasion, would at least reveal themselves to him this time as a golden rain, through which he could shoo away from himself his creditors, hunger, and the bailiffs. Today was the day on which the imprimatur of the most important censor, the publisher, had to arrive, and curiosity and the longing to see him at the merry banquet of the gods of earth impelled me upstairs to him. —Is it not sad that men keep their pleasure palaces so tightly locked and have them guarded by harnessed troops,* before whom the beggar unable to bribe them withdraws in terror!

Panting, I climbed up into high Olympus and opened the entranceway; but instead of one tragedy that I had not expected, I found two of them, the one coming back from the publisher and the tragedian himself, who had simultaneously composed and produced the second one ex tempore as protagonist.† Since he was lacking the tragic dagger, he had in haste (what in the case of an improvised drama can easily be overlooked) chosen in its place the

*A man in military harness is pictured on Dutch ducats.

†So the actor was called who in Thespis's day constituted, along with the chorus, the entire tragedy.

cord which had served as a travel belt for the manuscript while engaged in its return trip, and dangled on it above his work, like a saint traveling toward heaven, quite light and with all earthly ballast cast off. It was, moreover, quite still and quite chilly in the room; only a couple of tame mice played peacefully as sole house pets at my feet and squeaked either in good humor or from hunger; a third mouse nearby, which gnawed very zealously on the poet's immortality, his returned *opus posthumum*,[1] almost seemed to decide for the latter.

"Poor devil," I said looking up to him, "I don't know whether I am supposed to take your apotheosis comically or seriously. Droll it remains, nonetheless, that you have been engaged as a Mozartian voice for a bad village concert, and likewise naturally, that you've stolen away from it; in a land wholly peopled by the lame, a single exception is ridiculed as a queer, perverse *lusus naturae*; likewise, in a state full of no one but thieves, honesty alone would have to be punished with the rope; the only thing in the world that matters is juxtaposition and agreement, and since your countrymen are now used only to an abominably screeching clamor instead of song, they had to number you among the night watchmen precisely because of your fine, accomplished elocution; I too have become one for this reason. Oh, men are marching forward handsomely, and I would really enjoy poking my head into this asinine world for just an hour a century later; I wager I would see how, in antique collections and museums, they were copying nothing but the grotesque anymore and striving for an ideal of ugliness after they had long since declared beauty, like a secondhand school of French poetry, insipid. I would also want to attend the mechanical lectures on nature in which people are taught how they can completely assemble a world with minor expenditure of energy and the young students are being developed as world creators, whereas we are now only educating them as ego creators. Good God, what progress will not likely have been made in all sciences a millennium hence, since we are now already so far; we will have to have nature repairmen then in the same abundance as now watchmakers; conduct correspondence with the moon, from which we nowadays are already fetching down stones; work out Shakespearean plays in the lowest classes as exercises; no longer even tolerate love, friendship, loyalty, as now the clown, in our theaters; build madhouses solely for the rational; root out doctors as pernicious members of the state because they have found means against death; and be able to arrange storms and earthquakes as easily as now fireworks. —Poor swaying devil, what kind of a look would your immortality then acquire; you have done well to get out of the dust quickly." ...

I was, however, suddenly touched in my good mood, the way a violently laughing man finally breaks out in tears, when I looked into a corner where his childhood, as it were, mutely and significantly faced the expired one as his sole joy and at the same time as his sole remaining piece of furniture; it was an old, weathered painting, in which the colors were already half obliterated, much as according to the superstition the cheeks' flush fades on the portraits of the deceased. It presented the poet playing as a friendly, laughing boy at his mother's breast; oh, that beautiful countenance was his first and only love, and she had only become faithless to him by dying. Here in the picture childhood still laughed around him, and he stood in spring's garden filled with closed flower buds after whose perfume he longed and which burst on him but as poisonous blooms and brought him death. I had to turn aside, shuddering, when I compared the copy, the smiling curly child's head, with the original of the present, the swaying Hippocratic face, which looked blackly and terribly like a Medusa's head into its own youth.[2] He appeared to have cast his final glance upon the painting even in the last minute, for he hung turned toward it, and the lamp was burning close before it as before an altarpiece. —Oh, the passions are the insidious retouchers, who freshen up youth's blossoming Raphaelic head with the advancing years and deform and contort it with ever harder features, until a hellish Brueghelian mask has emerged from the head of an angel ...

The poet's worktable, this altar of Apollo, was a stone, for all available wood, right up to the loosened frame of the painting, had long since been consumed in his nocturnal sacrifices to the flame. On this stone lay the rejected tragedy, titled *Man*, and with it the poet's letter of refusal to life; the latter reads thus:

Letter of Refusal to Life

Man is good for nothing. Therefore I am striking him out. My Man has found no publisher, neither as *persona vera* nor *ficta*; for the last (my tragedy) no book dealer is willing to advance the printing costs, and even the devil doesn't care about the first (myself); and they are letting me starve, like Ugolino[3] in the greatest hunger tower, the world, the key to which they have cast before my very eyes into the sea forever. It's a lucky thing that enough strength remains in me to mount the battlements and hurl myself down. For this I thank, in this my testament, the book dealer who, although he did not want to help my Man out, at least did throw enough cord into the tower for me by which to be able to reach the top.

I think it is cheerful up there, with a good, free prospect; it is better in all ways, even if I should see nothing, than down here, for I'll no longer know anything about it—whereas old Ugolino, turned blind from hunger, groped about in his tower and was conscious of his blindness, and life still struggled powerfully in him so that he could not go under.

Like him, to be sure, while yet in my dungeon I too have toyed with gracious boys whom I produced alone in the night and who played about me as blossoming youth in bright golden dreams; in them, whom I wish to leave behind, I warmly embraced life—but they rejected them too, and the hungry animals that they locked in with me have gnawed them to bits so that they hover around me only in memory.

So be it; the door is slammed firmer behind me, and the last time they opened it was just to bring in the coffin of my last child; — I leave behind nothing now and go to meet you defiant, God, or Nothing! ...

These were the last remaining ashes of a flame that had to be stifled in itself. I gathered them up, and as many relics of *Man* as I could still tear from the hungry mice—carefully, because I was appointing myself by main force testamentary heir.

If heaven ever unexpectedly brings me into a better situation, I shall edit the tragedy *Man* at my own cost, as chewed up and incomplete as it is, and distribute the copies gratis among men. For now I will only convey something of the clown's prologue. In his own words as follows, the poet apologizes in a brief prefatory speech for the fact that he dared to introduce the clown into a tragedy:

"The ancient Greeks had introduced a chorus in their tragedies which through its general observations diverted our gaze from the single terrible action and thus soothed our hearts. I think that such soothing no longer suits the times, and one should rather violently provoke and incite, because otherwise nothing strikes home anymore, and men on the whole have become so flabby and spiteful that they carry on in a downright mechanical fashion and commit their secret sins out of sheer indolence. One should irritate them violently, like an asthenic invalid, and therefore I have introduced my clown to make them really wild; for just as the maxim goes that children and fools speak the truth, so likewise do they further the fearful and tragic, in that the former recite with innocent hardness while the latter make all into utter mockery and farce. Later aestheticians will grant me my due." ...

What I still want to communicate of the manuscript read thus:

The Clown's Prologue to the Tragedy: Man

I appear as introductory speaker of *Man*. A respective,[4] numerous public will more readily overlook the fact that by my gesticulations I am a fool, if I cite in my favor that, according to Dr. Darwin,[†5] the ape, which is incontestably more cloddish yet than a mere fool, is actually the introductory speaker and prologist of the entire human race and that my and your thoughts and feelings have only with time been merely somewhat refined and cultivated, although they ever remain, according to their origin, only thoughts and feelings such as could arise in the head and heart of an ape. Dr Darwin, whom I present here as my representative and attorney, maintains that Man as man owes his existence to a species of ape on the Medi-

[†]See his poem on Nature.

terranean Sea and that the latter, merely by learning to make use of their thumb muscle such that thumb and fingertips touched, gradually acquired refined feelings, made the transition from this to concepts in following generations, and finally donned the costume of judicious men, as we still see them now marching about daily in their court and other uniforms.

The whole matter has a lot to recommend it; for after millennia we still now and again find striking approximations and affinities in this regard; indeed, I believe I have observed that many respective and esteemed persons have not yet learned how to make proper use of their thumb muscle, such as a number of writers and people who presume to guide the pen; should I not be mistaken in this, that speaks very much for Darwin. On the other hand, we also find a number of feelings and agilities in the ape which obviously slipped from us during the *salto mortale* to man; thus, for example, an ape mother even today loves her children more than many a prince's mother; the sole point in contradiction might be if one sought to argue that the latter neglected them precisely out of superabundant love in order to accomplish what the former achieves only somewhat quicker by choking her young to death.

Enough; I am in agreement with Dr. Darwin and make the philanthropic suggestion that we learn to value more highly our younger brothers, the apes on all continents, and through thorough instruction in how to bring together the thumb and fingertips, so that they can at least guide a pen, we may educate those who are now only our parodists up to our level. For it is better, along with the first Dr. Darwin, to accept the apes as our ancestors than to wait too long until a second one makes quite different wild beasts into our antecedents, which he perhaps might document with just as solid grounds of probability, since most men, when you cover the lower part of their face and mouth with which they lavish dissembling words, acquire in their physiognomies a striking racial resemblance with birds of prey, for instance vultures, hawks, et cetera; indeed, since even the older aristocracy is sooner able to trace its pedigrees to the beasts of prey than to apes, a fact that, besides their predilection for robbery in the Middle Ages, is also still plainly evident from their coats of arms, on which they show for the most part lions, tigers, and eagles and other of the like wild beasts ...

The above may suffice to justify my person and mask before *Man*, the tragedy now to he performed. I promise a respective public in advance that I will be facetious until they laugh themselves to death, however seriously and tragically the poet may yet dispose things. —What is the point of seriousness anyway? Man is a facetious animal by birth, and he merely acts on a larger stage than do the actors on the small one inserted into this big one as in *Hamlet*; however importantly he may want to take things, in the wings he must still put off crown, scepter, and theatrical dagger and creep into his little dark chamber as an exited comedian, until it pleases the director to announce a new comedy. If he tried to show his ego *in puris naturalibus* or even only in a nightshirt and with sleeping cap, by the devil, everyone would flee from its shallowness and worthlessness; but hence he bedecks it with garish theatrical patches and holds the masks of joy and love before his face in order to appear interesting and to elevate his voice through the speaking tube attached inside; then the ego finally looks down onto these tatters and imagines to consist of them; indeed, there are actually other still worse dressed egos who admire and extol our patchwork scarecrow; for, seen in the light, the other Mandandane,[§6] too, is just more artfully sewed together, and has fastened on a *gorge de Paris*[7] in front to feign a heart and holds a more deceivingly worked mask before her death's-head.

The death's-head is never missing behind the ogling mask, and life is only the cap and bells which the Nothing has draped around to tinkle with and finally to tear up fiercely and hurl from itself. Everything is Nothing and vomits itself up and gulps itself greedily down, and even this self-devouring is an insidious sham, as if there were something, whereas if the choking were once to cease, precisely the Nothing would quite plainly make its appearance and all

[§]Goethe's *Triumph of Sensibility*.

would be terror-struck before it; by this cessation fools understand "eternity"; but it is the real Nothing and absolute death, since life, on the contrary, arises only through a continual dying.

If one were ready to take the like consideration seriously, it could easily lead to the madhouse; but I take it merely as Clown and thereby conduct the prologue up to the tragedy, in which the poet, of course, has taken it to a higher plane and even invented a God and an immortality in it, in order to make his characters more significant. I hope, nevertheless, to play ancient Fate, under which even the gods stood in the Greek view, and to confuse and scramble the acting personae quite madly so that they absolutely don't see through themselves and Man shall finally consider himself as God or at least, like the idealists and world history, form himself on such a mask.

I have now more or less heralded myself and in any case can now allow the tragedy itself to appear with its three unities: of *time*—to which I shall hold strictly, so that man does not perhaps stray into eternity; of *place*—which is going to remain fixed in space; and of *action*—which I shall limit as much as possible, so that man, that Oedipus, progresses only as far as blindness, but not in a second plot to transfiguration. I have not resisted the introduction of masks, for the more masks there are, one on top of the other, all the more fun it is to pull them off one after the other down to the penultimate satirical one, the Hippocratic, and the last fixed one, which no longer laughs or cries—the skull, hairless fore and aft, with which the tragicomedian departs in the end. —I have also had nothing to object against verses; they are only a more comical lie, just as the cothurn is only a rather comical pomposity.

Exit Prologus ...

Ninth Nightwatch

I am glad that among the many thorns of my life I did find at least one rose in full flower; she was, I grant, so entwined by the barbs that I was only able to draw her out stripped of her petals in my bleeding hand; but still I plucked her, and her dying fragrance did me good. This one Maytime amid the other winter and autumn moons I spent—in the madhouse . . .

Humanity is organized exactly in the manner of an onion; layer by layer, one is inserted into the other down to the smallest one, in which man himself then fits quite finely. So humanity builds into the great temple of heaven, on whose cupola worlds soar as wondrous holy hieroglyphs, smaller temples with smaller cupolas and aping stars, and into these in turn still smaller chapels and tabernacles, until at last the All-Holy has been completely enchased *en miniature* as in a ring; since it does hover round, great and mighty, upon mountains and woods and is lifted up in the sky in that radiant host, the sun, so that all the peoples fall down before it. Into the general world religion, which nature has revealed in a thousand characters, she in turn packs smaller folk and tribal religions for Jews, Heathens, Turks, and Christians; indeed, the latter are not even satisfied with this but are boxing themselves in yet anew. —So it goes likewise in the general insane asylum out of whose windows so many heads are looking, some partially, some totally crazed; even in here there are yet smaller madhouses built in for particular fools.

Into one of these smaller ones they now brought me out of the large one, presumably because they considered the latter to be too thickly populated. I meanwhile found things here exactly as there—indeed, almost better still, because the idées fixes of the fools locked in with me were mostly pleasant ones.

I cannot better portray my co-fools than by choosing precisely the moment when I had to present them to the visiting doctor, which happened now and again, because the overseer of the institute had appointed me vice or sub-overseer on account of my harmless fool-ishness. I did this the last time with the following speech:

"Doctor Oehlmann, or Olearius[1]—as you translate your name into immortality for dissertations and programs through a dead language—we are, of course, all laboring more or less under fixed ideas, not only private individuals but entire communities and faculties; of these, for example, many of the latter, along with marketing of wisdom, are dedicated to a simple trading in hats, and even believe they convert nonwise heads into wise merely by virtue of lightly capping them with such a hat from their factory; indeed, they often even clap one on a mere stump and thus seemingly shape philosophers, because the faces of the latter usually are accustomed to recede anyway from too much speculation deep under their hat brims—on account of the many examples that here crowd my memory, I have lost the thread of this periodic sentence and prefer to break it off entirely so as to begin anew."

Here Oehlmann shook his doctor's hat as if he doubted anyone would ever let a double of this bartered copy be traded for mine.

"Do you shake," I continued, "because heaven created me merely a fool, and the emperor did not create me a doctor later on? But let's put this aside for now and preferably speak of my madness and, last, the means to remedy it.

"Number 1 here is a proof for humanity, worth more than all the writings on the subject; I can never go past him without remembering the great heroes of antiquity, Curtius, Coriolanus, Regulus, and the like. His insanity consists in valuing mankind too high and himself too low; therefore, in contrast to bad poets, he retains all his body fluids because he fears bringing on a general deluge through their release. I often grow angry, when I observe him, over the fact that I do not really possess his imagined capacity—truly I would do it, I would take the earth in hand as my *pot de chambre* so that all doctors would sink and only their hats swim above in a throng. It is a great thought—the poor devil doesn't grasp it, for just see how he stands there and torments himself and holds back his breath, merely out of pure love of humanity, and if we don't provide him with some air on our part, then he is Death's. My recipe includes conflagrations, dried-up streams with windmills at a standstill, and many hungry and thirsty on the banks. A radical cure I think can be rendered by Dante's Hell, through which I lead him now every day and which he has earnestly proposed to extinguish. —He is supposed originally to have been a poet by trade who was not able to channel his fluids into any bookshop . . .

"Numbers 2 and 3 are philosophic antipodes, an idealist and a realist; the former is afflicted with a glass breast and the latter with a glass bottom, for which reason he never settles his ego, a mere bagatelle for the former, although he in turn avoids moral contemplation and therefore scrupulously covers his breast.

"Number 4 sits here simply because he has advanced too far culturally by half a century; a number of this type are still wandering around free, whom, however, as is fitting, people consider to be all mad.

"Number 5 held talks that were too reasonable and understandable, therefore they have sent him here.

"Number 6 became deranged through the derangement of taking seriously a potentate's joke.

"Number 7 had his brains singed by venturing too high in poetry, and

"Number 8, by pushing the emotion in his comedies too extravagantly in his days of reason, wholly washed away his reason. The former now imagines he burns as flame, just as the latter by contrast flows off as water. I have tried now and again to have the contending elements consume themselves in a mutual contest, but the fire fell so violently upon the water that, in order to separate them again, I had to call on

"Number 9, who thinks himself the world creator.

"This last number often holds the oddest soliloquies, and you can listen to one right now, that is, if you have the patience."

Monologue of the Insane
World Creator

"It's a queer thing here in my hand, and if I examine it through my magnifying glass from second to second—what they there call a century—things have got more and more crazily confused on the globe, and I don't know whether I should laugh or be vexed over it—if, moreover, either reaction even befitted me. The little sun speck, which is crawling around on it, is named man; when I created it I said, to be sure, on account of its peculiarity, it was good— that was, I concede, a little hasty; nonetheless, I was simply in one of my good moods, and anything novel is welcome up here in long eternity, where there is no amusement at all. —I am still, of course, content with a number of things that I have created; thus the gay flower world, with the children who play among them, delights me, and the flying flowers, the butterflies and insects, which parted from their mothers as light-headed youths but yet returned to them to drink their milk and to slumber and die on a mother's breast.* —But this tiny speck, into which I blew a living breath and called it man, does now and then annoy me with his little spark of godhead which I implanted in him in overhaste and over which he became deranged. I should have recognized at once that so little divinity could lead only to evil, for the poor creature no longer knows in what direction to turn, and the premonition of god that it carries about inside causes it to be more and more profoundly confused, without in the process ever reaching a clear decision. In the one second that it called the golden age, it carved figures lovely to look at

---

*Some naturalist or other has advanced the hypothesis that the first insects were only stamens on plants which separated themselves from them for some indefinite reason.

and built little houses over them, the ruins of which one marveled at in the next second and regarded as the dwelling of the gods. Then it worshiped the sun, which I had ignited for it as illumination and which, compared with my study lamp, has the relation of a spark to the flame. Finally—and this was the worst—the speck fancied itself to be god and constructed systems in which it admired itself. By the devil! I should have left the doll uncarved! —What am I supposed to do with it now? —Allow it to hop about up here in eternity with its buffooneries? —Even in my case that won't do; for since it has already grown more than exceedingly bored there below and often vainly endeavors to kill time for itself in the brief instant of its existence, how would it not be bored with me in eternity, at which even I am often aghast! I also feel bad about utterly destroying it; for the mote does often dream so very pleasantly of immortality and thinks, just because it dreams such a thing, it must come true. —Where shall I begin? Truly, even my understanding comes to a stop here! Do I let the creature die and die again and each time erase the little spark of memory of itself so that it can resurrect anew and wander about? That too, in the long run, will bore me, for the farce, repeated over and over again, must grow tiring! —Best above all is to delay the decision until it occurs to me to set a firm date for the Last Judgment, and come up with a cleverer idea . . ."

"What an infamous insanity that is," I interjected, as No. 9 came to a halt. —"If a rational man came out with the like, people would surely confiscate it."

Oehlmann shook his head and made some significant notations about psychic sicknesses in general.

The creator of the world, who was holding a child's ball in his hand during his speech and now began to play with it, continued after a pause.

"How the physicists are now wondering about altered temperature and will establish new systems concerning it! Indeed, this convulsion is perhaps bringing about earthquakes and other phenomena, and there is a broad field for the teleologists. Oh, the little sun speck has an astonishing reason and introduces something systematic even into the most arbitrary and muddled things; indeed, it often extols and praises its creator precisely because it was surprised by the fact that he was just as clever as it itself. Then it bustles about in confusion, and the ant people forms a great assembly and almost behaves as if something were being settled there. If I now employ my hearing trumpet, then I actually perceive something, and from pulpits and lecterns serious speeches are buzzing about the wise arrangement of nature, whenever I perhaps play ball and thereby a few dozen countries and cities collapse and a number of the ants are smashed, which otherwise, since they have invented vaccines, are multiplying only too much. Oh, since just a second ago they have become so smart that I can't even blow my nose without them seriously investigating the phenomenon. —By the devil! It is almost vexatious to be God when such people carp at you! —I'd like to squash the whole ball!" . . .

"Just look, Doctor, how wrathfully the fellow has plotted against the world," I continued when the creator of the world finished. "It is almost dangerous for us other fools to have to tolerate this titan among us, for he has his consistent system just as well as Fichte's[2] and basically has an even smaller opinion of man than the latter, who only sunders him from heaven and hell, but in compensation compresses everything classic round about into the little I (which any tiny boy can cry out), as into a pocket format. Anyone is capable now, if it please him, of drawing from his insignificant shell entire cosmogonies, theosophies, world histories, and the like, together with the little images pertaining thereto. That is grand and splendid, of course; if only the format were not so small! Even Schlegel[3] has been aiming for smaller images, and I must confess that a great *Iliad*, issued in sixteenmo, will never suit me—that means packing the whole of Olympus in a nutshell, and the gods and heroes must either accommodate themselves to a reduced scale or break their necks without mercy! . . .

"You look at me, Doctor, and shake your head for the second time! Yes, yes, you've hit it; all that pertained to my madness, and in the rational state I am of exactly the opposite opinion!

"Let us leave the creator of the world! . . .

"Numbers 10 and 11 here are evidence for metempsychosis; the first barks as a dog and formerly served at court; the second has changed himself from a state official into a wolf. One encounters curious ideas in them.

"Numbers 12, 13, 14, 15, and 16 are variations on the same street ballad, love.

"Number 17 has become absorbed with his own nose. You find that odd? I don't! For entire faculties are often absorbed with a single letter, whether they should take it for an alpha or an omega.

"Number 18 is a master accountant who's trying to find the final number.

"Number 19 is reflecting about a theft that the state committed on him—that, however, he may do only in the madhouse.

"No. 20 is finally my own little fool's chamber. Do come in and look around, for we are all equal before God and merely labor under different idées fixes, if not under a total insanity, merely with minor nuances. —That there is a bust of Socrates by whose nose you recognize his wisdom, just as you recognize Scaramouch's folly.⁴ This manuscript contains handwritten comparisons by me of the two and has turned out in favor of the fool. —The blemish will have to be cured, won't it? On the whole the most obdurate side of me is that I find everything rational absurd, just as vice versa—I cannot at all defend myself against this vagary!

"I have often tried to drag wisdom to me by the hair and have therefore, after brief academic nuptials with the muses, cultivated relations *privatim* with all three bread-faculties so as to have myself next publicly consecrated as a holy trinity for the best of humankind and stride in wearing all three doctors' hats piled one on top of the other. Oh, I thought to myself: Could you not then circulate as Proteus in practical and theoretical considerations merely through a slight, unnoticeable change of hats! Traffic in dissertations on the quickest method for curing sicknesses, and release the patient himself from his illness by the shortest way! Embrace the dying man, after a swift switch of hats, as a legal friend and set his house in order, and finally, merely by donning a robe, show him the right way to heaven as a divine friend? In this way, as in a factory through different machines, highest and ultimate things could be attained through different hats. And what a surplus of wisdom and money—a desirable combination of the two opposed goods, a highest idealization of the centaur nature in man, when the well-satisfied animal below allows the higher rider to strut about audaciously . . .

"But on closer examination I found everything vain and recognized in all this lauded wisdom nothing other than the cover that is hung over the Mosaic countenance of life so that it not see God.

"You see where that leads, and it is my idée fixe that I consider myself more rational than the reason deduced in systems and wiser than professional wisdom.

"I would truly like to associate with you in a medical consultation, if only so as to consider how this folly of mine is to be got at and what means one could employ against it. The matter is of importance; for tell me, how can one wish to rebel against sicknesses if one, as you know, is not even in agreement with the system, indeed perhaps even considers as sickness what is higher health, and the reverse?

"And who finally decides whether we fools here in the asylum are erring more masterfully, or faculty members in their lecture halls? Whether perhaps error might even be truth, folly wisdom, death life—exactly the opposite of how one at present takes it! —Oh, I am incurable; that I myself recognize."

After some reflection Dr Oehlmann prescribed for me much exercise and little or no thinking at all, because he was of the opinion that my delusion had come about through extravagant intellectual feasting, just as in the case of others indigestion arises through too copious physical enjoyment. —I let him go.

I am saving another nightpiece for my Maytime in the madhouse.

Tenth Nightwatch

This is a strange night; the moonlight appears and vanishes like ghosts in the Gothic arches of the cathedral. —A sleepwalker, with an infant in his arms, is climbing about on the tower light, it is the sexton; his wife looks from the dormer window, wringing her hands but mute as the grave, lest the sleeping wanderer, who passes over the most dangerous places safely, as a carefree man, plunge down into the deep grave with his boy by awakening at the call of his name and growing dizzy. —Across in the suburb a thief is breaking into a palace; but it is not my beat, and I am condemned to being silent; so let him break in! —Far away there is soft, scarcely audible music, as if gnats are humming, or Koch[1] is fantasizing at night on the Jew's harp; and above on the horizon skaters are turning with airy agility on the sheet of ice in the meadow and dancing the Basel dance of death to this funereal music.

Everything is cold and stiff and raw, and the limbs have dropped from the torso of nature, and it still stretches only its petrified stumps toward the sky without their garlands of blossoms and leaves. The night is quiet and almost terrible, and cold death is present in her as an invisible spirit that grips subdued life. Now and then a frozen raven plummets from the church roof, and a beggar with neither house nor home fights against slumber, which wants to lay him sweetly and enticingly in death's arms, as the mermaid invites the light-headed fisherman into the waves with song ...

Shall I cheat death of a beggarly life? By the devil, I really do not know what is better—to be or not to be! —Oh, those there in the imitation south of their bedrooms and the painted spring of the walls, when the real one outside is benumbed, they ask no questions and prepare nature for themselves as a tasty dish on their tables and like to enjoy her in sips and in pauses with interruptions, so that things retain their savor. But this man, free as a bird, still rests directly on our ancient mother's breast, who, capricious and peevish as any old woman, now warms her children and now crushes them. —But no, you, mother, are eternally true and unchangeable and offer your children fruits in the green bower that beshadows them, and flames and the remembrance of you when you are slumbering; but the brothers have cast out Joseph and maliciously conceal the gifts that you bestow on him, as on the other children. —Oh, the brothers are not worthy that Joseph walk among them! —Let him sleep away!

The face there is already still and cold, and sleep has laid the statue in his brother's arms;[2] I want to erect it here that it may gaze into the day as a frightful specter when the sun rises. —Oh murderous death, the beggar still had a memory of life and love—the brown locks of his wife here under the rags on his breast; you should not have choked him—and yet—

The Dream of Love

Love is not beautiful—it is only the dream of love that enraptures. Hear my prayer, serious youth! If you see the beloved on my breast, oh, then break her quickly, the rose, and cast the white veil over her blossoming face. The white rose of death is more beautiful than her sister, for she reminds one of life and makes it desirable and precious. Over the mound of the beloved's grave her figure hovers eternally youthful and garlanded, and reality never deforms her features and does not touch her that she grow cold and her embrace terminate. Youth, abduct her quickly, the beloved, for the one who has fled returns in my dreams and songs, she weaves the wreath of my songs and floats up in my notes to heaven. Only the living girl dies, the dead one remains with me, and eternal is our love and our embrace! ...

Hark! —Dance music and death chant—that shakes its bells merrily! Vigorously, on and on; he who drowns out his rival leads home the bride. Too bad, though; I see two brides, a white and a red—two weddings; for the one on the lower floor the female mourners are droning their dirge; a floor higher the musicians are piping and fiddling, and the ceiling over the death chamber and the coffin trembles and groans from the dance.

Do explain the nocturnal spook to me!

Lenore[3] rides by—the white bride here in the quiet wedding chamber loved the youth who is waltzing upstairs; and that is life's way, she loved, he forgot, she faded away, and he was enkindled for a red rose that today he leads home, while they are bearing the former away ...

That is the white bride's old mother at the coffin—she does not weep; for she is blind; the white one too is not weeping and slumbers and dreams very sweetly ...

Then the wedding procession, still dancing, storms down the stairs—and the youth stands between two brides. He does grow a little pale. Hush! The blind mother recognizes him by his gait. —She leads him to the slumbering bride's bridal bed.

"She has lain down earlier than you for the wedding night. Do not wake her; she sleeps so sweetly, but she has thought of you right into her slumber. That is your picture on her heart. —Oh, do not withdraw your hand so frightened from the cold breast; that night is the longest in which the frost is most bitter; and she lies lonely in her bridal bed without the bridegroom." ...

Look! Terror has also paled the red rose there, and the youth stands between the two white brides. —Away, away, that is the world's course. Oh, if I might only trumpet and sing!

Now the corpse floats through the streets, and the lamplight moves quietly behind on the walls, as if death passing by did not wish to betray himself to slumbering life. The frozen earth crunches under the footsteps of the pallbearers—that is the secret insidious bride's song! —And they conceal her in her little chamber.

But nearby, youths are still singing and carousing and squander life and love and poetry in a brief swift intoxication that by morning is dispelled—when their deeds, their dreams, their hopes, their wishes, and everything around them has become sober and grown cold ...

In the cloister of the nuns of St. Ursula⁴ there was still restless stirring late in the night, the bell struck soft and muted now and again, as if one heard a storming in dream, and at the church windows, whose bows looked down over the walls, an unusual luster often flared up only to go out again quickly. Alone I went around the wall, which like a charmed magic circle encloses the saintly virgins. —Suddenly I bumped into someone in a cloak—what I learned from him belongs in the following winter night; what I did still fits in this ...

The porter at the outer wall was a profound old misanthrope who was cordially attached to me as an object over which he could pour out his anger whenever he liked. I often visited him at night in order to let him vent his spleen; even now I was on my way to him. He sat in his hut by a lamp in the company of a black bird over whose head he had drawn a hood and with whom he was in conversation.

"Do you know that creature"—the porter spoke—"whose countenance laughs insidiously when its interposed mask gushes tears; which names God when it is thinking about the devil; which inside, like an apple on the dead sea, contains poisonous dust, while its peel, blossoming red, invites to pleasure; which utters melodic tones through its ingeniously twisted speaking trumpet, while screaming revolt into it; which like the sphinx smiles kindly only in order to mangle, and like the snake merely embraces so intimately for the purpose of pressing its deadly sting into your breast? —Who is this creature, Blackie?"

"Man!" croaked the animal in an unpleasant fashion.

"The black one doesn't speak one other word"—said the porter— "but for that reason he answers each of my questions right to the point. —Go to sleep, Blackie!"

The bird cried out Man three times more and stationed himself then, as if he were meditating profoundly, in a gloomy corner—but he was only slumbering.

"They're playing Let's-Bury-It in the convent," the old man continued; "do you want to watch? A chaste Ursuline became a mother today; in legend it would, of course, be recorded as a miracle; however, they have peeked so often at God's cards that nowadays they no longer believe in any miracle. The saintly virgin will be buried alive this night. —I'll let you in; take a look to pass the time!"

He took the key, the hinges creaked, and I went over graves through the cloisters. Torchlight often flew swiftly over the monuments, on which stone virgins slumbered in prayer with artfully molded faces, while underneath the originals had already cast off their masks ...

I placed myself behind a pillar; below was an open walled tomb —a lonely divestiture chamber for the exiting person; in the little chamber a pale death lamp was burning and, on a stone jutting forth, were located a loaf of bread, a jug of water, a crucifix, and a prayer book. In the church built over the tomb deep stillness prevailed among the saints, who looked down from the walls; only when now and then a gust of wind went through the organ works, a pipe would howl unpleasantly.

Finally the procession became visible through the columns— many silent virgins and in their midst the walking bride of death. The entire act would have had something horrifying for an onlooker of a poetically impressionable nature, precisely through the almost mechanically dreadful way in which it was executed; just as even the tragic muse, the less hand-wringing she does, the more profoundly she moves us. My heart, nevertheless (which is like a string instrument absurdly tuned on purpose, on which therefore nothing can ever be played in a pure key, unless it be that the devil might once advertise a concert on it), was little affected, and at bottom nothing further came to pass than a mad run through the scale, which went approximately through the following notes and was stalled in a disharmony:

Run through the Scale

"Life runs past man, but so fleetingly that he calls to it in vain to stand still for him a moment so he can discuss with it what it wants and why it is looking at him. Then the masks whisk by, the sentiments, one more distorted than the other. Joy, account to me—cries man—why are you smiling at me! The mask smiles and flees. Pain, let me look you firmly in the eye, why do you appear to me? It too is already passed. —Anger, why do you peer at me? —I ask, and you have disappeared.

"And the masks turn in a mad swift dance around me—around me, who am called man—and I reel in the midst of their circle, dizzy from the sight and endeavoring in vain to embrace one of the masks and tear the disguise from its true countenance; but they dance and only dance—and I, what shall I do in the circle? Who am I then, if the disguises should disappear? Give me a mirror, you carnival players, that I may once see myself—it's getting wearisome for me always to be looking only at your changing faces. You shake—what? Does no I stand in the mirror, when I step before it—am I only the thought of a thought, the dream of a dream—can you not help me to find my body, and will you always be shaking your bells, when I think they are mine? Hoo! It is indeed terribly lonely in the ego, when I clasp you tight, you masks, and I try to look at myself—everything echoing sound without the disappeared note—nowhere substance, and yet I see—that must be the Nothing that I see! —Away, away from the I—only dance on, you masks!"

Now the nun descends into the tomb. Oh, do end the play that I may find out whether it actually amounts to comedy or to tragedy. For a mask is still following the bride of death on her final path—it is insanity. The mask smiles secretly—does the true countenance behind it shudder, or is it transported—who will tell me?

To be sure, they are walling in as company for the bride a snake—hunger—which soon will twine about her breast and gnaw its way to her eye. If, then, the final mask also disappears and the ego is alone with itself, will it be able to beguile time for itself? . . .

Now the hammers of the Freemasons thud dully through the

vault, and one stone after the other is fitted into the vault of the tomb. Now I can only still espy the buried one's secret smile through a small hole by the light of my lamp—now merely a slight shimmer stealing through. —Now everything is covered up, and the living dead are singing a solemn Miserere over the buried one's head as a lullaby ...

I found the porter, when I returned, together as usual with his old gloomy mask. —"Do you hate mankind now?" he asked.

"I am practically alone with myself," I said, "and hate or love just as little as possible! I attempt to think that I think nothing, and that way I finally manage to get so far as to arrive at myself!" ...

"Take the worm along," the old man continued and lifted the cover over a slumbering child. "I don't want to keep him with me, for I still have attacks of human kindness when I could easily smother him in a frenzy!"

I took the boy in my arms, and this still dreaming life reconciled me again with the awakened.

"They handed the child over to me to get rid of it," spoke the porter, "for they tolerate nothing masculine among them, the pious virgins; the boy's mother you just saw buried; now seek out his father, or fling the citizen into the world; there is no danger about the breed of men, it won't go under."

"I know the father!" I answered and left the hut. Outside the cloaked stranger was standing and grabbed hold of me. —"The bride is buried—this is your son!" With these words I placed the boy in his arms, and wordless he pressed it to his heart.

Eleventh Nightwatch

The following is a fragment from the story of the cloaked stranger. I love the Self—therefore let him speak himself!

"What is the sun?" I asked my mother one day as she was describing the sunrise from a mountain. "Poor boy, you will never understand, you were born blind!" she answered, moved, and gently stroked my forehead and my eyes.

I was glowing—the description had enraptured me; between men and my love of them stood a dividing wall—if only I could once glimpse the sun, I thought, it would disappear and I would be permitted to enjoy a closer companionship with my mother . . .

From now on my fantasy toiled fervently, my longing mind strove violently to break through the body and look into the light. Beyond lay the land of my premonition, the Italy full of the wonders of nature and art.

They spoke much of night and day; for me there was but one, an eternal day or eternal night—they thought it was the latter! . . .

I sat in my darkness, and the wondrous great world dawned in my spirit, but the illumination was missing, and I only climbed about on life as on a sky-high cliff with bound eyes; I felt the flower's silk cheek, drank its fragrance—but I dreamed the flower itself was infinitely more beautiful than its fragrance and its silken cheek.

One night a vivid, wondrous dream allowed me to glimpse the light, and it was truly it; but when I awoke, I endeavored in vain to summon back the dream.

Around this time music climbed as a sweet genius into my dark dungeon and wound the tender wreaths of poetry about her strings. It was sacred ground that I now trod—the first Italy of my yearning.[1]

The angel who trafficked between the two muses and conducted them to me was a girl; the heavenly Madonna had left her earthly name behind for her—Maria was of the same age as I, and she enraptured the blind boy with her songs and notes and summoned love and hope from their dreams so that they looked clearly about themselves for the first time and stepped into life as the two loveliest vestals.

Maria was a parentless waif, and my mother had sworn a solemn oath, when she took her in, to dedicate the child to heaven if I should ever see the light. Now again I longed for the sun, though it took from me Maria and her singing.

Soon thereafter I frequently heard talk about a doctor in whose art people saw great promise to my advantage. —I wavered between opposed feelings—love for the sun and for Maria were equally fervent in my breast. They had to lead me to the doctor virtually by force . . .

He prescribed for me—and my heart heaved more stormily. I stood at the gates of life, as it were to be born a second time. Now I experienced a violent pain in my eyes; I cried out, for my dream returned to me—I saw light! —A thousand flashing rays and beams— and a swift look into the richest treasures of life.

The previous night then once more enveloped me. A bandage was placed around my eyes, and I was allowed to enter into the new world only little by little.

Nothing of intervening spaces—they showed me only a few objects, and no living being except the doctor approached me, until he finally considered me strong enough to bear the greatest.

He led me out into the night; over my head in the immeasurable distance the constellations were burning, and I stood like a drunkard under the thousands of worlds, sensing God without uttering his name. —Before me the old ruins of a previous earth, the mountains, projected into the night somber and rugged; a dull sheet-lightning out of cloudless air played about their heads. Woods reposed, deep and shrouded, at their feet and only softly shook their dark crowns. The doctor stood gravely and quietly next to me—a few steps further there was a motion as of a veiled form ...

I prayed! ...

Suddenly the scene altered; spirits seemed to draw up over the mountains, and the stars grew pale as if in terror, and behind me a broad mirror uncovered itself—the ocean ...

I trembled, for I believed God was drawing nigh.

And mists pressed against the earth and gently shrouded it—but in the sky the spirits marched on mightier, and as the stars were extinguished, golden roses flew up over the mountains into the blue heaven, and a bewitching spring was blossoming in the breeze— ever mightier and mightier—now a whole sea was billowing over, and flame upon flame burned into the floods of heaven. Then above the fir forest, beaming back in a thousand rays like a world light, the eternal sun climbed up!

I clasped both hands before my eyes and fell to the ground.

When I awoke again, the god of earth was hovering there in the airways, and the bride had torn all her veils and was revealing her supreme charms to the god's eye ...

All nature was a holy temple—spring lay like a sweet dream upon the mountains and upon the meadows—the stars of heaven burned as flowers in the dark grass, from myriad springs the sea of light plunged down into the creation, and all the colors in it ascended like wonderful spirits. A universe of love and life—red fruits and blossoming garlands in the trees, and perfumed wreaths around hills and mountains—burning diamonds in the grapes— the butterflies as fluttering, quivering flowers in the airways— song from a thousand throats, warbling, rejoicing, praising—and the eye of God looking back out of the endless ocean and from the pearl in the flower's chalice.

I dared to think the eternal one!

Suddenly there was a rushing behind me—new veils fell from life—I looked back quickly and saw—ah, for the first time—the weeping eye of our mother!

Oh night, night, return! I can no longer bear all the light and love!

Twelfth Nightwatch

In this world there occur, after all, the greatest irregularities; there-fore I interrupt the cloaked stranger here in the middle of his tale, and it would be no ill wish that many a great poet or writer might interrupt himself at the right time, likewise death the life of great men at the right hour—examples are obvious.

Often man raises himself up like an eagle to the sun and seems rapt from earth, so that all stare after the transfigured one's radi-ance in amazement—but suddenly the egoist returns, and instead of having stolen the sunbeam like Prometheus and bringing it down to earth, he binds the onlookers' eyes in the belief that the sun was blinding them.

Who does not know the solar eagle who soars through recent history! ...[1]

What's more, concerning my stranger, I give my word to authors hungering for romantic materials that a modest fee could be earned writing his life—they need only look him up and carry his story to its end ...

There was great commotion this night. Out of a famous poet's door flew a wig, and behind it hurried its owner, so that it was moot whether he was pursuing the good flying ahead or rather was being pursued by it. I held on to him on account of this ambiguity and had him confess …

"My friend!" he said, "I am pursuing immortality and am pursued by it! You yourself probably know how difficult it is to become famous, and how still infinitely more difficult to live; people are complaining in every field about a glutted market, likewise in the field of being famous and vital; in addition, they are complaining about so many bad subjects employed in both departments that they no longer are willing to take anyone at his word. They have placed especially great difficulties in my way, and I have absolutely not been able to get anywhere. Just tell me, what is a person supposed to do in this world who does not already wear a crown on his head in his mother's womb, or at least, when he's newly hatched, is not able to learn how to climb about on the branches of a genealogical tree—if he brings along nothing more than his naked ego and healthy limbs. I know of nothing more simpleminded in the time in which we are living, when the offices, the honors, the decorations and stars all are ready even earlier than the one who is supposed to wear or occupy them. Might a poor devil, who at his birth cannot immediately slip into a warm coat, not rather wish to issue as a stump from his mother's womb, to be marveled at and fed? I think you understand me, comrade!

"I have tried in every way to advance myself, but always in vain; until I finally found I have Kant's nose, Goethe's eyes, Lessing's forehead, Schiller's mouth,[2] and the backside of several famous men; I called attention to this and arrived; indeed, people began to admire me. Next I pushed things further, I wrote to leading spirits for old cast-off clothes, and fortune benevolently granted that I now stride about in shoes in which Kant once walked with his own feet, during the day set Goethe's hat on Lessing's wig, and in the evening wear Schiller's sleeping cap; indeed, I went still further, I learned to cry like Kotzebue and sneeze like Tieck,[3] and you won't believe what an impression I can often thereby bring about; a creature lives after all in its body and would rather have to deal with this than with the mind; it is no shadowboxing when I tell you that someone, before whom I once wandered in as Goethe, with hat set backwards and hands hidden in the folds of my coat, gave me the assurance that I amused him more than Goethe's writings. —People have been asking me since then to the most elegant tables, and I get on quite well at them.

"Only today I fared ill, for when I attempted to eavesdrop within his own four walls on a well-known great spirit, who makes an important impression publicly, he treated me as a thief, notwithstanding that what I purloined from him in haste with my eyes was really not very praiseworthy."

With these words he placed Lessing's wig on his head again and in so doing made the following sarcastic remark:

"Friend, what does one have of this immortality if after death the wig is more immortal than the man who wore it? —Of life itself I do not even wish to speak, for during his existence only the most mortal wretch struts about immortally, whereas people lash out with their fists at genius wherever it lets itself be seen—remember the head that filled this wig before me; good night!" ...

I let the fool run off ...

In the cemetery a young man was dawdling in the moonlight; I could come quite close to him, and he did not notice me, because he was busy inducing a moderate desperation in himself through vehement gesticulation and declamation—these are proven means, and I actually used to know an early morning preacher who could be moved to tears by nothing other than hearing himself speak very violently; gradually he succeeded in this; indeed, he finally drew a pistol and set it to his forehead several times until he had at last reached such a peak that he was bold enough to squeeze the trigger—it misfired, and at this violent motion, his false hairpiece slipped off. Since the matter finally appeared somewhat awkward to me, I leaped forward and handed the fallen object over to him, accompanied by an address suiting the situation. In the first heat he probably considered it to be a dagger and managed a few serious, although vain, thrusts with it.

I tried to bring him to himself with the remark that tragic situations were disturbed by comic nuances, as for example by a hairbag slipping off King Lear in passion and the like, and I succeeded to the extent that he sat down on the grave mound and agreed to let his false hairpiece be fastened on again by me. During this business I tried to convert him with an apology for life, which he had to listen to calmly, because I constrained him to it by his hair.

Apology for Life

"By God, life is beautiful though! —And whatever are you[4] capable of, young man, that you can cast it away as frivolously as this pigtail? —Hold the ribbon; I will attempt during the folding to unfold a few beauties for you as briefly as possible ...

"What is there on earth that you could expect improved in heaven—if, beyond the atmospheric one above us, still a second or even several should exist? —Don't you find everything here below tolerably arranged? Sciences, culture, and manners are in loveliest bloom and stride along quite modern; the typical state is like Holland, traversed by canals and ditches, in which all human abilities are cleverly diverted and divided so that there is no need to fear that they might suddenly, in too great a union, inundate the whole. There are people who are so advantageously placed that one can regard them as quite adequate hammers and tongs and who yet in no way suffer any impairment in their immortality on this account; just look at this colossus of mankind, how everything in it stirs and toils and traffics; the first climbs up over the second, and over this one in turn a third, like tightrope walkers; this one bears inventions, that one systems on high with him, and it cannot fail that this human race, which mounts higher and higher on its own shoulders or, like Münchhausen,[5] pulls itself up by its own pigtail, will finally clamber by mistake into heaven, and it will be quite unnecessary to think of another. —If only the braid on this head of humanity holds, and is not false as that which I am folding, why will it then any longer be necessary to transpose oneself into a higher world by some other way than this?

"Whatever do you think to gain there, friend? Better laws perhaps? The age speaks for ours here below! Better morals? We have risen so high morally that we have almost gone beyond and stand over them! Better constitutions? Don't you have a crowd of them lying before you like the different colors on a map? Go to France, friend, where constitutions change with fashions; there you can try them all on in a row; go from a monarchy to the republic, and from this in turn to a despotism; there you can be great and small, in short succession, and finally quite ordinary again, which, moreover, always remains the most interesting for mankind.

"Friend, against misanthropy there are excellent means; indeed, I have had the experience that a good meal even dissuaded me once from suicide, and I exclaimed satiated: 'Life is really beautiful!' As others the head or the heart, so I assume the stomach to be the seat of life; for the most part the stomach bears the guilt for everything great and splendid that ever occurred in the world. Man is a devouring creature, and if one only throws a lot to him, then in the hours of digestion the most splendid things issue from him and he is transfigured eating and becomes immortal.

"What a wise arrangement of the state, hence, to let its citizens—like dogs that one intends to train as artists—hunger periodically! For a meal, poets warble like nightingales, philosophers build systems, judges judge, doctors heal, priests howl, workers hammer, pound, carpenter, till, and the state eats its way upward to the highest culture. Indeed, if the Creator had forgotten the stomach, I maintain, the world would still lie there as crude as at its creation and not be worth talking of now.

"But what do you think then, of that life into which you are not going to carry over this inner soul of all culture, and where you intend to penetrate only spiritually! —Don't tear loose; I am now knotting the first bow by which I again attach your hair to the pigtail! —Friend, the mind without stomach is like the bear who indolently sucks on his own paws. He is but the treasurer of this sack suspended in him, and if you cut it off him, then he is done for. If there is a transmigration of souls, which I do not doubt, and if the departed spirits, as would then not be improbable, travel just as easily into flowers and fruits, et cetera, as into animals—where then does this connecting canal of spirits reside other than in the stomach swallowing them? Through it they ascend as vapors into the head, after the animal part has in turn gone its way, and it is as plain as day that we can absorb the great wise men, a Plato, Hemsterhuis,[6] Kant, et alii, in ourselves merely by contentedly eating our way into them.

"Think here of examples: Goethe, who unites in himself Hans Sachs, the romantics, and the Greeks, is just as good an eater as a poet and has apparently dined on these spirits beforehand; Bonaparte may have taken Julius Caesar as food, and only the spirit of Brutus still seems to sojourn there somewhere uneaten.

"How is it possible, friend, that you want to renounce this stomach and this life and, moreover, to fly out of this artful machine in which you are turning and driving a thousand wheels? How many stages there are, lying about you, on which you can act as hero! Battlefields, almanacs, literary papers, the greater and the smaller theater ..."

"I am at the court theater," the young man interjected, making a bow to express thanks for the once again attached false hairpiece. —"Besides, the pistol is unloaded, and I was only trying through a modest raging here on the grave to put myself into the character of a suicide whom I have to portray tomorrow. Sobriety is the tomb of art! I slip into the passions so far as possible as into a gauntlet; I play my characters with feeling and, at least, like the great masters, am miserly on a day when I have portrayed a miser, or mad when I played a madman."

He went away and left me standing there almost absurd and ridiculous. "Oh false world!" I exclaimed grimly, "in which nothing is any longer veracious, not even the hairpieces of your inhabitants; you empty, absurd playground of fools and masks, is it then impossible to lift oneself on you to some inspiration!"

For me it was as if I now spread out in the night under the shrouded moon and soared over the globe like the devil on great black pinions. I shook myself and laughed and would have liked to have shaken up all the sleepers under me at once and looked at the whole race *en négligé*, when it had not yet applied, put on, and changed any cosmetics and false teeth and hairpieces and breasts and backsides, in order to hiss maliciously at the entire absurd crew.

Thirteenth Nightwatch

I climbed up the mountain at the gate from the city—it was the vernal equinox, and outside lay the old fairy earth, and she was cooking her midnight magic herbs in order, after casting off silver hairs and smoothing wrinkles, to arise at morning beautifully tressed and garlanded as a young nymph and to carry her newborn children on her swelling bosom. —Below in the valley, a shepherd blew the Alp horn, and the tones spoke so alluringly of a far country and of love and youth and hope; I composed to their accompaniment the following

Dithyramb on Spring.

You appear, and frightened flees your gloomy brother, and the shields and armor in which he stood encased rattle crashing pellmell and shatter; and lo, blushing in morning's glow, the young earth steps forth as a budding virgin; and, youth, you kiss the beloved and weave the bridal crown in her locks. Then the last glacier sinks, and the frozen element becomes free and flows quietly down among flowers and clouded over by green bushes; the mountains hold their cow-herders' huts high in the blue air, and to their slopes cleave the spotted herds. Flowers bloom and dream love, and the nightingale sings of it in the shrubbery. The trees twine their branches in fragrant garlands and proffer them to the sky; the eagle ascends prayerfully into the sun's splendor as to God, and the lark swirls after him, exulting over the adorned earth. Every fragrant calyx becomes a bridal chamber, every leaf is a little world, and all sucks life and love from the hot heart of its mother! —Only man ...

Here the Alp horn suddenly grew mute, and the last note and the last word echoed slowly and dying.

Have you only written as far as this word, Mother Nature? And into whose hand are you delivering the pen for the continuation? —Can you never resolve why all your creatures are happy dreaming but man stands here waking and questioning—without receiving answer? —Where lies Apollo's temple—where is the voice, the sole answering one?[1] I hear nothing but echo, echo of my own speech—am I then alone?

Alone! the spiteful voice calls. Mother, mother, why are you silent? —Oh, you ought not to have written the final word in the creation, if you intended to break off there. I thumb and thumb through the great book and find nothing but the one word about me, and after it a dash, as if the poet had kept in mind the character, whom he thought to complete, and only let drop the name for me. Was the character too difficult of execution? Why did the poet not erase the name too, which now stands there alone, regards itself astonished, and does not know what he is supposed to make of himself?

Clap the book shut, name, until the poet is in the mood to write out in full the empty pages, before which you stand but as title! ...

On the mountain, in the midst of nature's museum, they had built another small one for art, into which several connoisseurs and dilettanti now drew with burning torches, so as to picture the dead inside as vividly as possible in the moving glow of light. I too now and again have my art whims, out of malice more or less, and often step out of the great art gallery into the small to see how man, even without being able to inspirit that chief part of all life, life itself, still rather nicely shapes and carves something that he afterward opines surpasses nature.

I shall follow the connoisseurs and dilettantes!

And before me the stony gods stood as cripples without arms and legs; indeed, some even with missing heads; the most beautiful and glorious thing to which the human mask had ever developed itself, the whole heaven of a great sunken race, dug up again from Herculanum and the bed of the Tiber as corpse and torso. An invalids' home of immortal gods and heroes, given shape amid a miserable humanity.

The ancient artists who had conceived and formed these gods' torsos marched shrouded before my mind ...

Now a little dilettante among those present was clambering up with effort onto a Medici Venus without arms, his mouth puckered and almost in tears, in order, as it seemed, to kiss her behind, this being by acknowledgment the most artistically successful part of this goddess. It enraged me, because in this heartless time there is nothing I tolerate less than the grimace of enthusiasm to which so many faces can contort themselves, and I climbed angered onto an empty pedestal in order to waste a few words.

"Young art brother!" —I addressed him. —"The divine backside is too elevated for you, and you cannot get up there, considering your puny stature, without breaking your neck! I speak out of human kindness, for I feel bad that you are trying to venture out of your depth under mortal danger. Since the fall, before which Adam, as is well known through the assurances of the rabbis, measured his hundred yards, we have become noticeably smaller and are shrinking more and more from age to age, so that one must gravely warn in our *saeculum* against all such neck-breaking attempts as the one in evidence is. What do you want anyway with this stone maiden, who at this moment would become an iron one for you if she were not missing genuine arms to clasp with? For with her restored ones there is no danger; they cannot even serve as a Berlichingen fist[2] and resemble only the wooden ones fastened on the bodies of shot-up soldiers. Oh friend, however much the art doctors of the newer period may heal and patch, they do not put the gods mutilated by malicious time, such as this torso lying here, back on their feet, so they will have to remain forever merely as invalids and emeriti retired here. Once when they still stood erect and had arms and thighs and heads, an entire great race of heroes lay at their feet in the dust; now the tables have turned and they lie in the ground, while our enlightened century stands upright and we ourselves endeavor to pass for middling gods.

"Art friend, where have we come that we dare to root up these great gods' graves and bring the immortal dead to light, when we know how severely proscribed the mere violation of a human tomb was among the Romans? Of course, enlightened men now regard these deceased candidly as idols, and art remains only a secretly insinuated heathen sect that deifies and worships through them—but how do things stand with her, art friend? The ancients sang hymns, and Aeschylus and Sophocles composed their choruses in praise of the gods; our modern art religion prays in critiques and has reverence in its head, the way genuinely religious people do in their heart.

"Ah, we should rebury the old gods! Kiss her behind, young man, kiss, and well done!

"On the other hand, friend, if you no longer want to worship, then you should also no longer admire at the expense of nature; for I resolutely oppose the humanization of these gods. You have the choice, either pray or bury! ...

"Don't look that way, dear fellow! Lead nature, genuine nature I mean, if possible in person, into this art hall once, and let her speak. By the devil, she will laugh over the comical human mask, which must appear to her as insipid as the scarecrow in Horace's epistles to the Pisos.[3]

"Let her say whether she ever really would have created this nose for this toe, that brow for this mouth, that backside for this hand—I bet she would become annoyed if you tried to talk her into such a thing. This Apollo would perhaps be a cripple had she continued him from the small toe, this Antinoüs[4] a Thersites[5] and that tragic powerful Laocoön[6] even a kind of Caliban, if everything were to be reformed according to laws of nature. Indeed, what might then well become of this Minerva which now stands before you worked up to the highest point of the ideal, in that precisely the head on her is defective wherein the wise spirit is enthroned, which in the manner of spirits has made itself invisible?

"This Minerva without head, moreover, excites my attention in a far greater measure than the Agamemnon with shrouded head in the well-known painting of Timanthes.[7] Just as the latter has given artists the rule to let the supreme infinite pain only be divined, so the former seems to indicate the same thing with regard to primal beauty. Our moderns aim at that too, and their heads are to be viewed from two perspectives only as surrogates of heads, for they stand on top, as it were, only as the knobs on towers, for the mere concluding of the figure. —The ancients, like that Prometheus there in the corner, baked their men out of clay to be sure, but they worked the sun spark in as well; we do not like to play with fire, out of fear of danger, and therefore leave the spark out; indeed, there exists now even a general fire police—a censorship and criticism—which quickly enough smothers each and every flame that seeks to flare up. Thus the sun spark cannot rise among us. A wise contrivance of the state, which suffers good, useful machines in preference to bold spirits among its citizens; which beats the fox out of his skin in order to use the skin; which values the hands and feet, as durable twisting and treading machines, more highly than the heads of its native children. The state, like Briareus,[8] has need of only one single head, but of a hundred arms—and well done then!" ...

I ended in fright, for in the deceiving shine of the torches the entire mutilated Olympus suddenly seemed to become animated; wrathful Jupiter wanted to get up from his seat, serious Apollo reached for his bow and ringing lyre, the dragons reared mightily around struggling Laocoön and his faint sons, Prometheus formed men with the stumps of his arms, mute Niobe shielded the youngest of her little ones from the sun arrows beaming down, the Muses without hands, arms, or lips stirred confusedly as if they were striving to sing and to play the old forgotten songs—but everything remained silent round about and only had the appearance of a violent, spasmodic motion on a battlefield. But deep in the background, without illumination, a choir of Furies stood rigid and petrified and watched the tumult darkly and hideously.

Fourteenth Nightwatch

Return with me to the madhouse, you silent companion who hovers about me on my nightwatches ...

You still remember my fool's cell—if you have not otherwise lost the thread of my story which, quiet and hidden, like a narrow stream, winds through the rocky and sylvan passages that I have heaped up all around. In this cell I lay, as in a den of the sphinx, shut in with my riddle and was almost on the happy pathway of truly professing madness as the sole tenable system, simply because I daily had opportunity to compare the results of this general school with those of the separate schools.

I want to go back some! writers say, when about to commence singing of the egg of the matter, and I too must submit to this, since on this night I intend to hatch the sole nightingale egg of my love; for around me the nightingales are warbling in every bush and branch and join as a choir in one single hymn to love.

Out of sullen rage over mankind, I was once playing Hamlet, in a guest role, in a court theater so as to have opportunity to discharge a part of my gall on the people sitting there in silence in the parterre. On this evening it came about that the Ophelia took her insanity from torment seriously and ran off from the theater unmistakably mad. There was an atrocious uproar, and in the way other directors are accustomed to preoccupy themselves with actors' immersion in their roles, so the present one, in contrast, toiled with full exertions to rehearse his prima donna *out* of the one she had played—but in vain: the mighty hand of Shakespeare, that second creator, had seized her violently and, to the terror of all present, did not let her loose again. For me it was an interesting spectacle, this prodigious intrusion of a giant's hand in an unknown life, this transformation of the real into a poetic person, who now earnestly walked up and down in buskins before the eyes of all rational men and emitted disconnected songs, like marvelous spectral utterances. However much one urged her with the most cogent arguments to return to reason, she protested against this just as vehemently, and finally no other means was left except to send her to the madhouse.

To my not slight astonishment, I met her there again. Her cell abutted directly on mine, and each day I heard her celebrate her beloved's wooden shoe and conch hat. A fellow like me, who is composed of hate and anger and, unlike other human children, seems to have been born not from his mother's body but rather from a pregnant volcano, has little sense for love and the like; and yet such a thing stole upon me here in the madhouse; to be sure, it was not expressed at first by the usual symptoms (love of moonshine, poetic congestion in the head, and the like) but, rather in an impetuous striving for the establishment of a fools' propaganda and propagation of an expanded colony of crazies, in order to have them suddenly disembark to the terror of the other rational men.

Yet the mad feeling meanwhile, which they call love and which has fallen down from heaven as a patch on the meager quilt of earth, in the end began to take on a more ardent complexion with me, and to my own horror I did several poems in verse, looked at the moon too, and even at times sang away when the nightingales piped outside about the madhouse. Once I truly detected some emotion on a so-called melancholic evening; yes, I was able in certain hours to peer out of a hole in my Caucasus cave and think less than nothing.[1] —I also incorporated observations at this juncture on my writing tablet, of which I will excerpt some here for tender souls:

To the Moon

Gentle countenance full of good nature and compassion; for you must unite both in you, because you never tear open your mouth, neither for cursing nor for yawning, when thousands of fools and lovers direct their sighs and wishes up to you and choose you for their confidant; so long even as you have already been roving around the earth as her companion and cicisbeo,[2] you have endured in constancy as a true confidant, and one finds not one single instance in world history, right back to Adam, when you might have grown reluctant, might have wrinkled your nose or assumed a spiteful mien, although you heard these sighs and plaints repeated a thousand and thousand thousand times already. You are still equally attentive; indeed, one sees you moved rather often, holding up the dishcloth of a cloud to conceal your tears. What better listener than you could a poet choose for reading aloud his works, what more intimate confidant could I choose, who waste away loving here in the madhouse? How pale you are, good friend, how sympathetic and at the same time how attentive to all who, besides me, are standing at this moment yet and looking at you! Your good-natured features one could easily take for simplicity, especially today when your face has waxed and is quite round and well-fed to look at; but you may wax as you will, I will not let myself be thereby deceived as to your concern, for you remain ever the old and wane again, too, and consume yourself—yes, do you not even shroud your face when emotion overpowers you, as the weeping Agamemnon did,[3] so that one sees nothing of you but the back of your head bald from grief!
—Farewell, dear, kind friend!

To Love

Woman, what do you want of me that you cling to me? Have you ever looked in my face? —You with your smiles and your gracious glad-eyed mien, and I with all the chagrin and anger on the head of Medusa! Dearest, reflect, we make a really too ill-matched couple. Let me go, by the devil! You are no concern of mine! You smile again and hold me fast? What means the interposed god's mask with which you gaze at me? I strip it from you to discern the animal standing behind it; for indeed, I do not consider your real face to be the most attractive. —Heaven, it is getting worse and worse, I am cooing and pining quite wretchedly—do you want to make me completely raving! Woman, how can you ever take pleasure trying to play on so shrill an instrument as I am? The composition is designed for a curse, and I must chant a love song to it. Oh, let me curse and not languish in such frightful tones! Breathe your sighs into a flute; out of me they sound as from a war trumpet, and I strike the alarm drum when I coo. —And now even the first kiss—oh, the rest could have been resisted, like everything that is bandied about merely in language and in sounds, and I would still have been permitted to think something else secretly all the while—but the first kiss—I have never kissed, out of revulsion for all moving and tender cant. —Demon, if I had known that you could mislead me to this I would have summoned all my strength and shaken you from me!

In such and the like fragments I wore myself down and sought to write myself out in a proper methodical fashion, like many a poet who spends his feelings on paper until at last they are all exhausted and the fellow himself stands there wholly gutted and sober.

Everything miscarried, however, for me; indeed, the symptoms grew more and more critical, and I began to wander about engrossed in myself and felt myself almost human and meekly disposed toward the world. Once I even thought it might be the best possible one, and man himself something more than the first animal on it, indeed, that he had his own worth and could perhaps even be immortal.

When things had gone this far, I gave myself up for lost and carried on just as boringly and tritely as any other lover. I even no longer revolted myself if I versified; indeed, I could remain moved for a longer time and accustomed myself to many expressions that I otherwise would never have permitted in my mouth. I launched my first love letter, which I here append for edification, together with the rest of the correspondence:

Hamlet to Ophelia

Heavenly idol of my soul, most charm-filled Ophelia! This introduction, with which I signed my first letter to you when we were
still loving each other in the court theater merely for the enjoyment
of the audience, could admittedly perhaps deceive you and serve to
persuade you that I am still laboring just as then under a feigned
insanity and all the metaphysical sophistries that I brought back
from the university. —But do not let yourself be deceived by this,
idol, for this time I am really mad—so very much does all reside in
ourselves and there is nothing real outside of us; indeed, according to the newest school we do not know whether we are in fact
standing on our feet or on our heads, except that we have assumed
the first by ourselves on trust and in faith. —This is quite abomi-
nable seriousness, Ophelia, and you must not perhaps believe I utter it as persiflage. —Oh, how everything has altered in your poor
Hamlet—this entire earth, which formerly seemed to him a desolate garden of thorns and thistles, a gathering place for pestilential
vapors, has now transformed itself before him into an El Dorado,
into a blossoming garden of the Hesperides; he was once so free
and sound to the core when he hated it, and is now a slave and almost sick because he loves it. —Dearest, —would that I could say
Most Hated; then at least there would be nothing that fettered me
to this inane ball and I could hurl myself down from it quite gay and
merry into the eternal Nothing—well, unfortunately, Dearest! I no
longer now say as previously to you: Get thee to a nunnery! for I am
mad enough to believe, if man loves, then the fool is something, although for that he only further hastens to encounter death and the
latter him, until they finally meet and embrace permanently and
eternally; whether this be at the rock where Saint Gustav[4] passed
away, on the scaffold where the beauteous Maria[5] bled, or in any yet
better or worse place.

I know for certain that the evil fiend hovers sneering over the
earth and has cast love down on her as a bewitching mask, over
which all human creatures are ravenous now to hold it up for a

minute long. Look, even I have unfortunately grasped it and am mincing right tenderly behind it with my death's-head and, by the devil, feel like propagating the human child with you. Oh, were it not for this cursed mask, then the sons of earth here below would certainly have played a joke on the Last Judgment through a law against population, so that our Lord God, or whoever else may care to look at the globe for the last time, would have found it to his amazement absolutely depopulated of people.

But let me finally come to the point, which, however much I endeavor, I cannot evade—to my declaration of love!

Things have not looked more angry, wild, misanthropic in me since my birth than in this moment when I write off to you, upset that I love you, worship you, and that—after the wish to hate and abhor you—I cherish none more earnestly than to hear the confession of your reciprocal affection. Until then your

loving Hamlet.

Ophelia to Hamlet

Love and hate stand in my role, and finally even madness—but tell me, what really is all this in itself that I can choose? Does anything in itself exist, or is all only word and breath and much fantasy? —See, now I will never be able to find out whether I am a dream— whether it is merely play or truth, and whether the truth in turn is more than play—one shell covers the next, and I am often on the verge of losing my mind over this.

Help me read my role backwards, till I reach myself. Am I then perhaps even moving outside my role yet, or is all only role, and I one to boot? The ancients had gods, and also one among them whom they called Dream; he must have felt odd whenever it occurred to him he wished to be considered as real, and yet he remained ever only Dream. I almost believe man too is such a god. I would gladly confer with myself for a moment to discover whether I myself love, or only my name Ophelia—and whether love itself is something, or only a name. —See, there I am trying to catch myself, but I am always running ahead of me and my name behind, and now in turn I am renouncing the role—but the role is not I. Do bring me but once to my I; then I will ask it whether it loves you.

Ophelia

Hamlet to Ophelia

Do not ponder over the like things so deeply, my dear, for they are of such intricate nature that they could easily lead you to the madhouse! It is all role, the role itself and the play-actor who is behind it, and in him in turn his thoughts and plans and enthusiasms and buffooneries—all belongs to the moment and swiftly flees, like the word on the comedian's lips. —All is even but theater, whether the comedian may be playing on earth itself or two steps higher on the boards, or two steps lower in the ground, where the worms pick up the cue of the exiting king; whether spring, winter, summer, or fall may decorate the stage and the theater master hang sun or moon in it or thunder or storm in the wings—everything vanishes again, though, and extinguishes and transmutes itself—including the spring in the human heart; and when the props are wholly removed, only an odd naked skeleton stands behind, without color and life, and the skeleton grins at the other comedians still dashing about.

Do you want to read yourself out of your role, to the I? —See, there the skeleton stands and casts a handful of dust into the air and now collapses itself; but afterward sardonic laughter resounds. That is the world spirit, or the devil—or the Nothing echoing!

To be or not to be! How simple I was at that time when I raised this question with my finger on my nose, how simpler still those who posed it after me and thought marvelous what was at the back of the whole thing. I should first have asked being itself about being; then afterward something sensible could be ascertained about nonbeing too. At that time I was still carrying the theory of immortality from the university and proved it through every category. Yes, I truly feared death on account of immortality—and by heaven, rightly, if after this boring *comédie larmoyante* yet another was to follow—I think nothing need be said here!

Therefore, dear Ophelia, put all this out of mind and let us love and propagate and play all the tricks together—simply out of revenge, so that after us roles must still appear which expand anew all these tediums, up to an ultimate actor, who grimly tears up the paper and falls out of the role, in order no longer to have to play before a parterre sitting there invisible.

Love me, in a word, without further pondering!

Hamlet

Ophelia to Hamlet

You stand once for all as cue in my role, and I cannot tear you out, as little as the pages from the play wherein my love for you is written. So I will then, since I cannot read myself back out of my role, read on in it to the end and to the *exeunt omnes*, behind which the actual I will then probably stand. Then I can tell you whether beyond the role something else exists and the I lives and loves you.

Ophelia

After this exchange of letters our exchange of words now occurred, and every succeeding exchange, from looks, kisses, and the like on, up to the exchange of self.

After a few months the cue for a new role was written. —I was almost happy at this time and detected some human love first in the madhouse, so that I earnestly brooded over plans to realize Plato's republic with the fools around me. But there the dream god again crossed out everything!

Ophelia became ever paler and more rational; although the doctor opined that her nonsense was on the rise in her; this was the moment when a great sense dawned in it ...

The storm raged wildly about the madhouse. —I lay against the bars and looked into the night, beyond which there was nothing further to be seen in heaven and on earth. It was for me as if I were standing close to the Nothing and cried into it, but there was no more sound—I was frightened, for I believed I had really called, but I heard only myself in me. A lightning flash, without subsequent thunder clap, flew arrow-swift but silently through the night, and the day appeared and disappeared hurriedly in it, like a ghost. Next to me, on the one side, a madman rattled his chains terribly; on the other, I heard Ophelia singing disconnected bits of her ballads; but the notes often became sighs, and finally everything seemed to me a grand disharmony, to which the rattling chains furnished the musical accompaniment. I imagined I was passing away. Then I saw myself with me alone in the Nothing; only the late earth was still flickering far out in the distance, as an extinguishing spark—but it was only a thought of mine that was just ending. A single tone quavered gravely and earnestly through the void—it was time chiming out, and eternity now set in. I had now ceased thinking everything else and was thinking only myself! No object was to be found round about but the great dreadful I, which feasted on itself and in devouring constantly regenerated itself. I was not sinking, for there was no longer space; just as little did I seem to float upward. Variety had disappeared simultaneously with time, and there reigned a horrible, eternally void tedium. Beyond myself, I tried to annihilate myself—but I remained and felt myself immortal! ...

Here the dream nullified itself by its own magnitude, and I awoke breathing deeply in relief—the light was extinguished, all about deep night; only Ophelia did I hear softly singing her ballads, as if she were rocking someone to sleep with them. I groped along the walls out of my chamber; near me madmen were still creeping outside through the darkness and hissing softly.

I opened Ophelia's door; she lay pale on her cot, endeavoring to lull into sleep on her breast a dead, just born child; by her a crazy girl stood and placed a finger on her mouth as if she were beckoning to me for silence.

"Now he's sleeping!" Ophelia said and regarded me smiling, and that smile for me was like looking into a freshly dug grave. —"Praise God there is a death, and afterward no eternity!" I uttered involuntarily.

She smiled on and whispered after a pause, as if language sought to dissolve gradually into breaths and gently disappear: "The role comes to an end, but the I remains, and they bury only the role.

Praise God that I am coming out of the play and can put aside my assumed name; after the play the I commences!" —"It is nothing!" I said, shaking. —She continued, scarcely audible: "There it is, already standing back of the wings and waiting for its cue; when only the curtain is first all the way down! —Ah, I love you! That is the final speech in the play and it alone do I seek to retain from my role—it was the most beautiful passage! The rest they may bury!" ...

There the curtain fell, and Ophelia exited—no one applauded, and it was as if no viewer were present. She already was sleeping quite motionless with the child on her breast, and both were now very pale, and one heard no breath drawn, for death had already laid his white mask on them ...

I stood by her bed stormily provoked, and in me there was a release of anger, as if for wild laughter—I was startled, for no laughter came, but the first tear that I wept. Near me, another was howling— but it was only the storm that whistled through the madhouse.

When I looked up, the insane were standing in a half-circle around the bed, all keeping silent but gesticulating and behaving weirdly, some smiling, others reflecting, still others shaking their heads or blankly regarding the white slumberer and her child; the Creator of the world was among them too, but he only laid his finger on his lips significantly.

I almost became uneasy in that circle.

Fifteenth Nightwatch

As much as everyday experience teaches that one tolerates fools in all places, the fact that I had experimented in propagating them nonetheless provoked indignation, and for this I was even told to quit my fool's cubicle as punishment.

Oh, it was very sad for me when I had to take leave of my brothers to mingle again with the rational; and as the bolts of the madhouse door rattled shut behind me, I stood there quite lonely and sought out in melancholy the cemetery where they had borne Ophelia. Oh, had I at least only been able to find a Laertes, to fight with him at the grave, for I had carried from the madhouse an aggravated hatred for all the men of reason who now once more walked about and beside me with their dull, insignificant physiognomies.

A rich man and a beggar have the advantage over other ordinary human beings that they may give full rein to their penchant for traveling. The rich man unlocks the splendors of earth with the golden key in his hand; the poor man has a free pass to the whole of nature, and he can occupy the highest and loveliest dwellings at his pleasure; today Etna, tomorrow Fingal's Grotto;[1] this week, the sage's[2] summer residence on Lake Geneva, and the next, the exquisite crystalline hall of the Rhine Falls, where instead of paintings on the ceiling the sun weaves rainbows overhead and nature rebuilds his palace for him amid perpetual destruction.

Show me a king who can lodge more splendidly than a beggar!

I traveled moreover with the advantage of nowhere being reminded of my bill or having to pay with thanks for my supper to anyone other than this ancient mother herself; for the earth still had roots in her lap which she did not deny me, and in the proffered rocky hollow she held out for thirsty lips the fresh bubbling drink of the plunging waterfall. —I was quite gay and free and hated humankind as I liked, because they crept so pettily and uselessly through the great temple of the sun.

Once I had just risen from my couch, a fragrant flowered sward, and was gazing into the glow of morning, which climbed like a spirit out of the sea, when, to unite the useful with the pleasurable, I bit into a root I had dug out. It is part of human greatness to carry on lesser business in proximity to sublime objects—for example, to look at the countenance of the rising sun with a pipe in one's mouth, or to eat macaroni during the climax of a tragedy; people have attained considerable success in this line.

As I now lay there so comfortably, I was seized by the urge for a monologue, which I delivered in the following fashion:

"Nothing really beats laughing, and I value it almost as highly as other refined people do crying, although a tear can easily be coaxed to light, merely by intense peering at a spot or by mechanical reading of Kotzebue's dramas,[3] yes, finally even by vehemently persistent laughter alone. Did I not recently see a rather emaciated man pour out copious tears at the sight of the rising sun, and others stood nearby and praised this as betokening a sensitive soul and finally cried over the crier. Only I stepped up and asked: 'Friend, is the subject so fervently moving?' —'Not at all,' he said; 'but according to more recent observations, besides bringing about sneezing and weeping, light rays also have an effect on procreation; and I was in Italy!' —I understood the man who looked the sun in the eye for some more real end than mere fantasizing. —When I turned around, laughing, the others, weeping, rebuked me in very harsh terms; I laughed all the harder over this contrast, and it lacked little but they would have stoned me out of compassion! ...

"Where, moreover, can a more effective means than laughing be found to bid defiance to the world's scorn and even to fate? The most redoubtable enemy is alarmed at this satirical mask, and even misfortune gives way in dread of me, if I dare to ridicule it! —What the devil is this whole earth along with her sentimental companion the moon worth anyway, except to be derided—indeed, she still has some value solely because laughter is native to her. Everything on her was so sentimentally and well arranged as to induce chagrin in the devil who once contemplated her for amusement; to avenge himself on the master builder, he dispatched laughter, and it contrived to slip adroitly and imperceptibly into the mask of joy; men willingly received it, until at last it removed its disguise and looked at them spitefully as satire. —Just leave me laughter my whole life long, and I will hold out here below!' ..."

"Hoho!" a voice now cried close to my ear, and when I turned around, a wooden clown was impudently and haughtily looking me in the face. "He is my patron!" said a big fellow, who held him out to me and had a big chest standing by him. "You have talent as a clown, and I can just use one, because mine died on me today. If you feel inclined, then shake on it; the job is lucrative and yields more than grubbing roots!" ...

All the while the wooden joker looked at me familiarly, and I felt myself drawn to him as to a friend. "The fellow was carved in Venice," the puppeteer said as if for encouragement, "and I wager he does his bit better than any other; just look, he walks and stands as on living legs, he puts his hand on his heart, drinks and eats if I pull on the strings, and can laugh and cry like an ordinary person merely through a slight mechanical pressure!"

"Done!" I exclaimed and took the chest on my shoulders, and the wooden company clattered inside under portage as if they were producing a French revolution for amusement.

At the inn we found the theater and already people who wanted to take a look at it; the director gave me fleeting theoretical instruction in tragic as well as comic art; also, for distraction, he opened for me a little side door where my predecessor in clownery[4] lay on straw in his winding sheet and had played out his role; the face was quite nastily twisted, and he said: "He died laughing, through which he contracted a choking seizure behind stage!"

"A lovely death!" I replied, and we now made ready to direct the wooden troupe. My companion's strong point was in both male and female lovers, the latter of which he spoke in falsetto. In contrast, my chief specialty was the clown, but I had to do the kings as well. When the curtain fell, the man embraced me ardently and said that I did honor to my profession.

How dearly, however, directing can cost one, that we had occasion to experience even among marionettes; the affair came about in the following manner:

We had set up our stage in a little German village near the French border. On the other side they were just giving the great tragicomedy in which a king made an unlucky debut and the clown, as Freedom and Equality, merrily shook human heads instead of bells. —We had the unfortunate idea of bringing Holofernes before the public and thereby inflamed the attending peasants so violently that they stormed the stage, abducted Judith from among our actresses, and with her and the severed wooden head of Holofernes straightaway marched before the bailiff's house and demanded nothing less from him than his head.[5] The head laid claim to turned pale when the rebels thrust the bloody wooden one at him, and because the matter seemed more and more critical to me, I quickly tried to give it a different turn. I took possession of Holofernes's head, jumped onto a rock and sought in my anxiety to articulate the following speech:

"Dear countrymen!

"Behold this wooden bloody king's head that I here hold up high. It used, when it still sat on its stump, to be governed by this wire, my hand in turn governed the wire, and so forth into the realm of mystery where the governing power no longer can be determined. This head is a regal one; I, however, who pulled on the wire so that it nodded or shook thus or thus, am a quite ordinary chap and am not accorded any consideration at all in the state. How could you then become so angry at this Holofernes, if he nodded or shook as I wished it? —I think you judge my speech to be reasonable, country-men! —Yet your anger over this wooden head still definitely seems to have transferred itself onto the head of your bailiff—and that I find unjust. —I will try to express myself figuratively: My Holofernes does not play according to your will; all right, then strike me, the common chap, on my hands so that my minister, the wire that I pull, assumes another direction and through this in turn the kingly head nods or shakes more amiably and sensibly. What has this poor head done to you that you bounce about with him so? He is the most mechanical thing in the world, and not even a thought lodges in him. But don't demand of this head any freedom, since he himself contains nothing analogous to it in him. —Also, there is something tricky about what you label freedom, for it is not only in the marionette play that you have seen today, where the wooden king's head is struck from his body without further issue, but I have in my chest materials of even faultier nature, where the writer was not equal to his materials and, in the manner of politi-cal poets, botched the republic, on which he was versifying, into a despotism. I can produce the like for you! Unjust it will always remain to exercise such monstrous punishments, such as to insist here on beheading when no head is available, for this wooden one is here merely for the eye, and luckily I know how to set it back on its torso, which might not work out in every similar case. And woe to my poor marionettes, if once it occurred to a real head to want to replace the wooden one here in my hand, and the former nod-ded and shook in his fashion and quite broke his wire—then a farce could easily revolutionize itself into a serious tragedy! —I believe I've said enough, countrymen!" ...

On the whole, whenever it happens not to be suffering from idées fixes, humankind is an honest, simple beast and easily accom-modates itself to absolute contraries; indeed, I believe it capable, though today it has rent the light bond that fettered it, of tomorrow letting itself be cast in chains with the same enthusiasm. And so to-day my peasants good-naturedly once more gave up revolutionizing and instead gave a cheer for their bailiff; unfortunately, however, this joy of the living actors was transformed into bitter suffering for my wooden ones.

We directors awoke in the following night from a persistent bustle that reverberated from the theater; at first we attributed it to jealousy over roles or a cabal broken out among the troupe, but when we sought to inform ourselves more exactly, we found the bailiff downstairs, whose head I had just resecured on its stump, with Holofernes in his hand and accompanied by servants of the court, who took the entire company prisoners in the name of the state, because they had been declared politically dangerous. All my protests were to no avail, and before my eyes they pulled several kings such as Solomon, Herod, David, Alexander, et alii, out of the chest to drag them away.[6] So inconsistently does the state proceed against its own representatives! —The last man was my clown; I abased myself for him virtually in supplication—only I was informed that all satire, without exception, was forbidden in the state by a strict edict of censorship and was already being confiscated in advance in these heads. With effort I managed to step aside with him for only a minute; I took him with me behind a wing, and there in the loneliness away from prying eyes, I pressed his wooden mouth to mine and shed my second tear, for besides Ophelia he was the sole being in the world whom I had ever truly loved. —My codirector wandered around the whole following day like a man in a dream, and because he did not want to renege on the announced tragicomedy, they found him that evening on stage hanging from a cloud.

So sadly did this undertaking end too, and I now sought in earnest, exhausted by life's hardships, to apply for a solid post among men. Nothing on earth excels the consciousness of being useful and enjoying a fixed salary—man is not a cosmopolitan alone, he is also citizen of a state! —The office of night watchman had just come vacant, and I thought myself in any case qualified to manage it with credit. The world is now very cultured, and great talents are with justification required of every single citizen ...

Well for him who has connections—I succeeded in gaining entrance to the minister's servant; he was just having his good hour and recommended me to his master; thus I was elevated higher and higher on the state ladder and passed from one hand to another, up to the top rung, where I wagered prostrating myself and was graciously given hopes for nightwatchmanship. —A closer examination in which I had to demonstrate whether I, for one thing, possessed a temperate delivery, so as not to wake the monarch from slumber if he slept, for another thing, however, an agreeable and cultivated diction, so as not to insult his musical sensibility on sleepless nights, did not turn out wholly unfortunately; and I had the pleasure, after further study had been urgently recommended to me, of seeing myself appointed night watchman.

Sixteenth Nightwatch

I wish my brush could complete this ultimatum and Hogarthian tailpiece[1] quite distinctly before every man's eyes; unfortunately, however, the colors needed are lacking in the night, and I can make nothing but shadows and airy nebulosities flit before the lens of my magic lantern.

Whenever I am in the mood to assemble kings and beggars in a truly merry fraternal company, I wander over their graves in the churchyard and picture how they lie peacefully side by side below in the earth there, in a state of the greatest freedom and equality, and in their sleep just have satirical dreams and grin maliciously from their eye sockets. Below, they are brothers; above at the most, only a mossy stone still rises out of the turf, on which the great man's old battered escutcheon hangs, while only a white flower or a nettle sprouts on the beggar's grave ...

On this night, too, I was visiting my favorite spot, this suburban theater, where death is director and produces crazy poetic drolleries as satyr plays to the prosaic dramas that are presented in the theater of the court and the world. The air was sweltering and oppressive, and the moon just looked down stealthily at the graves, and past it now and again blue flashes of lightning flew. A poet would have thought the other world was eavesdropping on that which lay below—I held it to be only a mocking echo and dull deceptive luster that impostures sunken life a while yet, as the expired rotting tree seems to gleam at night for a time, until it crumbles wholly into dust ...

I had stopped involuntarily at the memorial of an alchemist; an old, powerful head stared forth from the stone, and incomprehensible signs from the Kabbalah composed the inscription.

The poet was dawdling some time among the graves and conversing intermittently with skulls lying on the ground to fire himself up, as he put it; this got to be boring for me, and so I fell asleep at the monument.

Then in my sleep I heard the storm come up, and the poet wanted to set the thunder to music and compose words for it, but the tones eluded arrangement and the words seemed to explode and scatter in disarray as single incomprehensible syllables. Sweat stood on the poet's brow because he could inject no sense into his nature poem—the fool had hitherto tried poetizing solely on paper.

The dream became ever more profound and involved. The poet had seized his sheet of paper anew and endeavored to write; a skull served as his prop—he actually began, and I saw the title completed:

Poem on Immortality

The skull grinned insidiously beneath the sheet of paper, the poet saw no ill in it and wrote the introduction to the poem, wherein he invoked fantasy to dictate to him. Thereupon he launched into a grisly portrait of death so as to be able ultimately to summon immortality all the more brilliantly, like the radiant sunrise after deepest darkest night. He was wholly absorbed in his fantasies and did not notice that all the graves had opened around him and the sleepers below were smiling malevolently, without, however, moving. He now had reached the turning point and began to sound trumpet blasts and make many preparations for the Last Judgment. He was just about to wake all the dead when it seemed as if something invisible stayed his hand, and he looked up surprised, and below in their bedchambers they all were still reposing quietly and smiling, and none wished to awake. Swiftly, he grasped his pen anew and called more violently and added a powerful accompaniment of thunder and trumpeting to his voice—in vain; below they all merely shook indignantly and turned from him onto their sides as so to sleep more tranquilly and show him the naked backs of their heads. —"What, is there then no God!" he exclaimed wildly, and the echo gave him back the word "God" loudly and perceptibly. He stood there, now quite naïve, and chewed on his pen. "The devil has created the echo!" he said at last. —"One really can't tell if it is simply mocking or if someone is actually speaking!" …

He set swiftly to work once more, but the flourishes of his pen left no trace; then, tired and almost indifferent, he stuck it behind his ear and said in monotone: "Immortality is recalcitrant, publishers pay by the page, and honorariums are very slim nowadays; such scribbling brings in nothing, so I'll bring myself to drama again!" …

I woke at these words, and with the dream the poet too had disappeared from the churchyard; but at my side sat a brown Bohemian woman who seemed to be studying my features intently. I was almost terrified by her great gigantic figure and by her dark countenance in which seemed inscribed a strange baroque life with commensurately clashing traits. "Give me your hand, pale one!" she said mysteriously, and I extended it to her instinctively.

The more strongly and securely a person maintains his composure, the sillier does everything arcane and marvelous appear to him, from the Order of Freemasons to the mysteries of another world. I shuddered today somewhat for the first time, because the woman read my whole previous life to me from my hand as out of a book, up to the moment when I was raised as treasure. (See the Fourth Nightwatch.) Thereupon she said: "You shall also see your father, pale one; turn round, he is standing behind you!" —I turned quickly—and the serious stone head of the alchemist regarded me fixedly. She laid her hand on it and, smiling oddly, said: "It's him, and I'm the mother!" …

This produced a crazy, touching family scene—the brown Gypsy mother and the petrified father, who jutted half out of the earth as if he wanted to hug his son and press him to his cold breast. To round out the family group, I embraced both, and when I was thus seated between them, the woman recounted in the manner of a street minstrel:

"It was on Christmas Eve, as your father was attempting to conjure the devil—he was reading from the book and I was providing light for this with three charmed candles—underground there was a rippling, as if the earth were surging, and the light burned blue. We paused now at the passage where Heaven is renounced and Hell embraced, and looked at each other awhile in silence. 'Just for variety's sake!' this stone one then said and read the passage loudly and distinctly—something laughed softly between us, and we laughed loudly so as not to stand there like fools. Now it began to carry on around us, that night, in its fashion, and we noticed that we weren't alone. I cuddled close to your father in the chalked circle; we accidentally touched the sign of the Earth-Spirit[2] and grew warm next to each other. When the devil appeared, we glimpsed him only through half-opened eyes—it was exactly the moment in which you came into being! —The aforenamed was in quite a humor and volunteered to fill the role of godfather; he must have been an agreeable man in his best years, and I am astonished by the resemblance you bear him; only you look gloomier, something you ought to cure yourself of. When you were born, I had scruples enough to commit you into Christian hands and therefore conveyed you to that treasure-hunter who raised you. —That is your family history, pale one!"

What a clear light dawned in me after this speech, that only psychologists can imagine; the key to my Self was tendered me, and for the first time I opened with astonishment and secret trembling the long-barred door—the inside looked like Bluebeard's chamber,[3] and it would have strangled me had I been less fearless. It was a dangerous psychological key!

I would like to present myself as I am to skilled psychologists for dissection and anatomy-study in order to see whether they would read out of me what I now actually read—this doubt, moreover, is not intended as a challenge to science itself, which I truly esteem, because it never grudges spending time and effort on so hypothetical an object as the soul.

I might have expressed out loud some of the observations that I had made about myself in this moment, for the Gypsy spoke like an oracle: "It is greater to hate the world than to love it; he who loves desires, he who hates is sufficient unto himself and needs nothing beyond the hate in his breast and no third party!"

This statement served as her watchword, and by it I recognized that she belonged to my family. After a while she said rather secretively: "I would really like to see the old boy one last time down there in his final chemical experiment which he's conducting on himself; he has been lying in the ground a long time already—I wonder if anything is still left of him? —Come, let's take a look!" With these words she crept over skulls and dead men's bones toward the charnel house, returned with shovel and pick, and dug calmly and mysteriously in the earth.

I left her alone at her odd work, for beyond, someone was wandering about the graves with many twistings and turnings, as if he were avoiding shapes standing in his path; sometimes he appeared to smile, sometimes he turned aside terrified and trembling and fled a few steps, until he seemed to recoil from a new subject. —When I came near him, he seized my hand and said, breathing deeply in relief: "Praise God, a living person! lead me to that grave!" I deemed it madness and marched forward with him to see how it would end; he often restrained me, if I came too close to a grave, to prevent my touching the air over it; finally, however, he seemed to gather more courage and rested a while in the midst of three large monuments; they were toppled columns, and on their tablets stood the names of deceased princes.

"Here we can delay some," he said, "for nothing but stone and memorial stands over these graves, and in the ground beneath may still be found at the most a handful of dust along with the crowns and scepters; such great lords vanish swiftly because they enjoy in excess and in life already have absorbed a great mass of earthy parts."

I looked at him in amazement; he continued then: "You very likely think me mad; but in that you're mistaken! I do not set foot in these precincts cheerfully, for with me the world has gained a marvelous sense, and against my will I catch sight on graves, more or less clearly according to the extent of their decay, of the dead who lie under them.*⁴ So long as the defunct is still unscathed below, so long does his form stand distinct above the tomb for me, and only as the body decomposes more and more does the image too become lost in shadow and mist; it ultimately quite dissolves when the grave is empty. —The whole wide earth is, to be sure, a single God's acre, but the shapes of the decayed assume a kindlier form and blossom forth again as beautiful flowers—here, however, they still stand about distinctly and look at me so that I retreat from them in fright. Nothing could ever move me to enter this site, if an amorous tryst were not awaiting me here!"

"Then your darling should have picked a more cheerful spot for you!" I said disapprovingly about his unknown beauty, while he paused briefly.

"She is compelled to!" he answered. —"For she's taken up residence here."

Comprehending now, I understood when he pointed to a far grave. "She is resting there below—she died in her prime, and I can only wander here to her bridal bed. She is already smiling at me from the distance, and I must hurry; because for some time her form has been becoming more and more airy and only the smile about her lips is still quite perceptible." ...

"This is for once a somewhat unusual romance that I am experiencing," I joined in; "otherwise there is nothing on earth more boring than someone in love!" ...

We strolled on further now, and in walking he drew fleetingly some further sketches of the occupants by whose dwellings we had to pass.

"There a court fool has preserved himself well, he stands there

*An example of this odd power of second sight is given, if I'm not mistaken, in Moritz's *Magazine of Empirical Psychology*.

complete, right to the ridicule and satire in his expression. —Here a poet tarries in expectation of the resurrection, but there is hardly any of him still on hand for it, for I see merely faint dust and must constrain my imagination to discover anything clever in it. —Here I glimpse a mother with her child on her breast, and both smiling!" (This staggered me, for it was the grave of Ophelia!) "Here a financier and politician lie together, but both already show many defects. —That is said to be the grave of a famous miser, he is still holding fast to the end of his winding sheet with an already disappearing hand!" ...

We were now at the place, and he asked me to leave him; from a distance I saw only how he embraced the air and poured out hot kisses—it was indeed a queer tryst! ...

Meanwhile the fortune-teller had forced open my father's grave, and the rotten coffin was raised out of the ground; the curious moonlight was gliding over the half-weathered seals and decorations, and the crucifix on the lid gleamed bright and white. It was a rather strange feeling for me when the old gray past looked about once more in the present and my father's final cradle, which had cradled him into long slumber, rose up. I hesitated to lift the lid, and in this pause, to bolster my courage, I addressed a worm that I had seized just as it burrowed out of the soil by the casket:

"Besides the favorites and minions of grandees and lords, there is but one small group of people that actually finds comfort on majesty's breast; and to them you belong, miner. The king feeds on the marrow of his country, and you in turn on the king himself in order, as Hamlet says, to conduct defunct majesty, after a journey through three or four stomachs, back to the bosom or at least the belly of its loyal subjects. On how many kings' and princes' brains have you gorged yourself, you plump parasite, to attain this degree of corpulence? How many philosophers' idealisms have you reduced to this your realism? You are an irrefutable proof for the real utility of ideas, as you have crammed yourself valiantly with the wisdom of so many heads. —For you nothing any longer is sacred, neither beauty nor ugliness, neither virtue nor vice; you wind about everything, you Laocoön's serpent, and document your thorough sublimity on the whole human race. Where now is the eye that smiled so enchantingly or commanded so threateningly? —You, satirist, sit alone in the empty socket of bone and peer insolently and maliciously about and make the head into your dwelling (and something even worse), in which formerly the schemes of a Caesar and an Alexander were born. What now is this palace that can enclose a whole world and a heaven; this fairy castle in which love's wonders enchantingly delude; this microcosm in which all that is great and splendid and everything terrible and fearsome reside together in embryo, which brought forth temples and gods, inquisitions and devils; this tailpiece of the creation—the human head! —shelter for a worm! —Oh, what is the world if that which it thought is nothing, and everything in it only transitory fantasy! —What are the fantasies of earth, spring, and the flowers, if the fantasy in this little orb is scattered as dust, if here in the inner Pantheon all gods crash from their pedestals, and worms and decay take possession! Oh, do not vaunt to me in any way of the autonomy of the spirit—here lies its battered workshop, and the thousand threads with which it spun the tissue of the world are all rent, and the world with them. —Probably even the old man here in his chamber has cast off his theatrical costume, and this malicious fellow in my hand is perhaps just coming from the housecleaning he has attended in the paternal lodgings; —yet let it be—I will look fiercely into Nothingness and pledge fraternity with It, that I may perceive no further human traces when, at last, It seizes me, too!" ...

I was strong and wild enough now to lift the lid, even though I felt that this rage and anger, as all else, also pertained to Nothingness ...

How odd—when the quiet little bedchamber opened up in which I no longer expected any sleeper, he was still lying there unscathed on the pillow with a wan, serious face and black curly hair about his temples and forehead; this was still the bust copied from life, stored here in death's subterranean museum as an oddity, and the old necromancer seemed eager to bid defiance to Nothingness.

"That's how he looked when he was summoning the devil!" the fortune-teller said. —"Only afterward they folded his hands so he would have to pray down below against his will!" —"And why is he praying then?" I asked angrily; "no doubt countless stars are sparkling and swimming there above us in heaven's ocean, but if they have worlds, as many clever heads assert, then there are also skulls on them and worms, as here below; and that holds throughout the whole immensity, and the Basel dance of death merely grows all the merrier and wilder thereby and the ballroom grander. —Oh, how all those who rove about over graves and over the thousandfold layered lava of bygone races—how they all whimper for love and for a great heart above the clouds on which they might once find rest with all their earths! Whimper no longer—these myriad worlds roar through all their heavens only by the gigantic force of nature, and this terrifying spawner, who has spawned everything and herself with it, has no heart in her own breast, but for a pastime only forms little ones that she passes around—cleave to these and love and coo so long as these hearts still hold together! —I refuse to love and will remain quite cold and frozen so as to be able, if possible, to laugh away when the giant's hand crushes me, too! …

"The old necromancer seems to be laughing at my talk! Maybe you know better, devil-summoner—and above this demolished pantheon, a new more splendid one ascends which reaches into the clouds and in which the colossal gods, sitting about there in a circle, can really straighten up without knocking their heads on the low ceiling. —If it were true, that would be cause for praise, and it might be worth the trouble to witness how some immense spirits obtained a correspondingly immense scope for action and no longer needed to stifle and hate in order to be great, but could climb up freely into the heavens to spread their radiant plumage there. —The thought could almost make me hot! —Only don't let them all try and be resurrected on me—not all! —What would so many pygmies and cripples want in this great splendid pantheon in which only beauty shall reign, and the gods! Oh, we really are often enough ashamed of this company on earth; how could we share heaven with them socially! —Only you dare raise yourselves from slumber, you great regal heads who appear with diadems in world history, and you inspired singers who speak enraptured of royalty and exalt them. The others may sleep peacefully and very softly, even have pleasant dreams; these I grant them with all my heart! ...

"With you, old alchemist, I would gladly begin the journey; only you shall not beg for heaven—not beg—rather win it through spite if you have the strength. The falling Titans are worth more than a whole globe full of dissemblers who would like to sneak into the Pantheon through a little morality and thus and such comparative virtue! Let us go forth prepared to face the giant of the other world; for only when we raise our banner there are we worthy of dwelling there! —Leave off begging; I will tear your hands apart by force!

"Woe! What is this—are you too but a mask and deceive me? —I no longer see you, Father—where are you? —At my touch all crumbles into ashes, and there is only a handful of dust lying yet on the ground, and a few satisfied worms creep secretly away like moral funeral orators who have outdone themselves at the banquet of sorrow. I strew this handful of paternal dust into the air and it remains—Nothing!"

On the grave beyond, the visionary is still standing and embracing Nothing!

And the echo in the charnel house cries for the last time NOTHING!

Afterword: Authorship and Reception

The odd work titled *Nightwatches: By Bonaventura* (*Nachtwachen. Von Bonaventura*) did not enjoy any measurable success when brought out by the publisher F. Dienemann in the small Saxon town Penig in 1804 (but anticipatorily dated 1805). Yet an important early reader, the successful novelist Jean Paul Richter (1767–1825), launched a more than century-long tradition of false trails by speculating in a letter to a friend that the author was likely the romantic philosopher Friedrich Schelling (1775–1854), while at the same time noticing his own influence on the work. Other astute and influential readers such as Karl August Varnhagen von Ense (1785–1858) and his wife Rahel casually repeated this attribution to Schelling in their Berlin circle, although many traits of language and contents spoke against it. By the time Rudolf Haym published his major study of the German romantics in 1870, he cast doubt on Schelling's authorship, but other wrong leads were already being rumored about, and the urge to champion candidates was irrepressible. The notorious Caroline Michaelis, who ran away from her husband with the noted critic August Wilhelm Schlegel (1767–1845) and then next with Schelling, and is harshly mocked in the *Nightwatches*, was improbably proposed.

By 1903, Richard M. Meyer leaned toward E. T. A. Hoffmann

(1776–1822), whose later writing indeed offered some linkages, although his interests around 1800 did not match well. Rosemarie Hunter Lougheed attempted to reinstate the case for Hoffmann as late as the 1970s. By 1905–6 the minor figure Karl Christian Fischer was nominated without resonance, nor did a more sensible candidate, Gotthilf Heinrich Schubert (1780–1860), the romantic psychological theorist and author of *Views concerning the Nightside of the Natural Sciences* (1808), gain traction. When in 1909 Franz Schulz nominated Karl Friedrich Gottlob Wetzel (1779–1819), who was a friend of Schubert and student of Schelling, Wetzel excited more attention momentarily because he seemed to present more abundant related thematic material, but this attribution too had no sticking power.

Then in 1912 Erich Frank put forward the illustrious name Clemens Brentano (1778–1842) in a further new edition of the *Nightwatches*. Since Bonaventura draws on some influential motifs and themes from Brentano's brooding novel *Godwi, or the Stone Image of the Mother: A Bewildered Novel* (1800–1801)—for example, a repressed past, loss of primal innocence, Oedipal conflict, the haunting stone memorial—we would have to assume that Brentano is hiding his identity because of an anguished questioning of his own roots if we take him to be the anonymous author. In certain respects, in *Godwi* Brentano exercises an even wilder form of romantic irony going beyond the Sternesque and Jean Paulesque traits of the *Nightwatches*. But it is hard to square the pronouncedly Protestant tone in the watchman's sarcastic statements with Brentano's anxiety over carnal sin and his mystically colored Catholicism.

Two decades later, Hoffmann follows Brentano's lead more evidently than Bonaventura's in the way he manages the complexity of the layers and shifts in the narrative structure of his late novel *Tomcat Murr* (1819–21). The opening tumultuous scene of a storm that wrecks a festival and intimates the sudden arrival of the apocaplyse in *Tomcat Murr* indeed seems directly descended from the theatrical false apocalypse conjured by Kreuzgang in the *Nightwatches*; and the eventual suicide of Hoffmann's distraught noble composer Kreisler may distantly echo some accents in the piteous death of Bonaventura's rejected town poet. But the composer Kreisler remains a central figure in Hoffmann's work because of his heroic perseverance against the malice in the world, and Hoffmann ironically juxtaposes the smug tomcat Murr (who exhibits shifting public fads) as a hypothetical sentimental hero in order to magnify Kreisler's authentic nature as a tormented genius. The full title Hoffman gave this internally twinned, self-mirroring work hints ironically at the true balance: *Life and Opinions of the Tomcat Murr, along with a Fragmentary Biography of Kapellmeister Johannes Kreisler in Stray Printer's Sheets.*

A fundamental problem in seeking to establish authorship on the basis of a sharing of motifs and themes is that Bonaventura makes a grand satirical tour among the prominent writers of the age, openly mentions many of them, and does not hesitate to appropriate key moments or attributes for his own purposes. Thus the advancing of new and the repetition of some old candidacies in the first half of the twentieth century never achieved any level of reasonable certainty. That was thwarted despite many painstaking applications of thematic, structural, and linguistic analysis. Yet together these efforts have yielded valuable insights into the *Nightwatches*, deepening our appreciation of its complex way of reflecting its own age and offering clues to its potential to excite the interest of modernist writers and artists.

The surfacing of the threat of atheism in Jean Paul, and misunderstandings of Jean Paul's own personal position as a believer, had powerful repercussions in the opening nineteenth century and beyond. Germaine de Staël's translation of the "Dead Christ's Speech from the Roof of the Cosmos That There is no God" from Jean Paul's novel *Siebenkäs* (1796–97) in her famous treatise *De l'Allemagne* (1810) had double repercussions, because she omitted the ending frame in which Jean Paul's protagonist pulls out of the nightmare of God's death and rejoices in the creation as a believer. In the course of promoting wider awareness of the theme of the collapse of belief, Mme. de Staël influenced French romantic poets like Alfred de Vigny (1797–1863) and Gérard de Nerval (1808–55) to reconstrue Christ not as the traditional Savior (which he actually remained for

Jean Paul) but as a spiritual champion of the human mind. This latter approach enjoyed a long career in French nineteenth-century literature and reentered German modernism in the work of Rainer Maria Rilke (see Blume 1976). Bonaventura preserves the terrifying qualities in the dream of chapter 47 of Jean Paul's novel, in its full title *Flower, Fruit, and Thorn Pieces, or The Married State, Death, and Wedding of Siebenkäs, Poor Folk's Lawyer*, without letting his own narrator, Kreuzgang, recover from the trauma. For Kreuzgang, there is no Christ to look to as a martyr of the mind proclaiming the death of God; there is ultimately only the unlimited emptiness of the cosmos and the anguish of human consciousness posited in Kreuzgang's nightmare.

One of the most interesting and carefully argued proposals about the authorship and contents of the *Nightwatches* has been Linda Katritzky's study (1999) attempting to demonstrate why the documented interests, erudition, and temperament of the prolific Anglophile commentator and scientist Georg Christoph Lichtenberg (1742–99) make him a far more likely candidate than the current critical favorite, the theater director, playwright, and novelist August Klingemann (1777–1831). There is no doubt that Bonaventura drew heavily on Lichtenberg's treatment of English culture and notably on his Hogarth commentaries (see Gillespie 1973). Katritzky is helpful to all investigators of the *Nightwatches* through her meticulous efforts to highlight motifs and references in the novel. These evidence a considerable degree of commonality among Lichtenberg, the anonymous author Bonaventura, and the latter's known and likely sources. She focuses on "literary imprints" that can be documented in the year of Lichtenberg's death, 1799, when he withdrew to his sick chamber and was reliably reported to be engaged in feverish writing, writing that then mysteriously vanished. Katritzky acknowledges that there is as yet no concrete explanation of how the *Nightwatches*, if the book is Lichtenberg's, as she believes, was conveyed to the newly established publisher Friedrich Dienemann in Penig (whose operation started in 1802). She speculates, quite reasonably, that a printer could readily have inserted the few allusions to events that occurred soon after Lichtenberg's death in order to give the work an appearance of freshness. Even though her speculation is probably untenable, Katritzsky's *Guide* is indeed a very useful aid for readers who would like to explore cultural relationships in the intellectual history of the waning eighteenth century. She champions the case that no matter how disturbed the general direction of the book and many of its statements may seem, the *Nightwatches* is preponderantly an example of Menippean satire. Thus she rationalizes that many dire moments, harsh in tone (e.g., the bizarre Hamlet-Ophelia misery in the madhouse in Nightwatch 15), are somehow to be understood didactically as positive.

Andreas Mielke (1984) is among those who anticipated Katritzky in arguing that Klingemann's known writings do not exhibit artistic and intellectual gifts on a level readily equatable with the intensity of the *Nightwatches*, even if there are many scattered similarities in phrasing. Whereas Katritzky seeks to mitigate the importance of Bonaventura's struggle to cope with nihilistic ideas, Mielke views the head-on encounter with the new romantic philosophy in the novel as a major subject matter. In his estimation, this keen critique of romantic extremism eliminates Klingemann, who appears in his signed publications to be a more standard idealistic patriot. Mielke goes into great detail to demonstrate both overt and covert parallels between Jean Paul's writings and Bonaventura's views. He constructs the thesis that, under the guise of the pseudonym Bonaventura, Jean Paul was engaging in a clever, multipronged strategy to attack what he regarded as the absurdities and scary implications of romantic "idealism" or ego philosophy (most notably in the varieties pushed by Fichte and Schelling) and to champion what he regarded as fundamental human values (love, acceptance of death, belief, humor).

Although Mielke favors a different author, his choice resembles Katritzky's in two respects. He never asserts Jean Paul's masked authorship to be definitively proved, but he sees it as given in Jean Paul's stories and many authorial hints about appearing under other guises, and he draws an equation between the deeper purpose of the *Nightwatches* as he perceives it and Jean Paul's own documentable opposition to feared extreme consequences of romanticism. To arrive at this outcome, Mielke leads us through a delightful lining up of all the salient episodes and characters in the *Nightwatches*. This tour de force is indeed impressive, and, coincidentally, it demonstrates how by a slight paradigm shift we can assign alternate functions to the same narrative elements. The possibility of implementing such a shift in interpretation raises the very perplexing question whether the author Bonaventura was perhaps himself hovering between a positive and a negative worldview. In any event, Mielke's argument of a pervasive engagement with romantic ideas in the *Nightwatches* balances out Katritzky's argument in favor of a predominantly Enlightenment orientation. Neither interpreter is ready or willing to consider two alternate possibilities: (a) that the *Nightwatches* may be the single great life achievement of a minor author, a fortunate fusion of elements that benefited precisely from the protection of anonymity, which liberated the writer's mind; and (b) that the work not only "performs" the transition from Enlightenment to romanticism but also, in a leap ahead of its time, grasps the dilemma of romanticism as a dead end.

Debate over the status of the *Nightwatches* was reignited by Jost Schillemeit's claim in 1973 to have discovered the author in the theater director, critic, playwright, and novelist August Klingemann. Horst Fleig came to the same conclusion virtually simultaneously but delayed publishing his major statement until 1985. Though the consensus in favor of Klingemann remained somewhat unstable, most publishers have listed the *Nightwatches* under his name for the past four decades down to the present. In 1948, in a very detailed account of Klingemann's creative career and place in romanticism, Hugo Burath paid special attention to his seminal work in the theater and his critical writings but drew no connection to Bonaventura. Schillemeit's approach was to consider the range of collaborators connected with the *Magazine for the Elegant World* (*Zeitung für die Elegante Welt*), where in July 1804 an advance fragment of the *Nightwatches* appeared, the "Prologue of Hanswurst to the Tragedy Man," signed Bonaventura, and in March 1805 a pilot piece titled "The Devil's Manual: Introduction" alluding to the devil fantasies of the novel. In Klingemann's critical and imaginative writings Schillemeit found innumerable similarities of theme, phrasing, and fascination with particular figures old and new that could be matched up with salient moments and opinions in the *Nightwatches*. He found further associations with the *Nightwatches* in an excerpt from a romantic comedy by Klingemann, carried in the *Elegant World* in April 1803. This fragment also unmistakably reflects awareness of the irreverent fantastic comedy *Puss-in-Boots* by Ludwig Tieck, a friend of Klingemann when both were close to many key literary figures of the early Jena school of romanticism. Here we may surmise a link between the *Nightwatches* as a species of absurdist fiction and the early roots of theater of the absurd in Tieck (see Gillespie 2013).

The rival discoverer, Horst Fleig (1985), criticizes Schillemeit for using the less reliable approach of parallels restricted to one main author and boasts of having instead used a complex computer-assisted process for eliminating candidates out of a field of several hundred contemporaries of the ending eighteenth and early nineteenth centuries. Moreover, Fleig thinks that Schillemeit "banalizes" Klingemann because he does not pay sufficient attention to Klingemann's internal development up to the *Nightwatches*. Fleig discerns a deepening orientation to the great canonical works of the Western tradition. Of special interest in Fleig's alternate approach is its strong temporal dimension. While the language used in the *Nightwatches* and Klingeman's romances and plays may not match so well, there is a pronounced overlap with the articles he wrote while the *Nightwatches* was being composed. The similarity of habits of mind with the *Nightwatches* is even more striking after one sets apart specialized vocabularies (e.g., for jurisprudence and medicine) and evaluates prominent features along a trajectory of articles for some two dozen years, and especially during the key period 1802–5. Another important filter that affects how we perceive Bonaventura's language, according to Fleig, is the difference between writings couched in the third person and those couched as direct utterances of a first person. Fleig follows up his very instructive methodological refinement of Schillemeit with some hundred pages venturing into more complicated issues of interpretation of the *Nightwatches* and adduces possible clues in Klingemann's biography. Very valuable is that Fleig highlights intellectual interests that last from Klingemann's early into his late years, his main temperamental and artistic proclivities in theater, and the long-term development of certain themes and obsessions (for example, the night realm, decapitation, vampirism, masks and unmasking, Gothic spaces, Shakespeare, etc.).

Probably the most sensational attribution of authorship is Lothar Baus's assertion (1999) that the older Goethe, during a personally stressful period, composed the *Nightwatches* to ventilate his ennui and anger as a freethinker. Baus argues, moreover, that while Klingemann, here presumed to be Goethe's natural son, initially was ready to assist his father by posing as author, the socially dangerous character of the work constrained him, too, to have it issued anonymously under the cover name Bonaventura. With this ploy, Baus simply dismisses the discovery of a discreet note by Klingemann acknowledging the book (see Haag 1987). Much of the material that Schillemeit and Fleig ply for traces of Klingemann is interpreted by Baus as evidence for Goethe's covert personal confession. Baus speculates that elements of the book that attack cultural enemies and nuisances make more sense today in retrospect as serving Goethe's aims. This reading of the *Nightwatches* chapter by chapter correlates Goethe's biography, especially at the start of the 1800s, with events, details, motifs, and opinions from published and private sources both of the great poet himself and of his contemporaries. For example, the three boys whom the dying atheist embraces in Nightwatch 1 supposedly represent Goethe's alleged offspring Ludwig Tieck (son of Henriette Alexandrine von Roussillon), August Klingemann (son of Charlotte von Stein), and August Walter Vulpius (son of Christine Vulpius, legitimized after Goethe's marriage with the mother). Among Baus's many pieces of forensic reconstruction of hidden factors is his finding that the writer Johannes Falk, with whom Goethe for a while shared some common interests but then fell out, supposedly discovered Goethe's authorship of the *Nightwatches*. Falk's attempt to blackmail Goethe led to a mutually accommodative stalemate, and Falk's death eventually spared Goethe any public revelation.

The value of Baus's digging into possible backgrounds to details in the novel is the retrieval of a rich array of relationships in the era. What will, however, likely dissuade readers is that besides attempting to identify Goethe's love children in this study of the *Nightwatches*, Baus has elsewhere elaborated the thesis (Baus 1995) that the future Olympian was himself the natural son of the Holy Roman Emperor Charles VII and was placed with the family of the imperial councillor Goethe, who married his mother. Concealing illegitimate births was not at all unusual in the society Goethe knew, but this sequence seems too much of a good thing. It would be sensational if even a part of Baus's thesis should someday be validated—a doubtful proposition!

ARTISTIC RESPONSES TO BONAVENTURA

Today we can better understand why many characteristics of the *Nightwatches* as an example of "tantric" tomanticism would possess latent suggestive power for artists of later cultural moments, even though there may be no ascertainable chain of filiation over the many intervening decades, or even centuries, before some particular strand of thought or mode of expression resurfaces in a significant way. Some cultural forces are far more obvious than others—the enduring influence of Shakespeare being primary among factors in multiple feedback loops and lines of tradition in Western and indeed world literature. Besides the spell of Shakespeare, the renewed romantic interest both in Elizabethan and Jacobean and in Siglo de Oro and baroque literature and art was prominent notably in the work of Bonaventura's contemporary Ludwig Tieck (1773-1853), who translated and edited many leading figures of the late fifteenth through the seventeenth centuries, including Shakespeare and Cervantes. Thus we can recognize how important was the romantic urge to create linkages, as in the *Nightwatches*, between their own opening of the interior spaces of the self through theater and dream and the baroque period's impressive metaphoric complexes of life as "dream" and "theater." Not only does the *Nightwatches* explicitly refer to the puzzles of subjectivism in the ending eighteenth century and the dawning age of romantic psychology, but it posits several disturbing possibilities: that there are frightening forces in the underground of the self, as in nature; that experiencing the interior of the self qualitatively resembles captivity in the cosmos and time; and that aspects of the self, or exaggerated embodiments of these in one's fellow human beings, suggest our being in an insane asylum, whether we happen to be literally incarcerated or are living in alienation in the world.

It is a simple fact that we are looking in retrospect, from the afterlude of postmodernism in the early twenty-first century. Thus today's readers have a much more detailed record against which to read several preceding thresholds when artists could feel justified in being attracted to Bonaventura's work. Invaluable for appreciating the visionary theatricality of the *Nightwatches* today is our accrued knowledge of the romantic roots of theater of the absurd as this made its reappearance in the symbolist fin-de-siècle and early modernism and resurged during the heyday of existentialism (see Gillespie 2013). Bonaventura as an ancestral spirit fits partially within several of the major tendencies that were contending in the mid- to late nineteenth century and morphed variously in the twentieth. From our vantage today, we can say he is undeceived in advance of triumphalist positivism, is anticipatory of naturalism fraught with romantic anxieties, of symbolism as a neoromantic quest for spiritual values, of expressionism as an attempt at a radical break into modern reality, and of surrealism as a turn into the unconscious.

Important as background for us today are the numerous works in which several tendencies and artistic means converged after romanticism. For example, there is the cross between symbolism and expressionism as exemplified in August Strindberg's neoromantic *A Dream Play* (1901). There is the oppressive pall of night and terror in expressionist cinema, especially in postwar films like Robert Wiene's *The Cabinet of Dr. Caligari* (1920), in which we onlookers watch a protagonist searching for clues to killings amidst a jumble of old Gothic streets as if in a nightmare. We can never be sure whether the searcher is a patient in an asylum for the insane or the victim of insidious powers, nor even whether his story is part of a secret antihuman conspiracy stretching through the ages. The powerful vampire theme—which troubled preromantic and romantic writers, persisted throughout the nineteenth century, and was given new and forceful form by Bram Stoker (1847-1912) in *Dracula* (1897)—reemerges in the guise of Wiene's asylum director. James Joyce has his educational protagonist Stephen Dedalus dwell on the vampire theme passingly in the opening of *Ulysses*. When Stephen senses the possibility that some alien blood is working in him, this ambiguously conveys deep anxiety over the possibility of being unfree, thrall to a timeless life force, and yet, positively, also the promise of being related to ancestral archetypes as an artificer. Wiene and many other expressionist directors exploit the black-and-white technique intrinsic to the early movies to conjure our sense of being in the night condition, in an uncertain realm.

Another interesting strand that reaches all the way from Bonaventura and certain of his fellow romantics to many modernist writers is their interest in Dante. Reference to Dante's *La divina commedia* offered newer artists, too, a direct way to evoke the important romantic and nineteenth-century theme of the journey through hell. The association especially between modern urban life and traversing psychological, social, and historical kinds of hell evolved as a multilevel trope that largely displaced on a permanent basis the hopeful Enlightenment trope of the earthly paradise, that is, the promise that humankind's place in nature could be restored. We find many of these themes in such influential poets of the later nineteenth century as Charles Baudelaire (*Les fleurs du mal*) and Arthur Rimbaud (*Une saison en Enfer*). The romantic trope of the journey through hell persisted into modernism, and the world wars gave it increased currency despite all the countervailing arguments for believing in progress and the best of all possible worlds. Crucial to the poetic admiration for Dante across a broad spectrum of modernist writers—most of whom did not share his religious outlook—was their sense of his potent method of envisioning things in a mental space, a theater of the mind (see McDougal 1985).

Bonaventura extols the woodcut and black-and-white atmospherics in the *Nightwatches*. The logic of adapting analogous forms is evident in the response by the prominent expressionist artist Lovis Corinth (1858–1925). Corinth's collection of lithographs devoted to pregnant moments and prime motifs of Bonaventura's novel opens with a compelling etching of the poet in the moonlit cemetery of Nightwatch 16, fixated upon a skull he carries in his hand through the gloomy surroundings. It is a historical curiosity that Corinth died before he could finish hand-signing all the lithographs in this his final set of illustrations—an odd reminder of the connection that Bonaventura (like Lichtenberg) drew between the legendary death of Hogarth and his supreme final gesture as a truth-telling artist in his disturbing work "The Tailpiece." Jost Schillemeit, proponent of Klingemann as the author Bonaventura, has republished this very revealing document of expressionist sensibility (1994). We can reasonably conclude that the longer-term staying power of the *Nightwatches* is owed in considerable measure to the European audience's being conditioned by expressionism and then by existentialism. As Bram Dijkstra has pointed out (1986), without any reference to Bonaventura, Corinth in his early decades as a painter dwelled fulsomely on the antifeminine, antilife themes of decadence and symbolism. Corinth's career offers one clue among many that the psychosexual obsessions in the decadent and symbolist strains of much of pre–World War I art and literature provided one of the bridges between romantic and expressionist pessimism.

The launching of the journal *boundary* 2 at SUNY-Binghamton in 1972, explicitly as a vehicle for postmodernist theory and criticism, provides us with a solid historical marker for this movement. When *boundary* 2 moved to Duke University some twenty years later, it took on a decidedly neo-Marxian coloration, but in its heyday under its founding editor it pursued a blend of existentialist, Heideggerian, and Derridavian approaches. Kenneth M. Ralston's *The Captured Horizon: Heidegger and the "Nachtwachen von Bonaventura"* (1994) serves well to exemplify attempts to understand the romantic work as an ancestral foreshadowing of a modern atheism grounded in a philosophy of authentic Being. Ralston sees encounter with the "Nothing" in Bonaventura as central and elaborates a number of points in the *Nightwatches* which he believes reveal the work's spiritual affinity with especially Heidegger's thought about Western phenomena of nihilism. For Heidegger, nihilism in modernity refers both to the collapse of meaning embodied in the religious and metaphysical heritage of Europe over some two millennia and to the urgent project of positing meaning in response to this collapse. Ralston views Kreuzgang as an existentially unhoused person struggling to cope with the emergence of truth and seeking a new ground for the self. To the extent that the *Nightwatches* depends on theatrical metaphors, he deems that the text remains stuck in Platonic thought and thus in the nihilism of the expiring "theo-philosophic" tradition, that is, in the supposedly moribund Western tradition that doctrinaire postmodernists excoriate.

Yet Ralston opines that other metaphors in the work establish a more primordial and premetaphysical "horizon" that postmodernists can embrace; that is, Kreuzgang attempts to think his way through to the end of metaphysics. Ralston's interpretation of the scenes involving the unknown cloaked man of Nightwatch 11 is interesting, even if dubious. For Ralston, the cloaked man's story offers perhaps the strongest support to argue that there is a positive implication in Kreuzgang's observations about this figure, and that this positive moment offsets the negative impact of the aborted suicide of Don Juan in Nightwatch 4. Don Juan's inability to die supposedly indicates modern humanity's failure to break out of the spell of subjectivity and to claim an authentic self, whereas in Nightwatch 11, supposedly, the double heritage of Europe—the Greek-Judaic and Christian (in Ralston's reordering of the Greco-Roman and Judeo-Christian components)—is embodied in the concerned father and the doomed mother Maria, and these strands survive as a new synthesis in the rescued son. I find it regrettable that Ralston simply ignores the innumerable sharings of motifs with a wide swath of preromantic and romantic writers, out of his zeal to appropriate Bonaventura as a herald of postmodern consciousness.

He actually pauses late in his book to enumerate the qualities of Kreuzgang's character that he has omitted as "irrelevant." Being eager to fashion the narrator in the guise of the philosopher as liberator, he thinks one could apply a Nietzschean typology, except for the category "Übermensch," which even Ralston finds indisputably awkward.

Even if we must dismiss the general overreaching, Ralston's efforts do demonstrate that Bonaventura has struck enough chords to appeal to new generations of readers who naturally feel the urge to assimilate the precocious romantic work to their cultural moment and interests. Independently, using Friedrich Nietzsche as initial "orientation point" but quickly arriving at Martin Heidegger, Jacques Derrida, Paul DeMan, Michel Foucault, et alii as providers of newer terminology, Thomas Böning (1996) has offered a more detailed attempt to trace the intellectual history behind a now widely perceived spiritual affinity between Bonaventura and "postmodern" mentality. Böning starts from the obvious themes that many romantics cultivated (laughter, its connection to the devil, classic beauty versus modern ugliness, the carnivalesque, the terror in infinity, threat of nihilism, etc.) and seeks to demonstrate that the way in which Bonaventura treats these romantic obsessions in the *Nightwatches* anticipates how postmodern thinkers eventually will seek to make something "positive" out of the challenge they pose. Hence he views Bonaventura's subject matter and manner of narration, according to postmodernist cliché, as instruments for undoing "ontotheological" servitude. In effect, Böning's analyses of Bonaventura indirectly support the proposition that romantic irony, once turned upon itself, was indeed ancestral to today's "deconstruction"; that is, in the work of people like Derrida, DeMan, and Foucault we likely have witnessed a kind of epigonal resurfacing or late reception of "negative" romanticism in the French cultural stream. This epigonal stream has subsequently recycled, flowing back into the English-speaking, German-speaking, and other cultural streams and territories in the later twentieth century.

About a decade earlier than *The Captured Horizon* (and unmentioned by Ralston), K. Alfons Knauth (1976) undertook a careful analysis of spiritual affinities between the *Nightwatches* and the manifesto play of existential absurdism, Samuel Beckett's *Waiting for Godot*, and evaluated both works as tragicomic expressions of modern nihilism. In examining various transmutations of motifs that occur in Beckett's play, Knauth notices many fascinating correspondences that tempt us to suspect that the Irish writer, who was versed in several languages, including German, at some time earlier in his own career may have become aware of Bonaventura. At a minimum, it is clear that the two authors share many materials (for example, a fake apocalypse, world history as a tragicomedy, deeper identity of the watcher with the archetypal wandering Jew, the crushing ennui of time and waiting, the ambivalence of time and eternity, the fatuousness of the professional classes, the marionette as symbol of human alienation, a crippled and defective humanity and its analogous gods, laughter as weapon in response, parody of the classical unities and rules for literature, world devolution into chaos and nothingness). Naturally, if Knauth had wanted to expand his article, he could have devoted room to mentioning notable common sources for Bonaventura and Beckett (the obsession with clocks and clock time in Sterne's *Tristram Shandy*, the mockery of academic titles and hats in Goethe's *Faust*, cosmic tedium of the self in Jean Paul's "Speech of the Dead Christ," the obsession with the human head/skull in *Hamlet*, and so forth).

One of the finest studies written in English at the very close of the twentieth century was the comparative literature thesis by McKenzie Funk (1999) submitted to Swarthmore College. Funk does an exemplary job of contextualizing Bonaventura's work in its relationships to eighteenth- and nineteenth-century culture, mainly in Germany and Britain, and of showing how key traits bear analogy to moments in a variety of twentieth-century authors such as Franz Kafka. Funk deliberately avoids conditioning his interpretation in the light of signed works by Klingemann and instead argues that we must accept the text of the originally anonymous *Nightwatches* as a genuine expression of anguished rejection both of Enlightenment promises and of romantic hopes and wish-dreams. The thesis then turns to the novelist and playwright Ramón María del Valle-Inclán, whose play *Luces de Bohemia* (*Bohemian Lights*, 1924) is the foundational work of Iberian absurdism. Funk carefully contextualizes Valle-Inclán's writings in the modernist aesthetic milieu created by Spain's celebrated Ninety-Eighter generation and in the troubled society of Spain during the rise of fascism in the 1920s and the drift toward the civil war that was to engulf his country in the 1930s. In line with Martin Esslin, he distinguishes the Galician author's theory of the *esperpento* (grotesque-absurd) as a specifically Iberian approach. Funk pays attention to specific currents and attitudes in the two different cultural worlds and historical moments of Germany and Spain. On balance, he characterizes Bonaventura's antiromantic outlook as philosophical nihilism, versus Valle-Inclán's pessimism that is deeply colored by the harsh disillusionistic naturalism that descends in Spanish literary tradition from Cervantes and the baroque.

The work of the maverick Italian composer Gian Francesco Malipiero provides a good example of how certain impulses that twentieth-century artists felt Bonaventura was communicating could be adapted in a way that created a bridge from modernism over existentialism to postmodernism. Malipiero (1882–1973), an acquaintance of Pirandello, rejected many established musical conventions of the nineteenth century and, besides being aware of newer iconoclastic theater of the absurd, knew German literature well and had lived in Vienna. Thus when a colleague, Beniamino dal Fabbro, introduced the *Nightwatches* to him in 1950, he was predisposed to recognize enormous advantages in it for writing an opera for his own times, especially since the anonymous romantic novel had exploited such deeply rooted Italian and European traditions as the commedia dell'arte and Don Giovanni. The new work, with a title perhaps gesturing toward Kafka, *The Metamorphoses of Bonaventura* (*Le Metamorfosi di Bonaventura*), and using a libretto the composer himself based directly on the *Nightwatches*, premiered in Venice at the Teatro La Fenice in September 1996 and enjoyed a critical *succès d'estime*. Malpiero maintains the primary function of Kreuzgang as a protagonist-narrator by renaming him Bonaventura and having him, outfitted with his watchman's horn, narrate key incidents in compression in a long prologue.

The figures of these episodes or stories are conjured in the night space. We witness the actor's feigned suicide, the Hamlet-Ophelia encounter, and the ominous nunnery, while Bonaventura himself appears projected in dancing masks as Arlechino, Pulcinella, and Oedipus. Act 1 then brings Malipiero's version of the Don Giovanni story, including the murder of the sister, now named Eleonora, who dying sings of her love for Bonaventura, the brother of Giovanni. The act ends in a dance scene and in an inn where patrons discuss the odd event that has occurred at a just finished production of *El burlador de Sevilla* (the original Spanish title of the foundational baroque-era play about Don Juan by Tirso de Molina) in which the soprano actually died. Somewhat like the figure of the author Hoffmann in Jacques Offenbach's operatic suite of episodes, *The Tales of Hoffmann* (*Les contes d'Hoffmann*, premiere 1879), the pseudobiographical romantic soul whom Malipiero names Bonaventura, an ex-poet, limits his personal commentary to lamenting that he ever left his post as watchman and got caught up in such emotional turmoil. Act 2 switches us to the young Bonaventura, very poor and blind, thus identifying him directly with the mysterious cloaked man in the *Nightwatches*. Listening to a lady's song, Bonaventura reacquires his sight, which occurs during an orchestral passage with a show of lights, but he awakes to disappointment, for she has fled. Again surrounded by masks, he melts into the public that arrives for a show. This crowd includes a Hans Sachs and a subnarrator who recounts the story of a white and red rose. As the audience exits, Bonaventura is left marked with an emblematic wound, a red rose that the lady places on his bosom. Bonaventura's memory as a suffering consciousness provides the unifying thread; consciousness as existential pain is played out before our eyes in a theater of the mind in Malipiero's opera.

Symptomatic of the theatrical potential of the *Nightwatches* in the twenty-first century is that in autumn 2006 a "working group" called Representational Play (Darstellendes Spiel) in Berlin took the novel as its subject matter and conducted a semester of "Experiments and Improvisations toward a Transposition into Scenic Terms," under the Swiss director Marcel Kunz (Zurich). In December 2012 the German channel SDR (South German Radio) adapted the text of the *Nightwatches* for reading on the air. These sorts of efforts to translate the narrative moments into another medium and to realize the novel's performative and visual possibilities bear analogy to the instances in which troupes in more than one country have "translated" Kafka's modern fairytales into theatrical forms. Patrick Bridgewater (2003) has helpfully analyzed Kafka's treatment of modern themes by exploiting the gothic tradition and the artistic fairytale. We can expect more attention to the roots in "tantric" romanticism, to which a variety of generic transpositions and combinations can be traced. It seems self-evident today that the *Nightwatches* are suited to stir imaginative intermedic interpretations. It is hardly an arbitrary move to convert the novel's "voice" into performative exhibitions. Bonaventura's mobile narrator Kreuzgang explicitly compares himself to a protagonist in a fairytale in the very opening nightwatch, and this constantly morphing fairytale becomes episodic in a series of theatrical *scene di notte* in the original novel of 1804.

The highly theatrical and visual aspects of the *Nightwatches* also continue to invite a pictorial mode of adaptation, as we can see in a series of works by the Berlin painter and graphic artist Cornelia Renz, which she titled *Night.Tail.Pieces.* This set of key terms clearly picks up the important themes and imagery from Bonaventura's strange book: the nocturnal space of vision; the idea of the end of things, combined with emphasis on sexuality lurking behind the polite bourgeois facade, and in counterpoint to the tormented head; and the pervasive motifs of fragmentation and devolution. The collection, published in 2011, is based on an exhibition Renz mounted earlier that year at the Kunstverein in Konstanz, where she accompanied her various pieces with chunks of quotation both in the original German of Bonaventura and in English drawn from my translation. A longer-term historical echo is implicit in, that is, built into, her alignment of a sequence of works that use a variety of means. What still reverberates is Bonaventura's own attraction to a serial examination of the decadent eighteenth-century world in images such as those Hogarth created. The stellar romantic tribute to that perplexed post-Enlightenment vision occurs, of course, when Bonaventura explicitly names Hogarth's final work *The Tailpiece* in Nightwatch 16 as his model of models. Like the voyeuristic Kreuzgang, Renz takes us behind the curtain into strange places of human life, into realms of seeming contradiction, mixing charm and horror. The techniques include superimposing her own images on typically nineteenth-century subjects. It is no exaggeration to say that as our attention moves from one piece to another in Renz's assemblage, our experience is qualitatively enhanced if we know Bonaventura. It is as if we are engaged in a shadowy reenactment of the many suggestions in the *Nightwatches* of being caught in a feverish dance. If Corinth's earlier images captured a certain solemnity in the stark encounters with forces that challenge humanity, Renz often intensifies the encounter beyond shock to a virtually hallucinatory or psychedelic level.

It is anybody's guess when, where, or how Bonaventura may next serve as an inspirer of artistic expression.

Notes

The annotations ordinarily do not identify more commonly known mythological or biblical figures, nor titles or familiar figures from the works of Shakespeare.

FIRST NIGHTWATCH

1. In the original, *abenteuerlich*, "adventurous; odd, strange; fantastic, quixotic; wild." This term, formerly applied to adventure stories and romances, acquired ironic connotations with the advent of the modern novel.
2. In Greek mythology, Stentor was a herald of the Greek forces, renowned for his loud voice.
3. The writer Voltaire (François-Marie Arouet), 1694–1778, one of the foremost exponents of the Enlightenment, notoriously refused last rites when dying.
4. The Flemish painter Peter Brueghel the Younger, 1564–1638, was popularly given the name Hell-Brueghel because of his taste for terrifying and apocalyptic scenes.
5. Bonaventura refers to the *Inferno*, part 1 of *The Divine Comedy* by the Italian poet Dante Alighieri (1265–1321), who enjoyed a critical renascence in romanticism.
6. The Italian painter Correggio (Antonio Allegri), 1489–1534, renowned for his technique of interior illumination and modeling of the human body.
7. In Greek mythology, Tartarus was the pit of hell.

8. The phrase "Gott sei bei uns" in the original German ("God be with us!) was used, in either spoken or written form, as a popular charm to ward off the devil; it was often spoken while making a sign of the cross.

9. First direct reference to Jacob Boehme, 1575-1624, German theosophist and mystic, by trade a shoemaker; the earlier indirect allusion "aurora"—in contrast to the hellish threat—is to Boehme's famous *Aurora, or The Dawn Ascendant*. According to an account by his fellow mystic Abraham von Frankenberg, Boehme while dying was reported to have heard beautiful music.

SECOND NIGHTWATCH

1. The philosopher Plato, 429-347 BC, a student of Socrates, famously banished poets from his ideal state set forth in *The Republic*.

2. First of numerous allusions to the Don Juan theme in literature in general and to its treatment in particular in Wolfgang Amadeus Mozart's (1756-91) then new opera *Don Giovanni*, the premiere of which occurred close to the end of the composer's life.

3. First direct allusion to the works of William Shakespeare, 1564-1616, who throughout the *Nightwatches* represents the pinnacle of artistic genius.

4. In Greek mythology, Niobe epitomized motherly devotion in dying to shield her children against the arrows from Apollo's bow.

THIRD NIGHTWATCH

1. *Criminaliter*, "as in a matter of criminal law." Bonaventura uses the learned Latin term for ironic emphasis.

2. Franz Joseph Gall, 1758-1828, doctor and phrenologist, expounded the theory that human beings' intellectual and psychological faculties were localized in certain regions of the brain and were recognizable in external peculiarities of form of the skull and face; his teachings were very controversial during his lifetime, and only the first part of his theory was eventually proved right. He began to practice medicine in Vienna, then moved to Berlin, and in 1802, when an imperial edict denied him the right to spread his ideas, settled in Paris.

3. August Wilhelm Iffland, 1759-1814, famous actor and playwright, who directed the theater at Mannheim (1785-92) and Berlin (1796 to the end of his life). He regarded the theater, according to the Enlightenment principle of utilitarianism, as a moral educational institution; his works reflected the sentiments of the bourgeoisie and often depicted

family life with popular accuracy, though usually within the conventions of the *comédie larmoyante*—lacrimose or maudlin comedy.

4. August Friedrich Kotzebue, 1761–1819, prolific and popular playwright who became the butt of criticism of young German writers on account of his well-made plays based on social situations; he came to be seen as the epitome of bourgeois sentimentality. Suspected of being an agent for Russia, he was assassinated by the revolutionary student George Sand in 1819.

5. First direct reference to St. Crispin, the Roman shoemaker saint who aided the poor. Young King Henry V rallies his troops on Crispin's Day in Shakespeare's play about this popular monarch. Crispin was also the name of a figure in the commedia dell'arte.

6. Major compilation of laws under Justinian I, Eastern emperor from 527 to 565, who reconquered many of the Roman dominions lost after the empire's earlier height and built the great cathedral of St. Sophia in Constantinople.

7. This utterance travesties the moment in Mozart's *Don Giovanni* when the statue of the murdered Commendatore appears for supper at the antihero's lodgings in the final act.

8. In the original, *die Carolina*, for *Constitutio Criminalis Carolina*, the first general German codification of criminal law and trial procedures, which was promulgated under Charles V at the Imperial Diet of Regensburg in 1532 and gained recognition in most German territories. Its fusion of Roman and older German law formed the basis of legal development for three centuries; the Caroline system of harsh corporal and capital punishment was gradually modified and largely abolished by the end of the eighteenth century.

9. In the original, *Karolina*. In addition to the play on the Latin name of the criminal code, this is likely an allusion to the famous romantic woman Caroline, wife first of August Wilhelm Schlegel and then of Friedrich Schelling, with whom she ran away. Caroline's reputation for her liberal views on love was sufficient to provoke the association with the adulteress here.

10. In Greek mythology, Themis embodies divine order and law.

FOURTH NIGHTWATCH

1. The Kabbalah, a movement to create a system of occult theosophy or mystical interpretation of the scriptures among Jewish rabbis of the late Middle Ages and certain medieval Christians influenced by them, had appealed widely to the imagination of Renaissance philosophers

and poets. Having absorbed some elements of the Kabbalah, the pansophical and theosophical streams in Germany of the sixteenth and seventeenth centuries left a deep imprint, and the romantics had revived interest in the possibility of a unifying poetic interpretation of the natural and spiritual realms. They were fascinated with mysterious symbols or "hieroglyphs," such as the diagrams and Hebrew words used in theosophical books.

2. This mention of a Gypsy woman anticipates the moment of anagnorisis, that is, discovery of one's family relationships and identity in Nightwatch 16.

3. From the Latin saying *Ne sutor ultra crepidam*: The shoemaker should not go beyond his last—that is, should not venture judgments beyond his competence.

4. Hans Sachs, 1494–1576, shoemaker and master singer, author of numerous short comedies and Shrovetide farces (*Fastnachtsspiele*) in which the clown is often a central figure and foolishness the theme.

5. See n9.

6. The narrator's name, Kreuzgang, refers here directly to a "crossroads" or "crossway" but suggests "going crossways" or "bearing a cross." The word can signify a cross-aisle in a church, cloisters in a convent, or a vaulted archway as in church architecture, as well as a procession with a cross. The novel's pervasive cross leitmotif reinforces our sense of the ambiguity of Kreuzgang's nature, beginning with the phrase *durch ein Kreuz*, "with (a sign of) the cross," in the opening paragraph of Nightwatch 1. The watchman's name is echoed in the gruesome burial scene of Nightwatch 10 in the term *Kreuzgang*, "cloisters," and the pun on the cross concept in *lex cruciata* in Nightwatch 7 explicitly interprets it.

7. *Salto mortale*, Italian for a deathly or desperate leap.

8. "Tailpiece," in the original *Schwanzstück*, is a favorite phrase of Bonaventura's, doubtless because it combines reference to something final in art and drama and sexual and eschatological implications. Mentioned several times in the novel is the painter and social satirist William Hogarth, 1697–1764, some of whose most famous engravings depicted poverty, squalor, crime, and also vices of the affluent in eighteenth-century England, often with savage indignation.

9. The legendary figure of the wandering Jew in romantic literature often pictures modern unhoused, alienated existence and here reinforces the theme of an inability to die, that is, to find peace and meaning.

10. The rebel Titan Prometheus, who challenged the gods by himself shaping human beings and was condemned by Zeus, was a favorite figure of Sturm und Drang and romanticism. Here he presages a defiance that devolves into nihilism.

11.   Such a revolt against the author, doubtlessly known to Bonaventura, occurs in Ludwig Tieck's fantastic comedies *Puss-in-Boots* and *The Topsey-Turvey World* in the last years of the eighteenth century. By the early twentieth century, the Spanish writer Miguel de Unamuno will have developed this same theme in his novel *Niebla* (Fog), and at mid-century the Irish author Flann O'Brien (Brian O'Nolan) carries the idea to remarkable lengths in his novel *At-Swim-Two Birds*.

12.   In the original, Hanswurst (Jack Sausage), the dumb but sly servant figure of German Shrovetide plays, then in the seventeenth and eighteenth centuries the principal comic personage; later applied to any simple-minded joker or fool.

13.   The puppet play now told may be a parody of Friedrich Schiller's neoclassical tragedy *Die Braut von Messina*, in which incest and fratricide occur under the aegis of fate.

14.   The Latin expression *forum externum* in canon and international law regards the right to practice one's religion publicly. It is often paired with *forum internum*, the freedom to hold a religion or philosophical conviction privately.

SIXTH NIGHTWATCH

1.   *The Last Judgment* by Michelangelo Buonarroti, 1475–1564, was a favorite painting of the German romantics.

2.   The Latin term *caput mortuum*, literally "dead head," is used in alchemy to signify a useless substance that remains after a chemical operation.

3.   The philosopher Immanuel Kant, 1724–1804, had dealt with categories of perception in his epochal *Critique of Pure Reason*.

4.   *In puris naturalibus*, "in a state of nature; stark naked." Besides referring to the body politic, here the Latin term may also suggest sardonically the wretchedness of the human body after the spark of life is extinguished.

SEVENTH NIGHTWATCH

1.   *Lex cruciata*, referring to biological crossing as a factor of inheritance, is another pun on the term *cross*; compare NW4n6.

2.   In the original, *Stifts- und Taborshütten*. The word *Stift* refers to a religious foundation endowed with property and investments, an establishment attached to a church college or serving ecclesiastical purposes, e.g., a cloister; accordingly, also an educational institution (often for girls) or an old-age home (for noblewomen). *Tabor* means a fortification or fortified place or camp; in Austrian usage, a fortified building near

or on the edge of a locale, usually near a church or around it. (The word is further associated with *Taborit*, a follower of the radical movement within the Hussites, after the city Tabor, south of Prague, founded in 1420 as a camp by Hussites.) The compound with *Hütten* (huts, cottages) is tinged with irony. The motif of "poetic cottages" is a commonplace from German eighteenth-century lyrics, especially the writings of the sentimentalists following the poet Friedrich Gottlieb Klopstock, 1723–1803.

3. Fabled people of giants in Canaan (Numbers 13:28–34).

4. After their defeat by the forces of Zeus, the Titans were consigned to the abysses of Tartarus.

5. *Advocatus diaboli*, "devil's advocate."

6. *corpora delicti*, "bodies of evidence."

7. *in praxi*, "in practice."

8. This is apparently a facetious reference to a nonexistent provision of the *Lex de injuriis*, Latin for the law regarding slander.

9. *Culpose*, "negligently, heedlessly at fault, culpable"; Kreuzgang uses a term from Roman common law.

10. *Foro privilegiato*, "privileged forum"; Kreuzgang sardonically claims that only the court of heaven has jurisdiction in his case.

11. Probably refers to the jurist Adolph Dietrich Weber, author of *Über Injurien und Schmähschriften* (Concerning slanders and defamatory writings, 1793), although he actually rejected such a position.

12. In the original, *Trillhaus*: a revolving cage into which birds or small animals are put and which they turn through their hopping; a little house in the marketplace containing an upright revolving drum on which public offenders are turned while standing.

13. In the original, *spanischer Mantel*: a wooden implement of torture so named because of its resemblance to a cloak of Spanish cut, and consisting of a cylindrical jacket or casing with apertures for the head and arms.

14. *Mente captis*, "those whose minds have been seized, i.e., deprived of sound sense."

EIGHT NIGHTWATCH

1. *Opus posthumum*, "posthumous work."

2. Bonaventura alludes here to the condition known in medical Latin as *facies Hippocratica*, that is, changes that are produced in the face by impending death, long illness, and other major systemic stress. In mythology, the hideous head of Medusa could turn to stone those who looked directly at her.

3. The moving story of the imprisonment and starvation of Count Ugolino della Gherardesca with his sons and grandsons in Pisa is narrated by Dante in canto 33 of the *Inferno*. The drama *Ugolino* (1768) by Heinrich Wilhelm von Gerstenberg, 1737–1823, a forerunner of Sturm und Drang in its treatment of their dire suffering, is the more immediate reference in Bonaventura's mind.

4. Hanswurst's deliberate malapropism "respective" for "respectable," occurring three times in his prologue, plays ironically on a term central to the bourgeois audience's concept of itself. *Respektiv(e)*, "respective(ly)," immediately suggests both *respektabel* (respectable) and *respektierlich* (respectable, important, considerable) in a ridiculous way. Bonaventura's thrusts against Enlightenment sentimentality and neoclassical expectations, assignment of important functions to Hanswurst, mocking of Schiller as well as Iffland and Kotzebue, and predilection for horrific fairytale motifs with psychological implications recall the young Ludwig Tieck. (See NW3nn3–4, NW4n13, NW12n3.)

5. Erasmus Darwin, 1731–1802, English doctor and poet, an early advocate of the theory of evolution, and grandfather of Charles Darwin, 1809–82.

6. Mandandane is the queen of an ironically depicted court in Goethe's comedy *Der Triumph der Empfindsamkeit* (*The Triumph of Sensibility*). Prince Oronaro, a sentimentalist, dotes on her image in the form of an identically attired puppet that he drags about with him; she switches places with the puppet; after some confusion, the jealous king is reconciled, while the prince remains satisfied with his mere copy of the queen.

7. *Gorge de Paris*: article of clothing like a dickey or shirt top covering the breast and throat; false bosom.

NINTH NIGHTWATCH

1. Olearius is the Latinized form of the common German name Oehlmann (Oilman) and is representative here of the pretentiousness of the professions. The double name is probably modeled on that of the Frankfurt lawyer in Goethe's early drama *Götz von Berlichingen*, set in the ending Middle Ages.

2. Johann Gottlieb Fichte, 1762–1814, an important philosopher for the German romantic movement, argued that both the form and the content of knowledge were subjectively apprehended by the mind and derived from the creative ego. The "self," finding itself confronted by the "nonself," manifests its freedom by gradually overcoming all that seems to delimit it and render it finite. The evolution of the ego through ever-increasing clarity of consciousness will eventually result in the virtual

identity of the individual self with, or its effective submersion in, the universal infinite reality or "transcendental self."

3. Probably an allusion to the ideas about illustrating great classical works that August Wilhelm Schlegel advances, for example, in "Über Zeichnungen zu Gedichten und John Flaxman's Umrisse," *Athenäum* 2 (1799): 193–246. Or perhaps an allusion linking the well-known ideas of Friedrich Schlegel concerning the fragment as art form and the theme of reduction to a miniature format through ineluctable fragmentation (physical and spiritual entropy) in the cosmic process.

4. The commedia clown Scaramouch or Scaramuzza had an outsized nose and was noted for crudity.

TENTH NIGHTWATCH

1. Franz Paul Koch was a celebrated traveling virtuoso of the early nineteenth century who played the jaw-harp or Jew's harp (*Mundharmonika*). There was a vogue in the first decade of the century for strange instruments with jarring or grating qualities.

2. "In his brother's arms": in the arms of Death, brother of Sleep.

3. Named after the girl in the ballad "Lenore" by Gottfried August Burger, 1747–94. When her beloved Wilhelm does not return from war, Lenore falls prey to despair and quarrels with divine Providence; Wilhelm then appears in the night to fetch her, but he is a ghostly rider who carries her into the realm of death and hell.

4. According to legend, Ursula, daughter of Deonatus, king of Brittany, led eleven thousand virgins on a pilgrimage to Rome and on the return journey was martyred with them at Cologne when she opposed the Huns; however, their spirits rescued the city, and Ursula fulfilled the mission of which she had dreamed. The Ursulines are members of the order for women named after her and founded in 1535, which follows Augustinian rules.

ELEVENTH NIGHTWATCH

1. Here and elsewhere in the work, Italy stands for an earthly paradise and land of fulfillment. There may be a measure of irony in this usage, which reflects the German obsession with Italy as a realm with both classical and romantic significance. Goethe's cultural pilgrimage through Italy (1786–88) was one of numerous examples that contributed to the general magic of the name.

1. Kreuzgang alludes to the wonder of the times, Napoleon Bonaparte, confident that he does not need to name him outright.

2. Kant, see NW6n3; Johann Wolfgang von Goethe, 1749–1832, poet, playwright, novelist, and dominant figure of German letters; Gotthold Ephraim Lessing, 1729–81, Enlightenment critic and dramatist; Friedrich von Schiller, 1759–1805, critic and dramatist.

3. Kotzebue, see NW3n4; Ludwig Tieck, 1773–1853, leading author of the Jena group of romantics and, with August Wilhelm Schlegel, Germany's major translator of Shakespeare, who became part of the standard German repertory in the Tieck-Schlegel version.

4. In the course of the sentence Bonaventura switches from the older polite, singular form of address *Er* (masc.) or *Sie* (fem.) to the then more distinguished, and now standard polite, plural form *Sie* (masc. or fem.).

5. The pretended author of *Baron Münchhausen's Narrative of His Marvellous Travels and Campaigns in Russia* (Oxford, 1785), by Rudolf Erich Raspe, an exiled Göttingen student, became synonymous with a teller of extravagant fictions. Raspe had based the adventure stories on an actual nobleman who had fought in the service of Duke Anton Ulrich of Braunschweig-Wolfenbüttel. Through the German version by Burger (1786), the Baron entered popular lore as the epitome of a liar and fabulous figure.

6. Franz Hemsterhuis, 1721–90, who contributed to the formation of German transcendental idealism, was highly regarded as a philosopher in the late eighteenth and early nineteenth centuries.

THIRTEENTH NIGHTWATCH

1. The allusion is to the Delphic Oracle pertaining to the god Apollo; the "voice" emerged in the vapors from a fissure in the earth, thus out of Mother Nature.

2. The sixteenth-century Free Imperial Knight, whom Goethe immortalized in the historical drama *Götz von Berlichingen mit der eisernen Hand* (1773), symbolizes the genial individual living out of his own nature. Berlichingen asserts his rights against artificial encroachments and political pressures as a new age of statecraft is ushered in. In addition to manly hardness, his iron fist suggests the principle of *Faustrecht* (prevailing through strength) and the mutilation of noble forms—both themes in this nightwatch.

3. Horace, *Epistolae* 2.3.

4. Antinoüs, a young Bithynian of great beauty, was a slave and lover

favored by the emperor Hadrian, 117–38, and became regarded as the model of plastic beauty.

5. Thersites, a character in the *Iliad*, who came to typify insolent cowardice.

6. Laocoön, the Trojan priest who distrusted the Greeks' wooden horse and was destroyed along with his sons by serpents sent by Athena. Lessing's analysis of the intrinsic properties of the famous statue versus those of Vergil's poetic treatment of the subject, expounded in *Laokoon oder Über die Grenzen der Mahlerey und Poesie* (1766), deeply influenced German aesthetic thought.

7. Timanthes, a late fifth-century BC Greek painter of the Sikyonian school famed for his *ingenium*; in his *Sacrifice of Iphigenia* he showed degrees of grief culminating in the veiled Agamemnon. In chap. 2 of *Laokoon*, Lessing cited Timanthes to illustrate the principle of subtle suggestion of emotion in painting and sculpture.

8. Briareus, son of Heaven and Earth, a giant with fifty heads and a hundred arms, was cast into the sea by Poseidon and chained by Zeus under Aetna in the company of his brothers in punishment for his revolt against the new order of the gods.

FOURTEENTH NIGHTWATCH

1. Kreuzgang thinks of himself as a confined Titan, in the fashion of Polyphemus or Prometheus.

2. *Cicisbeo* (from Italian), a *cavalier servente* in eighteenth-century Italy: a male companion, the recognized gallant of a married woman.

3. Another allusion to the subject as treated by Timanthes; see NW3n7.

4. Gustavus Adolphus, 1594–1632, king of Sweden; the rock is the Schwedenstein near Lützen.

5. Mary Stuart, 1542–87, Queen of Scots, who was beheaded by her cousin Elizabeth I.

FIFTEENTH NIGHTWATCH

1. Celebrated cavern on the Isle of Staffa in the Hebrides, penetrated by the sea that splashes on its basalt walls creating a musical effect; this inspired Felix Mendelssohn to write an overture. Fingal was a legendary Scot hero, reputedly the son of Ossian, king of Mowen, an Irish bard and hero (third century); through the vogue of James Macpherson's purported translations (1760–63), the Ossianic materials left a deep impression on German Sturm und Drang literature that is still resonant in this passage.

2. "Sage" probably refers to Voltaire, who has been mentioned in Nightwatch 1, or to Jean-Jacques Rousseau, who was a citizen of Geneva.

3. See NW3n4.

4. I.e., in the fixed role of Hanswurst.

5. The Apocrypha story of Judith and Holofernes was a favorite subject of German biblical drama in the sixteenth and seventeenth centuries and became part of the puppet show repertory as well; after it had ceased to be of importance in the high tradition, the story remained alive in the popular tradition.

6. The three biblical kings and the world conqueror Alexander were protagonists in the older German biblical and folk romances and drama and continued to appeal to the popular imagination as figures in puppet plays.

SIXTEENTH NIGHTWATCH

1. See n31.

2. This is an ironic allusion to the moment in the opening scene of Goethe's *Faust, ein Fragment* (1790) when Faust is attracted by the sign of the Earth-Spirit and summons him. He appears in terrifying aspect in flames, representing the driving forces of nature, and rejects Faust as unequal to the dynamic power of the creation. Here Bonaventura invokes the Faust tradition as renewed by Goethe. Kreuzgang's deceased father had wanted to be a Faust (the originally Latin name Faustus, when spoken as Faust in German, is cognate with English *fist*).

3. The fairytale figure of Bluebeard, a knight who killed his wives because they disobeyed his command, stands here for the horror of a monstrous nature in general and was made an important literary motif with pronounced psychological implications by Tieck's often nightmarish play *Blaubart* (in his *Volksmärchen*, 1797), taken from the French fairytale collection of Charles Perrault, 1628-1703. See NW12n3.

4. Karl Philipp Moritz, 1756-93, educator and aesthetician, befriended Goethe, edited Γνοθι σεαυτον, *Magazin der Erfahrungsseelenkunde, als Lesebuch für Gelehrte und Ungelehrte* (Know thyself: Magazine of empirical psychology; a reader for scholars and nonscholars, 1783-98). His interest in psychological delineation had some impact on literature through his autobiographical educational novel *Anton Reiser, ein psychologischer Roman* (1785-90) as well as his scholarly writings.

Select Bibliography

Arendt, Dieter. 1972. *Der "poetische Nihilismus" in der Romantik: Studien zum Verhältnis von Dichtung und Wirklichkeit in der Frühromantik.* Tübingen: Niemeyer.

Arnold, Barbara. 2006. "*Night Watches* on the Computer: Creating an Author's Dictionary with Computational Means." *Literary and Linguistic Computing* 21, no. 1 (January).

Baus, Lothar. 1989. *Goethes Schattenehe mit Charlotte von Stein: Die wahren Eltern des romantischen Dichters und Theaterdirektors August Klingemann (1777-1831).* Homburg/Saar: Asclepios Edition.

———. 1995. *Der Illuminat und Stoiker Goethe; Eine chronologische Zusam-menfassung der neuesten Goethe-Entdeckungen: Karl VII.-Urania-Tieck-Illuminaten-"Nachtwachen"-Komplex.* Homburg/Saar: Asclepios Edition.

———. 1999. *Nachtwachen von (des) Bonaventura, alias Johann Wolfgang Goethe: Eine Goethesche Autobiographie.* Part 1: The Text Corpus; Part 2: Final Deci-phering of the Pseudonym. 6. Auflage. Homburg/Saar: Asclepios Edition.

———. 2004. *Wolfgang Goethes und Uranias Sohn, Ludwig Tieck.* 4. erw. Auf-lage. Homburg/Saar: Asclepios Edition.

Berns, Ute. 2012. *Science, Politics, and Friendship in the Works of Thomas Lovell Beddoes.* Newark: University of Delaware Press.

Blume, Bernhard. 1976. "Jesus, der Gottesleugner: Rilkes 'Der Ölbaum-Garten' und Jean Pauls 'Rede des toten Christus.'" *Herkommen und Erneuerung: Es-says für Oskar Seidlin,* edited by Gerald Gillespie and Edgar Lohner, 336-74. Tübingen: Niemeyer.

Böning, Thomas. 1996. *Widersprüche: Zu den "Nachtwachen. Von Bonavetura"
und zur Theoriedebatte.* Freiburg im Breisgau: Rombach Verlag.

Bridgwater, Patrick. 2003. *Kafka, Gothic and Fairytale.* Amsterdam: Rodopi.

Brinkmann, Richard. 1966. *"Nachtwachen von Bonaventura": Kehrseite der
Frühromantik.* Pfullingen: Niske.

Brzović, Kathy. 1990. *Bonaventura's "Nachtwachen": A Satirical Novel.* New
York: Lang.

Burath, Hugo. 1948. *August Klingemann und die deutsche Romantik.* Braunschweig: Im Vieweg-Verlag.

Burckhardt, Sigurd. 1968. *King Lear: The Quality of Nothing.* Princeton, NJ:
Princeton University Press.

Butler, Erik 2010. *Metamorphoses of the Vampire in Literature and Film: Cultural
Transformations in Europe, 1732–1933.* Rochester, NY: Camden House.

Corinth, Lovis. 1925. *Die Nachtwachen des Bonaventura.* Illustrated by L. Clovis.
Berlin: Propyläen.

Cornwell, Neil. 2006. *The Absurd in Literature.* Manchester: Manchester University Press.

Dijkstra, Bram. 1986. *Idols of Perversity: Fantasies of Feminine Evil in Fin-de-
Siècle Culture.* New York: Oxford University Press.

Ellenberger, Henri. 1970. *The Discovery of the Unconscious: The History and
Evolution of Dynamic Psychiatry.* New York: Basic Books.

Feger, Hans. 2007. "Das Groteske in Bonaventuras *Nachtwachen.*" *Athenäum:
Jahrbuch für Romantik* 17:51–77.

Fleig, Horst. 1985. *Literarischer Vampirismus: Klingemanns "Nachtwachen von
Bonaventura."* Tübingen: Niemeyer.

Frank, Erich. 1912. "Clemens Brentano, der Verfasser der *Nachtwachen.*"
Germanisch-Romanische Monatsschrift 7:417–40.

Frye, Northrup. 1969. *Anatomy of Criticism: Four Essays.* New York: Atheneum.

Funk, McKenzie.1999. "The *Nachtwachen von Bonaventura* and Valle-Inclán's
Luces de Bohemia: A Comparison in the Satiric Grotesque." MA thesis,
Swarthmore College.

Gillespie, Gerald. 1971, 1972. *Die Nachtwachen des Bonaventura / The Night
Watches of Bonaventura.* Austin: University of Texas Press; Edinburgh:
Edinburgh University Press.

———. 1973. "Night-Piece and Tail-Piece: Bonaventura's Relation to Hogarth."
Arcadia 8:284–95.

———. 1976. "Kreuzgang in the Role of Crispin: *Commedia dell'arte* Transformations in *Die Nachtwachen.*" In *Herkommen und Erneuerung: Essays
für Oskar Seidlin,* edited by Gerald Gillespie and Edgar Lohner, 185–200.
Tübingen: Niemeyer.

———. 1981. "Romantic Oedipus." In *Goethezeit: Studien zur Erkentnis und*

Rezeption Goethes und seiner Zeitgenossen; Festschrift für Stuart Atkins, 185–200. Bern: Francke Verlag.

———. 2013. *Ludwig Tieck's "Puss-in-Boots" and Theater of the Absurd: A Commentated Bilingual Edition*. Brussels: Presses Interuniversitaires Européennes / Peter Lang.

Haag, Ruth. 1987. "Noch einmal: Der Verfasser der *Nachtachen von Bonaventura*." *Euphorion* 81:286–97.

Haym, Rudolf. 1928. *Die romantische Schule*. 5th ed. (orig. 1870). Berlin: Weidmannsache Buchhandlung.

Hunter, Rosemarie. 1974. "*Nachtwachen von Bonaventura* and *Tristram Shandy*." *Canadian Review of Comparative Literature* 1:218–34.

Hunter Lougheed, Rosemarie. 1985. "*Die Nachtwachen von Bonaventura*": *Ein Frühwerk E. T. A. Hoffmanns?* Heidelberg: Winter.

Katritzky, Linda. 1999. *A Guide to Bonaventura's "Nightwatches."* New York: Lang.

Klingemann, August. 1828. *Errinnerungsblätter*. 3 vols. Braunschweig: Bei G. C. E. Meyer.

———. 2012. *Theaterschriften*. Edited by Alexander Košenina. Erlangen: Wehrhahn Verlag.

Köster, Heinrich. 1956. "Das Phänomen des Lächerlichen in der Dichtung um 1800 (Jean Paul, E.T.A. Hoffmann, Bonaventura)." PhD dissertation, Freiburg im Breisgau.

Knauth, Alfons K. 1976. "Luckys und Bonaventuras unglückliche Weltansichten: Ein Vergleich von Becketts *En attendant Godot* mit den *Nachtwachen von Bonaventura*." *Romanistisches Jahrbuch* 26:147–69.

Kohl, Peter. 1986. *Der freie Spielraum im Nichts: Eine kritische Betrachtung der "Nachtwachen von Bonaventura."* Frankfurt am Main: Lang.

Lichtenberg, Georg Christoph. 1966. *Lichtenberg's Commentaries on Hogarth's Engravings*. Translated by Gustav Hardan and Innes Hardan. London: Crescent.

Malipiero, Gian Francesco. 1970. *Le metamorfosi di Bonaventura*. Milano: Ricordi.

McDougal, Stuart Y., ed. 1985. *Dante among the Moderns*. Chapel Hill: University of North Carolina Press.

Michel, Hermann, ed. 1968. *Nachtwachen. Von Bonaventura*. In *Deutsche Literaturdenkmale des 18 und 19 Jahrhunderts*, vol. 133. Berlin: Behrs, 1904. Repr., Liechtenstein: Kraus.

Mielke, Andreas. 1984. *Zeitgenosse Bonaventura*. Stuttgart: Hans-Dieter Heinz Akademischer Verlag.

Neuswanger, R. Russell. 1970. "Investigation of Some Central Motifs in *Die Nachtwachen des Bonaventura*." PhD dissertation, Ohio State University.

————. 1976. "On Laughter in Bonaventura's *Nachtwachen*." *German Life and Letters* 30:15–24.

Pfannkuche, Walter. 1983. *Idealismus und Nihilismus in den "Nachtwachen von Bonaventura.*" Frankfurt am Main: Lang.

Praz, Mario. 1970. *The Romantic Agony*. Translated by Angus Davidson. 2nd ed. London: Oxford University Press.

Pribić, Rado. 1974. *Bonaventura's "Nachtwachen" and Dostoevsky's "Notes from the Underground": A Comparison in Nihilism*. Munich: Verlag Otto Sagner.

Ralston, Kenneth M. 1994. *The Captured Horizon: Heidegger and the "Nachtwachen von Bonaventura.*" Tübingen: Max Niemeyer Verlag.

Renz, Cornelia. 2011. *Night. Tail. Piece*. Edited by Axel Lapp. Berlin: Green Box. (Forty-two illustrations, with commentary by various hands and excerpts from the *Nightwatches*.)

Rouché, Max. 1969. "Bonaventura ne serait-il pas Jean Paul Richter lui-même?" *Études Germaniques* 24:329–45.

Sammons, Jeffrey. 1965. *The "Nachtwachen von Bonaventura": A Structural Interpretation*. The Hague: Mouton.

Schillemeit, Jost. 1973. *Bonaventura: Der Verfasser der "Nachtwachen.*" Munich: C. H. Beck.

————, ed. 1994. *"Nachtwachen" von Bonaventura*. Illustrated by Lovis Corinth; afterword by Jost Schillemeit. Frankfurt am Main: Insel Verlag.

Schultz, Franz. 1909. *Der Verfasser der "Nachtwachen von Bonaventura": Untersuchungen zur deutschen Romantik*. Berlin: Weidmannsche Buchhandlung.

Sölle-Nipperdey, Dorothee. 1959. *Untersuchungen zur Struktur der Nachtwachen von Bonaventura*. Göttingen: Vandenhoeck & Ruprecht.

Thiele, Joachim. 1963. "Untersuchungen zur Frage des Authors der *Nachtwachen von Bonaventura* mit Hilfe einfacher Textcharakteristiken." *Grundlagenstudien aus Kybernetik und Geisteswissenschaft* 4:33–44.